What To Do Until
Enlightenment

Healing Ourselves...
Healing The Earth

Revised and Expanded Edition

STUART W. ALPER, Psy.D., LCSW

DEDICATION

This revised edition is dedicated
to Frank Howell and Antonio Mendoza.

To Frank: Gone these many years, I still get messages from your
spirit. Even from the other side you managed to provide me
with the cover image of this book, taken from a serigraph you
created entitled Reunion.

To Antonio: The passion you bring to your life, your music and
your art has been an inspiration. Time and again you have
encouraged me to expand the limits of my creativity.

What To Do Until Enlightenment
Copyright Revised Edition © 2006, Stuart W. Alpert
First Edition, Published as a part of the Frontiers of Psychotherapy Series
by
Ablex Publishers, 1990

ISBN 10: 0-97855792-0-8
ISBN 13: 978-0-9785792-0-3

Published in 2006 by:
Wolf Song Publishing
200 N. Beacon St.
Hartford, CT. 06105
Email: stuart-naomi@comcast.net

TABLE OF CONTENTS

Introduction to the Revised Edition

I CAN'T REMEMBER THE NUMBER OF TIMES I'VE LEARNED THAT the future often does not turn out the way we think it will. Anticipating what might happen can be a waste of time and energy. It's one of the reasons why living mindfully in the present grounds us in reality. The past is over and the future hasn't arrived yet. It's the here and now, the present, where the real action is. When I decided to revise this book I expected the revised edition would basically be the same as the original. I expected that minor editing would make the book clearer and more readable. I believed that I would be correcting spelling and grammar and, at times, doing slight modifications in order to clarify awkward sentences that reflected some formlessness in my thinking. In actuality, I did this and much more. I found that my writing style has changed, hopefully for the better. I also discovered that in the original there were times that my writing had a "chasing my tail" quality to it where I went round and round the same point without deepening or adding to the clarity of what I was presenting. Therefore, in this revision I found myself often deleting redundancies and cutting and pasting in order to rearrange sections to improve the book's overall readability.

I deeply appreciate all of you who read the original and gave me such positive feedback, sharing with me that it had deep meaning for you. Like so many of us, certainly I am my own worst critic. Also, I deeply appreciate all of the encouragement and support I received to reprint this book after it has been out of print for past few years.

My intent in revising this book is to continue to present the view that as humans, we have an emotional/energetic/body process that is always sending us messages to expand our consciousness. Whether we are aware of these messages or not, they are available to us. We simply need to learn how to read their code. For my life's work, I have chosen the path of awakening my and others' consciousness and learning the code. I hope that what I have learned can help point the way to your own awakening and help you enter a transformational process, thereby, providing you with more emotional and energetic ground to stand on.

In this Introduction and in the first chapter of this book, I have included personal information about my history and the emotional issues that were a result of my childhood. I share some of my story in order to help readers understand how I've come to understand my own process of growth, my path of discovery, as I move toward deepening my consciousness. It has been fourteen years since the first printing of *What to Do Until Enlightenment*. During these fourteen years I have continued "working on myself" in order to clear out abusive energies that still live in me from my childhood.

The phrase, "working on myself" is the way the practitioners of Body-Centered Gestalt Therapy refer to deepening the connection to life and spirit. It refers to the process of continuing to clear out the old assault energies from childhood that are still embedded in the cells of our psyche and body. These assault energies interfere with a free flow of energy. "Working on myself" also means building in new supports that allows all of what I feel to emerge into consciousness. In this way I can live into what is true and real, rather than living from denial, illusion, and a role of how I believe I should appear.

The way that I had to defend myself in relation to the abusive energies in my childhood created places of darkness and alienation in me. These experiences were like a veil that separated me from my life energy and prevented me from feeling more alive. The impact of these energies also created feelings of isolation and of "no self."

They prevented me from being able to clearly form my anger and my need. In order to lift the veil and feel more alive I have continued to deal with knowing when I'm angry and being able to share my anger in a clear and non-blaming way. An interesting thing has occurred through my life as I have learned to know the signals that tell me that I'm angry and be able to share it more clearly. There are fewer things that touch my anger and the times that I am angry, my anger is much less intense. I feel that my anger is being transformed into understanding and compassion. I have also brought my attention to being more in touch with what it is that I need at any given moment and allowing need to become a simple and non-controversial part of me.

I continue to become more conscious of how I am emotionally wired as I allow myself to feel my sadness and suffering that is a result of how I was treated as a child. I increasingly make room for these feelings and support them when they open in me. Part of what I mean by support has to do with bringing compassion and understanding to whatever I feel. When I do this I don't have to tighten, space out, or collapse my body in order to block these feelings. I have learned through experience that blocking feelings causes them to be locked in my muscles and organs. These blocked feelings then backup and clog my system just as plumbing that is clogged doesn't allow water to flow freely. Being unblocked, I can build a connection to my deeper places of knowing, allowing for a connection to spirit and the profound and universal knowing that this connection affords me. As I have been involved in this process of "working on myself" I have experienced an increase in my compassion, peacefulness, and joy.

The result of my continued work during these fourteen years is that I've become softer and more emotionally accessible. I believe I blame less and am less emotionally distant and arrogant. I find that I take more responsibility for myself after I have lost my sense of center and I have "acted out." In general, I feel stronger and more balanced. This is how it feels inside of me and it is also the feedback that I have received from my friends, colleagues, clients, and students.

I feel a deeper sense of connection to my body in general, to my heart in particular, to the ground, and to spirit and universal truths.

This does not mean that I consider myself enlightened. Rather, I feel more alive and intact. I feel more accepting that I am on a life-long journey. At times, I feel integrated with my emotions and my body. When I have brought enough compassion and support to what I have been feeling there are more times that I experience a deep sense of oneness. Other times, I'm dealing with the minutiae of life and the trench work of my own issues that still exist inside of me. Most of the time, I feel excited to be alive and feel separate from more of my emotionally inherited familial suffering. Having separated from more of the suffering, I stand a little straighter and feel stronger.

On this journey toward feeling more alive I have had to become conscious of my defensive structures that were developed to survive the abuse in my childhood. These defensive structures had become organized in my body as areas of tension, dissociation, blankness, and collapse. In the process of learning to relax into these experiences, rather than fighting them, I found that I began to integrate my softness with a different sense of power. I softened by relaxing the tension, came more into my body out of disscociation, became perceptually and intellectually clearer as blankness let go, and expanded out of the suffering of being collapsed.

As I had more of myself, the feeling of increased self-possession produced a heightened feeling of power. It was not power that came from controlling myself or others. I found that the more that I could create a flexible container for all of my feelings and emotions, the stronger and more powerful I felt. To build a container for my experiences, rather than to live in tension, dissociation, blankness, or collapse, meant that I had to live through the specific experiences of how I had developed these defensive organizations.

At times, the traumatic childhood memories that were stored in my body intensified as I worked to reach a deeper place of alive-ness. At other times, the battle between my life force and my old defenses caused physical breakdowns. In living through these experiences I discovered how tension and stress develops by living from a defensive structure. I also discovered how this tension and stress creates physical pain and illness. I learned that supporting my emotions and living through my childhood trauma brought both a physical and an emotional healing.

It was as if the tension created in my childhood assumed that it knew the outcome if I let go and softened. My body was organized to believe that the old memories of humiliation, rejection, abandonment, violence, and craziness would still be waiting for me if I took another step toward aliveness. In truth, the only way that these assaultive experiences were waiting for me was in my reliving how as a child I had been humiliated, rejected, abandoned, and treated with violence and craziness.

As I rewrite my life script by allowing more of myself to exist, I am aware that if anyone is emotionally abusive with me today, I am now more able to hold my ground and remain clear. It is not that as I grow the world becomes free of abuse; rather, there is now more of me that feels assured that I can deal with whatever comes my way. Therefore, I am less defensive. This does not mean that I don't get thrown off center at times and live as if I am still a defenseless child. However, when this occurs I can return to center more quickly and take responsibility for having acted out as if I were a victim, rather than having to continue splitting off and defending myself in the old stereotypic ways that I adopted as a child.

As you read parts of the first chapter to the book that I wrote fourteen years ago, you will note the difference between what I felt then and what I feel now about having to deal with my inner abusive voices. I can look back at where I have come from emotionally and revel in the trip. I feel excited about the possibilities that await me as I continue bringing awareness to my process. It is this sense of hope for the new lives that we can create for ourselves that I want to pass on to you. The process of transformation is unlimited as we allow ourselves to unfold.

Stuart Alpert
Hartford, CT. September, 2005

Acknowledgements
for the Revised Edition

Acknowledgements for the Revised Edition

WHEN I WROTE THE ORIGINAL ACKNOWLEDGEMENTS BACK IN 1991, I considered them an integral part of the book. I felt that they spoke to the feeling of heart and connection that is at the center of Body-Centered Gestalt Therapy. The list has grown. In fourteen years many new people have entered my life and contributed to who I am today. I do want to thank my eight partners, two associates, and twenty Independent Practitioners who make up Hartford Family Institute. Although conflict is a part of any group, we have grown to be an alive and caring group of individual thinkers and practitioners.

I would also like to acknowledge all of the people in my New York City Group. I appreciate your eagerness to grow and how all of you have also become a part of my life.

Especially important to my development in the past fourteen years has been my practice of mindfulness that has been enhanced by Thich Nhat Hahn, and my learning and practice of Chi Lel Qi Qong with Luke and Frank Chan. I want to thank all of the healers, teachers, and authors that have been a part of my journey during the past fourteen years. Pat Sigel: Your thoughtful and caring editing of the revised manuscript was important in its clarity and organization. It was a pleasure working with you. Don Pogue: Thank you for your suggestions about the manuscript and all of the typo and spelling errors that you picked up on.

Acknowledgements from the First Edition

My acknowledgments speak to those who have touched me in some special way regarding the writing of this book. At times, the acknowledgments are for the heart and support that I received from my friends and colleagues, which allowed this book to come together. At other times, they are for the thoughtful and caring teachings that have come my way. If I fully give into the desire to make room for all the people who have touched my life and give them all the room that is their due that in itself would be a book. I know all of you have brought stimulation, meaning, love, and support to my life. I have absorbed what you have meant to me so that you reside inside me. At times I can hear your teachings, the way you turned a phrase, a certain intonation that was yours that is now a part me. I can recall your way of thinking, your support for me in who I was and who I have become.

First and foremost to Naomi Lubin-Alpert, my partner in life, who is also a co-founder and partner of Hartford Family Institute and a co-developer of Body-Centered Gestalt Psychotherapy. You are the person who has been the major editor and emotional support for my writing this book. You are the most important person in my life. Your love and faith in me is beyond my ability to measure. It has carried me through many rough times and also added to the beauty of the sweet times. The way that we have balanced our personal and professional lives together feels amazing. We are certainly never bored.

Our early years together of endlessly attempting to find the similarities and differences between Bioenergetics and Gestalt Therapy became the cornerstone of Body-Centered Gestalt Therapy. As we grew, so did the therapy. Much of what I have written we have worked out together. For all the various reasons that we have discussed, I happen to be the one who has written the book. The editing you have done is invaluable and is a testimony to how we have decided to live our lives. Thank you for being able to share with me how much you didn't like the early, unformed parts of the manuscript. Knowing that I would feel terrible, you decided that the truth was more important than my temporary hurt, frustration, and disappointment.

We love, learn, travel, and grow together. You have always brought your honesty, courage and deep desire for life to our relationship. And we have both needed all of it as we have sought to find all the ways that we have brought our unresolved childhood issues to our relationship. We have devoted ourselves to breaking all the negative fusion with one another, so that we can seek out greater aliveness. It has been, and continues to be, quite a trip. I love you.

To Dori Gatter: We are family and ground for one another. You inspire me to be more of myself as you become more of yourself.

To Arlene Alpert: In grammar school when I had an essay or book report to write I always asked you to give me a first sentence to start me on my way. At times you responded quickly to my asking for help. At other times you weren't so forthcoming. My asking would then reach a feverish pitch, where pleading and whining felt like my only alternative. It felt like the laws of inertia had been developed particularly for my first sentence dilemma. Whether you started me on my way immediately or finally gave into my panicked entreaties, you always helped me. As I began this book those memories of my first sentences with you created a warm feeling that helped me on my way.

To Joan Reuter: I honor and value our relationship. As children, our relationship was a refuge from all the family craziness. We found a precious way to care and support one another.

To all the excellent and caring teachers that I have had and the professional and personal bonding which took place with you: I want to honor all of you and let you know how important you have been in my life. To Virginia Satir: Thank you for being the person to introduce me to love and congruence. To Alexander Lowen: for your pointing me toward my body and the ground, both with your therapy and teachings. To Carl Kirsch: You set a fire under me with your excitement for learning and your special way of seeing and working with energy. To Stanley Keleman: You taught me about process, containment, and how to start giving up pushing myself. To Marilyn Rosannes Berett: You introduced me to the concept of supports, at times directly, and at other times through my discussions with Naomi. To Steve Gallegos: You guided me on the path of spirit, helped me find my connection to the earth, showed me more about the use of imagery, and introduced me to "the chakra animals." To Berniece Falling Leaves: You are a never ending source of information, magic and excitement.

To Brent Harold and Andrew Mason: Whether I was excited or depressed about my writings, I always felt your support, caring, and encouragement. The memory of the time I cursed the two of you because you supported me through a difficult time always produces a warm smile.

To Sherry Osadchey and Dina Fisher: Thank you for your permission to use material from your personal journals and the emotional support that came with the permission.

To mention my partners, associates, and secretaries at Hartford Family Institute in a sentence does not do justice to a group of people that greatly add depth, color, humor, support, caring, and intellectual stimulation to my life. So thank you, Karen Caffrey, Dori Gatter, Sylvia Gingras-Baker, Peggy Guay, David Gilroy, Donna Baker-Gilroy, Sherry Osadchey, Gail Rosenfeld, Denise Soucie, Eileen Stecker, Terry Wolfe, and Leona May Price. I feel your place in my life very deeply.

When I finally had the courage to give a copy of what I considered to be a fairly polished draft of the original manuscript to someone, I hoped that you would read it, Elizabeth. When you read it and were enthusiastic about the content and then offered me your editorial comments, I was so excited I could have screamed. If I remember correctly, I did. Almost immediately, I wondered if you had lost your mind because you enjoyed what I had written. I cherish that meeting with you and the help you have given to me about the use of language. So thank you, Elizabeth Kincaid-Ehlers.

To all of the HFI Independent Practitioners: We continue to challenge ourselves so that we can come together and still hold our separateness. I commend all of our creativity and individual power.

To Diane DeArmond, Nancy Swafford, and Pennie Cohn: Thank you for your reading and the suggestions you made about the chapter on faith. That was a wonderful weekend you spent together with Naomi and me, you with your writings about Daniel and Maggie, and me with my musings about faith.

To Garth and Sam Matthes: Your comments about an early draft of Chapter One also helped me on my way. Perhaps more important for me is the connection that we have, in heart and humor and in sharing our lives together. Sam, your creativity is an inspiration for mine.

To all the students and friends in the Kansas City training program: I look forward to coming each time and find your openness and eagerness to learn a rich and exciting part of my life. I also feel very cared about and feel that our relationships that have grown over the years are truly nurturing. Arriving in Kansas City feels like I'm home, even though I have just left home.

To Helmut Pauls: Thank you for sharing your thoughts about destructiveness and suicide with me. Your ideas were alive in me as I wrote about children bonding with their parents in the energy of hate and death. To all the other members of the training program in Germany: After twenty-one years of being with you, I no longer come to Germany. I still value our connections and hold all of you in my heart.

I have a special thank you for all the students in the Hartford Training Program. Being a part of your desire to grow professionally and personally is exciting and is a constant stimulation for my own growth. Working with you is a very special part of each week. As in most intimate relationships, you are more likely to see me in all of the various ways that I can feel and be in the world. I appreciate your feedback through the years.

My own personal therapy has been an important part of my life. It has helped me discover and come to terms with much of the darkness that resides inside of me. It has enabled me to know and open to the world in a way that is still expanding. To my first therapist, Arne Welhaven: You were a gentle support when I didn't realize how very frightened I was. You guided me toward my body and fully accepted all the ways that I was not yet a man. To Alan Lopez: You added your microsurgery ways and helped me gain more support for each moment of my existence. To Rozanne Hauser: When you said to me after our first session that I had come to you to learn more about bonding, I reserved judgment. As it has turned out, you couldn't have been more correct about your sense of what I needed. I appreciate how you have met all the facets of who I am, both my light and my darkness, so I could continue on my path toward enlightenment. You still continue to be with me through this revision.

To all my clients: Your wanting more of your life brings courage to my life. As you choose to live the ordinary with integrity and make room for the extraordinary, you are constant reminders to me about my faith in process. A special thank you to all the clients and students I have included in this book. My hope for you is that, as you read about yourself, it will add to your personal growth and under-standing.

The original edition of this book was published by Ablex Publishers in a series entitled "The "Frontiers of Psychotherapy." Ed Tick was the editor of that series and along with his wife, Kate Dahlstedt, edited the original manuscript. Your careful and caring reading has been an important part of polishing the rough edges. Your appreciation and caring for what I had written helped me see the end of the tunnel. A special thank you for helping me release an infinite number of commas into the universe for other people to use.

The Human Condition

THERE ARE MANY TIMES WHEN WE ACT IN WAYS that are not necessarily in accordance with what we want for ourselves. For example, we long for love and intimacy, yet we often withdraw from it. We want to feel full and satisfied, yet we often feel empty and alienated. We want a life full of meaning. Yet, no matter what we do or how busy we may be, we can be filled with an underlying feeling of meaninglessness. We may be unable to clearly understand why we are feeling meaninglessness, unending need, sadness, hurt, anger, and fear. We may either live in denial of these feelings or live as if we can't remove ourselves from the suffering that being stuck in these feelings causes us. We learn to cope with them the best way that we know how, but we may never find a satisfying resolution. We want a life full of pleasure, yet we often find ourselves stuck in various forms and shades of dark, unknown, and uncomfortable feelings. We want to be connected to our bodies, to the earth, and to the natural order of things, yet we abuse our bodies and the planet we live on.

These are the conditions in which we find ourselves. In fact, we may be confronted with these realities on a daily basis. Whether we meet them actively or passively, they stand in the way of our reaching a place of beauty, harmony, joy, compassion and loving-kindness. Despite these dilemmas, we find the courage to survive. We find ways of living the heroic in the ordinary and the ordinary in the heroic. Our human spirit finds a way of helping us make a life for ourselves that possesses degrees of pleasure, power, and caring.

LONGING FOR ENLIGHTENMENT

All I want is all out
no holds barred
self commitment.
Less thinking
more action
A stronger connection
between head and heart.
To be.
All I want is action without the
tediousness of
    planning
        thinking
            fearfulness
A reaching without
    wondering
        pondering
            belaboring consequences.
Why do I hold back

FANTASY

Perhaps if I place a bellows
    to my ear
I can blow away all the
unnecessary thinking
And with the fresh breeze
    feel
        free...

WHAT TO DO UNTIL ENLIGHTENMENT:

Enjoy a sunset
Cry when you're sad
Feel your anger when you're angry
Get to know your negativity and don't treat it like it's bad
Move when you're happy
Forgive yourself for not being perfect, then recognize that you are
Respect the earth
Know that pain is a part of life. Suffering is optional[1]
Learn to breathe into the feeling of craziness
Get to know your defenses and make friends with them
Start to live like everything about you makes sense
Appreciate that moving slowly is as useful as moving fast
Understand that feelings are neither good nor bad
Honor your life
Sing, and if you don't know any words, improvise
Do nothing at all or anything you want to do
When you're lonely, tell someone
Reach out to someone and tell them when you need
          mothering or fathering
Appreciate your capacity to grow and change
Appreciate your capacity to remain stuck
Look up at an evening full of stars and wonder
Then, honor your life again—Enjoy the way.

As we move along our life's journey I'm reminded of the following:

A Navajo Night Way Chant

As you wander, beauty is before you
As you wander, beauty is behind you
As you wander, beauty is above you
As you wander, beauty is below you
As you wander.

A note about remaining balanced:

Much of this book is about a human condition in which all parents can kill the aliveness of their children. It is not my intent to blame parents. Since all parents were children, they too were the victims of this condition, as were their parents. Thus I invite all parents who read this book to see themselves as the children we are talking about; for only by living this process from the child's point of view can we unlock the trapped life within us and become better parents to ourselves and to our children. **Therefore, as we wander let there be no blame.**

What To Do Until
Enlightenment

CHAPTER ONE

The Transformational Process: Accepting Our Humanness

WE* ARE ALL PART OF WHAT IT MEANS TO BE HUMAN. I AM NOT defining the various forms of the human condition as sick or pathological. Rather, I want to honor our humanness and come to a deeper understanding and appreciation of all the forms that our humanness can take given the multitude of combinations of supportive and abusive energies that we have internalized throughout our childhoods.

My hope is that in reading this book we will develop a heightened awareness of how we have learned to cope with our inner life, our relationships, and the world. With this heightened awareness we can deepen our understanding of how personal transformation occurs, thereby supporting and nurturing our growth. Perhaps this book will be like a good therapy session where there is an immediate impact. To this end, what if after each paragraph, or page or section, you stop and let yourself become aware of what you are experiencing in your body? *Breathe!* Allow yourself to know if you are reading this book simply collecting information, or if you are allowing yourself to be touched beyond thought and intellect. This is also what I want for myself. The best of what I write comes from my heart and spirit, not merely from my intellect. When I allow for this connection, it initiates personal transformation.

*Throughout the book I use the pronouns we and our. This is because I include myself in all that I write.

My intent regarding the transformational process is to clarify:

- **how emotional, energetic, spiritual, and physical change takes place**
- **how we can grow to become fuller and more alive**
- **how to allow for self expression that is simple, direct, and full-bodied**
- **how listening to our body provides us with the information that we need to keep ourselves balanced**
- **that all unresolved emotional trauma can manifest itself as physical pain and illness**
- **how understanding the roots of our mental critics (our victimizers) helps us to develop compassion for whatever it is that we are feeling**
- **how to soften the rigid need for control so that we can become more relaxed and flowing**
- **how to be receptive to messages from our own deep sense of knowing and wisdom**
- **how to follow our life force to deepen our creativity and life's meaning, rather than living from old stereotypic forms that limit aliveness and creativity**

GIVING UP THE ILLUSION OF CONTROL

I believe that from conception through our formative years, we internalize the family and societal energies to which we have been exposed. Understanding this, we can begin to understand the transformational process. Revisiting my own childhood illustrates how we absorb and bond with the energies from our families and from society. We are definitely products of those childhood years.

My professional training as a therapist began when I was four years old. This training started as I took on the role of arbiter to stand between my parents during their constant arguments. As a lightning rod, I would act to draw their attention to me, away from whatever they were arguing about. Humor was one of the ways that I achieved my mission. Because of this, later in life my humor was much more than an expression of pleasure. It was also a way that I dealt with intense emotional situations.

I developed other ways of separating my parents. When my mother felt hurt because of my father's violent verbal explosions, I would go to her with love and understanding for her pain. I soothed my mother's contempt for my father by becoming her "good boy" and dutiful son. When my father exploded and then acted as if nothing had happened, I alternated between attempting to get close to him so that he would calm down and keeping my distance when I felt that his energy was too dangerous. I learned never to reach toward my father for anything that I needed. All of these ways of being, these "roles," helped me later in life to have radar-like sensitivity to other people's moods and needs.

These early experiences, which were continually reinforced, lent themselves to certain careers. I could have become a comedian, labor negotiator, diplomat, lawyer, or a psychotherapist. Ultimately, I chose to become a psychotherapist. What pushed me in this direction was my attempt to understand the depths of why people feel and behave the way they do. I felt that if I understood enough, I could mend my own and my family's wounds.

After college I decided, at first, to go to law school. I was accepted but postponed my admission for a year in order to earn enough money to pursue my law degree. During that year I visited a cousin of mine who was a social worker at a community center. My visit with him opened me to two realizations. The first was that I wasn't aggressive enough to be a successful trial lawyer. Being a "good boy" and dutiful son had blunted my assertiveness. The second, as I stated above, was that I felt drawn to wanting to be a psychologist and practice psychotherapy so that I could understand more about human behavior. All of the reasoning that went into my career choice was part of a complex decision that had to do with the energies of abuse and support that I had absorbed growing up. Although I thought about my decisions in a conscious and rational way, they were engrained in my emotional/body structure, rather than in my conscious and rational mind.

At the same time that I took on my childhood role as arbiter and lightning rod, I was not supposed to know what was really going on between my parents. I was dealing with something I wasn't supposed to understand nor see clearly. This crazy paradox caused a layer of blankness and denial in my perception and intellect so that I believed that I wasn't intelligent. I was unsure that I would be successful enough in school to continue and be able to graduate with a Doctorate in Psychology. I graduated as a social worker in 1963, then became one of the first social workers practicing as a psychotherapist in Connecticut and have been practicing ever since. After forty years in practice I received my Doctorate in Psychology in May, 2002. The decision to return to school after all those years was for my own personal satisfaction, learning, and completion of an old dream.

It seemed natural that my first job after graduate school was working as a therapist with emotionally disturbed children and their families in residential treatment. I felt that I instinctively knew the territory. My supervisors gave me the highest evaluations. What they didn't know is that I felt safer working with children than with adults. I felt frightened of grown-ups, especially men. At that time I didn't feel that there was anything that I could do about my fear. My way of dealing with fear during those early years as a therapist was to act brave, use my sensitivity to understand people's feelings, and at the same time, be distant and intellectual. I could draw people out, stay in control, and deny that my fear existed. This was my protection. I possessed a combination of sensitivity and woodenness. It was a long and hard road for me to feel alive and be spontaneous.

My need to be in control had its roots in how I had learned to become my own family's therapist. I had learned to be an expert at listening to other people's emotions and repressing my own. I had learned to remain in control of my emotions and to hold my body rigidly to cover up how collapsed I felt in order to cope with the violence and craziness that surrounded me. Without this adaptation, I would have lived in constant terror. I was supposed to believe that I could alter the violence and the craziness in my family. This was also a child's magical thinking that I was all powerful. In reality, I was helpless to change how my parents related and felt toward one another, or how they treated my sisters and me. I was simply a part of the family drama.

Looking back, when I first worked as a therapist, I would have been considered a workaholic. I would see 40 or 50 clients each week. I felt most alive when I was working. As I began my journey through my unfinished childhood issues and grew emotionally, I slowly worked less and developed more outside interests. Each time I gave up a piece of my compulsivity and resistance, I had to deal with an underlying layer of suffering, depression, and craziness that had always been with me. I had learned to effectively cover up these feelings with my "dedicated schedule." I also began to realize how much I was like my parents, while at the same time defending against being like them.

As I gained therapeutic experience, I realized that denying my helplessness by trying to be in control was based on illusion. In reality, there were times I was helpless to do anything more than express what I saw and how I felt in a clear, direct, and open manner. It was up to the client to consider or reject my efforts. It began to make more sense to recognize when I felt helpless and to learn to accept it. As I learned to accept my helplessness, in fact, as I began to accept all of my feelings, I felt more powerful and it was easier to work with adults as well as children. The process of acceptance freed up energies that had been employed in the service of denial and stuffing my feelings. I felt more in the world as I felt less of a need to deny and repress my emotions. In this process of giving up control, I began to replace control with an acceptance of my whole self that led to a feeling of power and self-possession.

After seven years of working in my first job at a residential treatment center, I began to work with children, adults, and couples in a variety of outpatient agencies. During that same time period I practiced as a consultant and psychotherapist in schools and in a teenage drop-in center. I also taught undergraduate students and lectured in graduate courses in psychotherapy. I began a part time private practice, where I focused both on marriage and family therapy and working with adults in individual psychotherapy.

During those years I started to learn how very frightened I actually was and about the basis of my fears. What had changed for me was that I was able to recognize that my fears were based on old childhood experiences that I was projecting onto present situations. I began to understand that there were many things that touched my childhood fears. In becoming aware that I was frightened and beginning to be larger than my fear I was able to start making decisions that were neither fear-driven nor meant to avoid my fear.

As I discovered the depth of my fear, I also began to feel more alive. I did not have to use so much energy denying my fear. **Living my fear with awareness had become the doorway to my life.** These early years of dealing with childhood issues helped me develop an "Equal Opportunity Fear." I was now no longer just afraid of grown-ups. I realized that my fear was actually about allowing for the feeling of aliveness to exist in my body. Learning to accept my body being alive and to share and express my aliveness has been a life-long journey.

For many years now I have worked as a therapist in private practice with adults and couples. I have also led training and therapy workshops for professional therapists and the general public as a part of my private practice. Since 1969, my work has been centered at Hartford Family Institute, which I co founded with Naomi Lubin-Alpert and George Rogers, III. Hartford Family Institute is a private, outpatient, mental health group and training institute in Body-Centered Gestalt Therapy. I am one of the co-developers of this therapy.

Although I feel very confident that I help the clients that come into therapy with me and that I have never done a workshop that hasn't turned out well, I still can feel frightened, especially at the beginning of a workshop. It now feels like vestigial fear, like the tail that was once there and is now only a protrusion of bone at our coccyx. This vestige presents itself as the voice of my own worst critic. Through this voice I can assault myself for being <u>only</u> sensitive and believing that I don't have any intellectual competence, reliving my role in my family dynamic. As I mentioned above, while my family encouraged my sensitivity, they discouraged my intellect by not wanting me to see the truth of what was going on. In this way, they encouraged perceptual blindness and denial, rather than perception based on reality. As a result, my mind became blank and fogged. At certain moments, which are becoming rarer with each passing year, I still carry pieces of that legacy of blankness and fogginess when I want to express myself clearly, especially in the face of someone questioning what I am saying from an energy of cynicism or contempt.

That's the bare bones and some of the sinew of my professional career. I am more successful and have more esteem from my peers, colleagues, and clients than I ever dreamed would be possible when I started out over 40 years ago. I have a waiting list of clients who want to see me and am sought after to lead workshops and training programs for therapists. Although much, much less, there are times when I still need to balance my sense of self-acceptance and self-possession with remnants of that old insecurity left over from my childhood.

Through the years I have criticized myself for not being a risk-taker. In truth, my life has been full of the risks that always lead me to the next step of my professional and personal growth. At those times, some deeper place of wisdom has guided me. A feeling from the depths of my being told me what I had to do, what my next step was to be. No matter how I tried to fight this feeling with arguments about potential disaster and my lack of readiness, I ended up giving up the illusion of control. Even without knowing how my life was going to turn out, giving up something that once felt secure and had grown stale, in order to remain fresh and alive, has always led me to the next step on my path. This is how transformation takes place. Like winter making room for spring and regeneration, we need to let go and make room for the budding of new growth.

Just this kind of opportunity awaited me when I had started to become known and valued within the larger residential treatment center community. As a result of this recognition, I felt that it was only a matter of time before I would advance in the field and become a director of an agency. But institutional work no longer touched my life and creativity. So, instead, I chose to follow my internal wisdom and start a private practice while working part time in social service agencies. I would never have known at the time that starting this practice with Naomi and two other partners would evolve into Hartford Family Institute.

Leaving the residential treatment center made room for me to continue to expand my vision of my professional cutting edge. Over the next few years, this choice led to continuing my professional training in family therapy, Satir's work with communication and families, and in Bioenergetic Analysis. Naomi and I began to discuss her training in Gestalt Therapy and mine in Bioenergetics. It was these early discussions that led to the development of Body-Centered Gestalt Therapy.

Often, we do not realize how our current experiences will enhance our life in the future. When I was at the residential treatment center, I had begun to do some teaching for the professional staff of the agency. I enjoyed teaching and leading workshops and training groups for other psychotherapists and this is what I began to do in addition to my seeing individuals, couples, and families in my clinical practice. The training groups that I led in the United States and Europe, in turn, produced the need for a text that would describe the Body-Centered Gestalt Therapy process and Naomi and I responded to that need by writing a self-published monograph entitled, RECLAIMING ALIVENESS: A MATTER OF HEART.

The thought of writing a book had been floating around inside me for some time. Given how I had come to understand my early childhood experiences, and with my then 27 years of experience as a therapist and trainer, I believed that I did have something important to share. There were moments that I seriously considered writing a book, although I always felt that my busy clinical schedule prevented me from writing.

Also, I never considered myself a writer. Imagining seeing my thoughts and ideas in print touched both my excitement and my old fears about my having limited intelligence. The fear of humiliation was like a low weather front gathering strength for the storm to come. Besides wanting to inform others, I also felt that writing a book would more clearly define who I was. Writing would help me take my next step into the world. Once my beliefs were published, it felt like there was no taking them back and that I would be giving up some old hiding place. Though there are many clinicians who dream of a book they might write, for most it remains at the dream stage and that was where I felt my interest in writing would remain. Even thinking about writing touched off my old victimizing voices. I believed those old voices would have a field day if I actually did begin. The following is a part of the story of what happened that made room for me to write.

In the early 1990's Naomi and I were invited to lead a series of training workshops for professional psychotherapists in New York City. I was born and raised in Brooklyn, New York, had completed some of my post graduate training in "The City," and believed that New York was the place where the most sophisticated therapists practiced. For me, this invitation meant that I had reached the height of my career. It was like taking "my show to Broadway." Naomi and I agreed to lead these workshops the following year.

As the time to lead the workshops drew nearer I began to feel that these workshops would feed my ego but otherwise leave me empty. I already had enough satisfying work that I was doing. After leading an introductory workshop for these therapists, I realized that they were simply human, like all the other therapists I had trained and that I did not need to inflate myself with a New York City identity. Even though I had learned to say no to other requests on my time, it felt like an uncharacteristic move for me to turn down what I had so treasured. Yet this is what Naomi and I did. We wrote to the therapists in New York and cancelled the workshops. We shared with them that it did not feel right to lead the workshops at this point. Our life forces seemed to be moving us in another direction. At the time, I didn't know what I was going to be doing. I just realized that leading these workshops did not feel right.

Along with Naomi, here was another risk that I decided to take. Taking the risk meant following my intuition and my body sense of where my life was and wasn't. It meant allowing aliveness and spirit to lead, rather than trying to control how life should be and always playing it safe.

Within about a month of this decision I suddenly realized that not leading the New York workshops had been the first step in making room for my writing this book. The next step came when I spontaneously decided to drastically reduce my practice in order to write. I was giving myself the time that I needed. I thought that between six months to one year would be enough time. I was stepping off into the unknown not knowing if would have any clients to work with in my practice when I returned It turned out to be more like eighteen months that I kept my reduced schedule.

During the eighteen months it took to write this book, I had to deal with many unexpected experiences that occurred because of the lack of structure in my life. I felt I had grown to be a fairly centered person prior to this time. I felt very powerful and open-hearted at times, and was deeply respected by my peers, clients, and trainees. Even with all of these "emotional credentials" and professional applause, the time spent writing became a continuation of my journey into my unfinished issues.

Internally, I felt held to the fire regarding how much I believed in what I was writing. I was asking myself the question: If I truly believe that every experience is here to help us take our next step toward enlightenment, then am I prepared to live in this way when the going gets tough? I was constantly telling clients, and other therapists, to understand the importance of supporting each and every moment of their lives. Did I really believe that we need to support and appreciate ourselves no matter what we experience in order to live each moment to its fullest?

Daily, I was being confronted with whether I would be able to support myself through the intense negative feelings that arose in me as my life became centered on writing. Throughout the process of writing this book I became aware that I needed to learn more about dealing with the unknown and the unformed. At times the unknown and unformed felt exciting and free. At other times the lack of structure opened up a level of horrible feelings and emotional abuse from childhood that I had previously found ways of resisting.

One particular day illustrates both polarities. I started out feeling calm, centered, and focused. By the end of the day I was feeling horrible; dark, agitated, and negative. At the end of this day I wrote the following entry in my journal.

"I have given up much of the usual form of my life. During this year I have often struggled with the feelings that emerge from my formlessness. Today, I came to my writing feeling good after yesterday's revision of Chapter Four. Naomi was reading and editing some work that I had just completed and Elizabeth (a colleague of mine) was reading some earlier material that I had written. The work was going well and I was getting the support that I needed. I felt light and expansive about continuing my writing this morning. My thoughts and words came easily to me.

"Then the computer wouldn't work. I spent an hour trying to figure out what had happened. I still can't make any sense of why the computer won't work. The point of all of this is that the frustration about the computer changed the calm and centered way I was feeling. Suddenly, I felt like I had walked into a storm of critical energy that I had not seen or expected to be there. I did recognize the symptoms from previous times; I felt agitated, my nose started to run, my eyes teared, and I starting to unmercifully pick on myself. I felt that everything I had ever written was stupid and meaningless. I believed that the way that I felt earlier in the day was an illusion and that my belief that I was writing something worthwhile was ridiculous. What had happened with the computer felt like it had pushed me into a totally different reality. I couldn't cope with the frustration of the computer not functioning. I had lost all perspective. I lived this morning as if it were a major "life and death" catastrophe. The feeling of catastrophe spread to everything that I was thinking and doing. I had reached the end of my support to keep writing with any equanimity and grace."

That's the way life is for all of us. **We move between feeling integrated and alive and then having to deal with the next difficult feeling that opens inside of us.** I have spent my career trying to understand how to help others develop a balance between dealing with their negative voices and negative energies that are a part of traveling the path toward enlightenment and being able to focus on their life and the world at large.

If I could have fully lived each moment with the computer as it unfolded during that day, totally accepting everything about myself and the world, I would have been in an enlightened state of consciousness. I would have been alive and at one with the universe. Love and acceptance for me and all those around me would have emanated from my body, my soul, the very center of my being. I would have felt empowered, connecting to the power, energy, and wisdom of the universe. All experiences would have been simply part of the flow of life. I would have been able to keep perspective and realize that everything is energy, that the only thing that changes is how the energy manifests itself. The incident with the computer would have been experienced as a blip in time. Therefore, I would not have felt the frustration and suffering that came from the computer event touching old childhood feelings of being a victim. The computer incident wouldn't have been the catalyst that would disconnect me from my center.

There have been times in my life that I have felt that kind of equanimity in the face of external difficulty. I have felt at one with my surroundings, centered and loving. At times like this I don't become uncentered because of any external difficulties that might arise. Many people I have known and have worked with also have times in their lives where they too feel a sense of oneness. At these times, all problems take on a different perspective. The actual circumstances behind the problems may not change. However, feelings about the circumstances change, because we are now living with the fullness of our heart and power. We are living in the moment. Therefore, we don't approach the situation in the same reactive way we might when we are off-center.

Living with the need for things to be different, and with feelings of powerlessness that they aren't, creates a different reactive set than when we are at one with ourselves and the world. At moments of oneness we feel totally in possession of our own lives and destinies. Unfortunately, for most of us, this state of enlightenment doesn't last. We might worry our way out of the feeling of oneness by wondering how long it will last. Or without our knowing why, like what happened to me with the computer, we feel something shift in us, returning us to an old, familiar way of feeling and living in the world.

Each time I come to a centered, more enlightened place, I carry something back with me to the less settled reality of my everyday existence. I carry back some piece of understanding that has been transformed into emotional and embodied knowledge. It is like reclaiming a piece of ancient wisdom. Because of what I have brought back, I feel a little bit more balanced and in harmony even during my difficult times. This makes my life easier to deal with and I feel more committed to supporting myself in each moment of my existence. The more committed I am to support each moment, no matter what I may be feeling, the more I am not being dominated by the assaultive energies from my childhood and the more conscious and enlightened I feel.

I have come to realize that giving up attempting to control what I feel has always led to the next place of aliveness and embodiment. However, giving up is easier said then done. It is one thing to say we need to accept everything about ourselves and not get caught up in attempting to defend our old emotional structures. We might pay lip service to the idea of relinquishing our egos and giving in to the flow of life rather than attempting to control what we feel at any given moment. All spiritual traditions contain some version of surrendering the ego to higher powers. It is another thing altogether to put this into practice.

I had often said to myself and to my clients that we had to give up "trying" and fully accept what we considered to be our weaknesses or our faults. Long ago I thought that I recognized the importance of breathing mindfully in order to take fuller responsibility for who we are and how we live in the world so that we can build a base for living in the moment. I saw how our current feelings and attitudes are based on old childhood learnings that are stored in our body that are now outdated. I understood that, if we didn't interfere with any of our feelings and fully accepted ourselves, we would be living "in the moment," without our negativity overpowering us. I told myself and my clients that all the answers we needed about life were inside us, and that, if we allowed our deeper place of wisdom to emerge, we would feel stronger, clearer, more open-hearted, and be able to have more fulfilling relationships. And finally, I was increasingly feeling that there was a universal consciousness that we could all tap into if only we gave up trying. All of this has felt wonderful and worthwhile to pursue when I was connected to these views. However, I needed to find a way of dealing with myself and my clients when I felt disconnected from this reality and this way of living and instead, was dealing with the assault energy that had opened in my own body.

Even knowing that the total acceptance of who we are in the present can open us to a deeper personal power and allow us to feel more alive and complete does not necessarily change how we feel or how we live. Like many things that we feel are good for us, there can be a force that keeps us away from what we need to do for ourselves. What helped me through the times when I was disconnected from the power of letting go was my sense that the disconnection was my spirit's way of leading me back to the next piece of "unfinished business" that I needed to understand. I felt that, in this way, my spirit was showing me the next step along the path of enlightenment.

SPIRIT'S PLACE IN OUR LIFE: LOSING AND FINDING THE JEWEL WITHIN

What I mean by *spirit* is that part of us that is all-knowing; the force in us that knows how to live in balance and harmony in ourselves and is part of the universal spirit. It is also the part that births and "grows" us. Our spirit helps us move in the direction of being more fully who we are and who we can become.

All living things have a life force, and our life force provides us with our connection to all human, animal, and plant life, and also our connection to a universal energy. I use the words *spirit* and *life force* synonymously. Our spirit is connected to a universal knowledge, a Higher Power, a center that is connected to all; and it is constantly providing experiences and situations for us to deal with, and to learn from, that will return us to enlightenment. Our spirit helping us return to enlightenment means that we were once enlightened. I believe we are born in an enlightened state as spiritual beings. As children, we are not consciously aware of this, nor do we have the cognitive skills to organize our thoughts and verbal expression to explain this state of being. However, as children, our spontaneity and our wise, innocent voice is the indication that we live directly from our spirit, directly from our life force.

If the grown-ups in our lives are caring, they will be in awe of the wisdom that emerges from us. They will nurture the depth of our knowing that is beyond our years. Their own hearts and spirits will be touched by ours and they will met us in oneness. Our aliveness and our spirit will be welcomed into the world.

Early in our life, before we were met with abusive, victimizing, energies, nothing stood between our spirit and its expression. We were fully open to ourselves and to others. In the process of our growing up, to varying degrees we were tamed like wild horses might be tamed and broken. Although we need to be brought into some form of acculturation, this does not have do be done with the emotional or physical whip, threats of or actual abandonment, humiliation and contempt, over-protectiveness or threats to our very existence. Like a blanket covering a precious jewel, our life force and our connection to spirit is covered with a defensive structure that we unconsciously created to survive the threats to us as alive and vibrant beings. Although operating on our behalf, for some of us our spirit had to go far away in order to help us survive our parents' victimizing energies. Deeply encoded within us, our spirit contains these programs for survival.

We are born that precious jewel, pure of spirit, and wind up as adult psychological beings not knowing we are jewels. This does not mean that as adults we are devoid of spirit. Depending on how deeply we were abused, we may remain out of touch with our spirit. In fact, if we were abused as children for being "too spirited," we may grow up doubting spirit exists. This becomes our safe place. Hidden, though still active, our spirit helps us adapt and survive the abuse and the acculturation process.

We learn to adapt for love, for approval, for safety, for nurturance. The adaptations become habitual as we develop ways of avoiding emotional and/or physical abuse. Our adaptations are ways that we learn to modify the direct feeling and expression of our spirit. The way that we adapt becomes our personality, our character structure, our way of being with ourselves and being in the world. We learn to identify ourselves with our adaptations rather than with our life force because of how ingrained and safe the adaptations have become.

When we lived directly from spirit as children, our light touched the defensive structure and the darkness that separated our parents' connection to their spirits. This took place because the negative energies that were stored in their bodies from their childhoods were touched by the life that was in our bodies.

For us the connection with spirit breaks when being one with spirit brought an intensity of assault that brought us to the edge of death. Why else would our spirit have to go so far away? As if hiding in the jungle or among the stars, our spirit is still sending us encoded messages and guiding our path so that we may return to it some day and be more embodied and alive.

As we gain the power and consciousness to understand that how we feel and express ourselves as adults is based on ways of being that were adaptations we learned in childhood, we become more aware of how spirit has been and still is operating to help us return to a connection with it. Spirit shows us the path through all the issues of our adaptive personality that stand in the way of our

complete awakening. Every way we react, every dream, every inter-
action, involves a message from spirit. The path toward
enlightenment is there for all to walk. All that is necessary for us to
be on the path is simply an awareness of it. Then, as we live every
moment of our lives with ever increasing awareness, we move along
the path.

What do we do until enlightenment? We still have to live and
breathe the air of our everyday existence with all its suffering, difficulties, and frustrations. We still need to cope with all of our feelings
of vulnerability, need, loss, anger, and fear, and hope to find some
peace and satisfaction as we travel through our lives. Unfortunately,
most of us are not taught how to support our feelings of joy, fear,
anger, loss, need, vulnerability, or for that matter, our deep feelings
of pleasure and sexuality. We either become impulsive and act out
these feelings or become compulsive in our suppression or repression of them. When we are impulsive or compulsive we move away
from a more direct experience of aliveness. Impulsivity can lead to
various addictions, compulsivity to depression. We become alienated from our aliveness with the result that life feels meaningless.
To add insult to injury, we have been taught to victimize ourselves
for not feeling more alive and being able to develop a life that has
meaning. For the most part, we are unaware that we are victimizing
ourselves and that it is the assaults and their impact, not the feelings
themselves that cause the distress that we feel in our lives.

A personal example of this is that my being the mediator, the
sensitive listener, in my family meant that I learned to disregard
my sadness and my protest and anger in the face of what was going
on between my parents, as well as how they were treating me. I
learned not to protest what was abusive — what didn't feel harmonious and balanced. I learned to hide my sadness. In effect, I found
the place in my family where I could survive with the greatest degree
of body integrity. For me it was in being the "good boy" and dutiful
son who was not supposed to feel sad, angry, negative, and upset. I
learned to appear loving and compassionate. Yet because of my role
of understanding, part of that love and compassion was an act, it

didn't come from my heart. It came from learning how to survive in the war zone between my parents and the various assaultive energies that were directed toward me.

Underneath my role layer I was sad and angry. I developed an underlying attitude of withholding — a form of hidden spite and revenge. The more that I was split off from being able to acknowledge and support these deeper feelings, the more these various forms of anger and sadness kept me split off from the deeper connection to myself. I came to understand in my own therapy that to feel these deeper emotions was to accept how deeply impacted I was by the assaultive energies that were my daily emotional and energetic diet as a boy. I needed to believe that I was above the fray. Not to live in this way would have been too overwhelming for me to bear.

I also believed that if I experienced sadness and anger I had failed. I learned that this sense of failure, this turning away from my anger, spite, revenge, and sadness and need to always be attentive and caring, was created by my spirit helping me organize myself against my parent's abuse and the resultant pain. My spirit was helping me find the crack in the emotional universe of my family were I could survive.

I absorbed my family's victimizing energies into my body where they produced my belief system. The belief system was that I needed to be distant from myself and my own aliveness in order to survive. Learning to act out the role of caring when actually I felt sad or angry not only separated me from myself, but in so doing, I withheld myself from others. Being alienated from my authentic self I was not present for connections with others.

As I have come to understand as an adult, it was never all of the feelings that I had to hide from myself that were my problem. Rather, it was the feelings that I had absorbed from the assault energy in my childhood, and as a result of these energies, the beliefs that I had developed that created the anguish and suffering that I often felt in my life. Through therapy, I learned my spirit's code and in turn, the way back home to myself.

Through my "working on myself," my postgraduate training, and working with my clients, I learned how we all have come to the point of being unable to listen to our spirit, where we need to hold onto a less alive and less vibrant self. I have learned how we all have built emotional and body structures that interfere with the way in which we live and feel. These structures also impact the way that we understand the world and relate to it. As an example, as I have faithfully continued to live my own process, I have become more connected to nature and to all living things. Having been born and raised in a large city, without being guided into a connection with the earth and with all living things, it was not until later in life that I felt the importance of a connection to nature in supporting my own and my clients' growth. Nature was outside of me, rather than my feeling a direct participation in all that was alive.

Feeling my connection to nature has helped me experience the way my spirit, my life force, is a part of all that is alive. Nature is in us and we are in nature. This is our direct link with God. I have come to understand how our spirit helps us form in whatever manner is open to us in order to survive and guide us toward the magic that is life. When we allow for the connection to the natural world we are living in a state of wonder, awe, and grace.

Having the ability to be connected to our spirit and to the universal, harmonious life force is truly incredible. Like a shaman, shape-shifting into different life forms, if we work at clearing out the old abusive energies from our system, we reform into a more sensitive being who feels a deeper connection to our own life force, to spirit, and to the world at large. When we continue to work through our adaptive body structure, we learn to shift our beliefs, our emotional reactions, and the very form of our body. As with the shaman's ability to learn from nature and shift from human form to animal form, we can learn about the magic of life and spirit. We can feel the truth of our connection to nature and to all of life and can learn to harness the power and energy of life and spirit.

ALIENATION: LIVING IN OPPOSITION TO OUR SPIRIT AND TO NATURE

There is a split in our culture regarding our connection to the essence of spirit as it is manifested in nature. There are those among us whose spiritual and emotional connection have been damaged. The damage is manifested in only wanting to use nature and tame it, severing themselves and us from the magic of life and the earth that supports all of us emotionally, energetically, and spiritually. When our connection to nature has been severed, we are not the earth's steward. We live removed from the spirit and magic of the interconnectedness of all of life. The depth of meaning in this connection removes depth and meaning from our lives. This perpetuates the cycle of living severed from the connection to our own spirit and then being moved further away from consciousness into unconsciousness.

Just as we may try to get rid of parts of ourselves in ways that are ultimately self-destructive, when we don't honor our connection to the spirit of the earth we treat it in violent ways that are equally self-destructive. When government and business treats nature as only an enhancement to profits, rather than something that is a profit to our spirit and our soul, the earth itself is being victimized. Our sensitivity and spirit is also assaulted by this. For example, we need the food, clean air, and water, as well as the beauty, the sense of wonder and belonging that the earth can provide for us — yet so often we treat our planet in uncaring and unthinking ways. **Through pollution, we kill the source of what keeps us alive.** We need to come to the center of the interdependence between ourselves and our environment. Serge King, in *Kahuna Healing*,[1] states that for a person " to heal him/her self is to heal the world, and to heal the world is to heal him/her self. This is not a loss of individuality, but an understanding that individuality itself is a relationship with the environment."

To the degree that we are alienated from ourselves, we are alienated from everything around us. Conversely, to the degree we are alienated from our environment, we are also alienated from our bodies, our emotions, and our spirit.

HOW DO WE GET THERE? A ROAD MAP

In this chapter I have begun to present myself and some of my beliefs. At its beginning I listed what I wanted to elucidate about the transformational process. As the book unfolds I intend to do this by:

1) describing and deepening our understanding of how we are all survivors of abuse;

2) exploring how the bonding process is the vehicle for the child's internalizing abuse;

3) looking at how all abuse turns us against our own life force and stops us from being more open to ourselves;

4) presenting new ways of understanding and appreciating our defenses as supports, and understanding how at the same time, our defenses create much of the chronic suffering, discomfort, and frustration that we live with;

5) exploring and honoring how our spirit, our life force, perfectly guides us through our lives;

6) discussing and illustrating how it is the acceptance of who we are in every moment of our lives, not the conscious attempt to give up ego, moves us toward meaning and the awakening of our consciousness;

7) examining how we have become increasingly bonded with technology, rather than with human values and thereby, are moving away from being in touch with our natural biological and planetary rhythms;

8) investigating the connection between our emotional/physical processes and the physical world around us;

9) and finally, presenting the importance of absorbing and accumulating an appreciation and heart for ourselves.

FROM THE MUNDANE
TO THE TRANSFORMATIVE

In presenting the nine points that have just been listed, the book is meant to be a link between our mundane, everyday existence and our desire to transcend ourselves in order to discover and feel at home with our true nature. It is possible to link the ordinary nature of our lives with the core of harmony and balance that exists in each of us and in the entire universe.

It is through the exploration of the nine areas I have just presented that I will also demonstrate the uniqueness of Body-Centered Gestalt Therapy, for what I am writing about in the nine areas above is the theory and practice of this therapy. In Body-Centered Gestalt Therapy there is a way of understanding and living life so that a continual process of growth and change continually produces a shift toward living more fully in our bodies and in the embodied appreciation of our experiences. The shift is toward being more humane and effecting the way that we experience and treat ourselves, other people, and the planet.

While writing, there were times when I felt that simple discussions about life can become complicated, for at times the subject, like the living of life itself, is ethereal, difficult to pin down and put into neat categories. I knew that in writing about the nature of the human condition I was trying to describe something that was both simple and complex at the same time, like trying to describe the taste of chicken. In order to understand the multifaceted nature of how we have moved away from our aliveness and how we can return to it, we need to build a picture of the various aspects involved in this process. Like the children's game where we connect the numbered dots to eventually complete a picture, along the way we may not be clear how all the numbers connect to create the entire picture. I know that these times can produce a feeling that there is nothing to hold onto, nothing to anchor yourself to.

I'd like to suggest that this isn't a problem. As I have been saying throughout this chapter, our emotional life is full of unexpected experiences that at first we may want to reject. We go along feeling simple and clear, and then all of a sudden we can find ourselves mired in some confusing and obscure experience, not knowing how we got there. No matter how hard we try, it doesn't seem that we really can control and avoid certain feelings and experiences. At times like this it can be essential for our continued growth to not move prematurely toward closure. It can be important to allow our mind and body to remain open for what may follow. I hope that this is the way that you will approach reading the rest of this book. Breathe and allow your experience to build on itself.

CHAPTER TWO

Our Perfect Spirit In an Imperfect World: Self-Acceptance Heals

AS WE BEGIN TO CONNECT THE DOTS, LET'S START WHEN WE came into the world. Since birth, we have had to make our way through an imperfect world. And we have done so. We have survived everything that we have needed to, in order to be here in our adult bodies and personalities. Now we need to accept and have heart for who we *have* become in order to grow into who we *can* become. I'm talking about acceptance and heart that can radiate through our bodies, not an acceptance that is intellectual and hard, which justifies the way that we are and how we live. We need acceptance that is warm and alive, that can melt our chronic muscle tension and provide us with a greater sense of aliveness and clarity. Self-acceptance, appreciation, and compassion allow us to balance those adult personality characteristics that were born from our experiences as children and then trapped within our inner child and frozen in time along with the delight, innocence, and spontaneity of the child we were before we were met with abusive energies. Heartfelt acceptance and appreciation can allow us to reweave these characteristics into a more alive and satisfied adult self.[1]

Self-acceptance and feeling meaning in our lives go hand-in-hand. The more acceptance we have for ourselves, the more meaning we feel in our lives. We need to celebrate how we learned to exist and have tried to make a life that has meaning and happiness for ourselves in an imperfect world.

Building a deeper sense of self-acceptance will also lead us to a fuller understanding of how deeply affected we were by how we were treated as children. We are often unaware of what the impact of being unloved as children has on how unloved we feel as adults. Living unaware of the impact of our childhood, it is more automatic to blame our feeling unloved on our present lives than to deal with the impact of the non-loving aspects of our families and our society. This is especially true if we don't know how to do the work that is necessary to free our hearts.

Love warms us, validates our existence, allows us to feel our own hearts, power, creativity, spirit, and sexuality. Love supports our living fully in our bodies, without the tension we produce to cope with emotional and physical abuse. Love says 'yes' to feeling our emotions, dreams, and desires. The imperfect world of our family and society, where we are not unconditionally loved all the time and are emotionally and/or physically abused at other times, creates endless variations and complications as opposed to what love would have allowed for us.

HOW DARKNESS AFFECTS OUR LIVES: UNDERSTANDING OUR ABUSIVE ENERGIES

The world is full of emotional, physical, and mental distress. Child abuse, sexual assault, teenage suicide, general anxiety, depression, and the fear related to terrorism are increasing in alarming proportions. Our society is burdened with mounting problems of alcoholism, drugs, crime, and homelessness. Over-consumption and overpopulation are eradicating plant and animal species at an alarming rate. Where to dispose of our ever-increasing mountains of garbage, issues of acid rain, the pollution of streams, rivers, and oceans, the wreckage of our pristine wilderness areas through over-development and industrial overuse, and the health and environmental problems caused by the increasing hole in the ozone layer are all adding to the world's distress and its population being at risk. All of these anti-life aspects of our world cast a pall on our life and on our spirits. The pall becomes an assault to our aliveness and creates a darkness that we all live in, and have to cope with, in order to survive.

At times we are angry with the darkness and the people we hold responsible for what feels wrong with our society. We may rail against what seem to be the untouchable enemies behind the mounting crime statistics, emotional problems, terrorism, and environmental issues. Or we may feel compassion for the victims we don't personally know and the individual stories that they represent. At other times our lives are more personally touched by emotional abuse, crime, drugs, alcohol, death, and environmental problems.

Darkness and abuse are not just outside of us. We all contribute to the darkness. None of us grew up in perfect families and therefore, the darkness of the imperfect world around us also touches the darkness left over from our own childhoods that still lives within us. This inner darkness, that we now have to contend with, includes an endless variety of feelings that are the emotional baggage that remains with us from the negative, uncaring aspects of our childhood.

The darkness that is a part of the world we live in and our own unresolved emotional issues combine to profoundly affect our lives. We often feel so influenced and overwhelmed by the darkness that we numb ourselves to it and live in denial of its immediate impact. Having learned to numb ourselves, it is difficult to recognize and support our emotions, senses, and intuition. When we consider all of our personal and the social issues, we can be left feeling lost along with searching for meaning. Living peacefully and joyfully without denial may feel entirely beyond our ability and our comprehension.

PEACE AND HARMONY ARE POSSIBLE: OUR TRUTH IS IN OUR BODIES

Yet here we are. Whether we are conscious of these issues or not, we are living and dealing with them and doing our best to survive and cope with our everyday existence while searching for a life filled with meaning and happiness.

Our world can either feel devoid of meaning in a frantic, addictive search for peace and pleasure or hold out the prospect of superficial meaning in an accumulation of wealth and power.

Even if we believe that meaning will come to us by searching outside of ourselves, our spirit is still sending us messages about coming home to our bodies and spirit. It is constantly showing us the direction toward enlightenment. It is trying to help us realize that we are looking in the wrong direction, that it is the connection to ourselves through being at one with our spirit and the world around us that ultimately provides the happiness we are seeking.

What is essential to understand is that despite the darkness that exists, peace, calm, and joy are possibilities for everyone. Deciding to actively deal with our personal issues that are based on the unresolved trauma from our childhoods can bring us through the inner and outer energies of darkness that surrounds our aliveness. It would be like releasing a cloud of dark energy surrounding us, just like the dark cloud that follows Pig Pen in the Peanuts cartoon. Releasing our trauma brings us to a quiet, peaceful, and joyful center inside of us. It is possible to build our own personal power so we feel our feet on the ground, our connection to the earth, and a sense of oneness with all of life, both light and dark.

In order to build this kind of personal power we need to learn how to return to a deep sense of respect for our biological/emotional/energetic/spiritual processes. We can begin building this respect as we look at how, beginning at conception, our life force provides our cells with instructions to divide, individuate, and grow us. As both children and now as adults, if we are able to listen, free of our inner assaultive voices, our biology tells us when we're hungry or thirsty, tired or ready to engage the world and express ourselves. In every way we are being told how to remain in balance.

The spirit that is contained in our life force, along with our biology, leads us to create the exact emotional, energetic, and body organization that is necessary for us to survive the combination of abuse and support we received in our childhoods. This body organization allows us to experience the greatest degree of happiness with the least amount of pain. This organization enables us to feel as safe as is possible and to have as much of our aliveness and center as is available to us, rather than decompensate to an even lower level of functioning. Our body organization helps us maintain some form of balance and integrity between the adult that we are and the abused child who still resides within us. It is our spirit that allowed us to survive while having the maximum amount of emotional, physical, and energetic organization that was available to us. Our spirit is now also constantly highlighting the exact physical and emotional experiences we need to deal with to help us heal our inner abused child.

It is worth repeating that if we know how to listen deeply, our spirit, our body and our emotions are constantly moving us toward balance and the integration of our childlike qualities of playfulness, spontaneity, softness, vulnerability, and innocence with our adult qualities of strength, sexuality, intelligence, and awareness. We are being provided with all the necessary information and experiences to live fully conscious lives.

Perhaps our intent is the most important part of being able to listen and hear the messages. When we feel our heartfelt desire to want our spirit, body, and emotions to inform us, we can directly ask them to tell us what we need to do to bring them more directly into our lives. Our spirit will tell us. We can ask it to send us an image of what needs to happen next to feel more centered and alive. The more we talk to our spirit, our body, and emotions, the more we reinforce that channel of communication.

As we listen deeply to our spirit and become more conscious, this in turn, impacts the way that we live in the world. We experience that there is a universal energy, a universal consciousness, that we are all a part of. Our life force is a part of that universal energy, and we come to experience how everything that we do impacts that universal energy, that universal life force, and in turn, how we are affected by it. We become aware that we are living in a quantum field that holds all the information and wisdom that ever was.

As we become more sensitive to how everything in the universe is connected and interrelated, we can feel our common bond with all of humanity, and transcend our usual belief that we are totally separate beings. Feeling our common bond provides us with meaning, for who we are becomes a part of all that is alive.

As we deepen our experience of our common bond, we naturally feel more passionately about the injustice in the world. And as our consciousness expands, it provides us with the ability to stand against injustice without getting lost in the world's darkness. This is the path toward inner peace and toward each of us in our own unique way working to spread peace throughout the world. This is the path to living mindfully, the path toward living in the here and now.

Through the balancing of our bodies and our emotions we are paying more attention to our life force, our spirit, and allowing our spirit to continually point the way toward meaning, toward aliveness, toward helping us accept the light and the darkness that is in each one of us. We need to understand how to listen for the messages, and then learn to decipher them. However, so often, we fight our spirit by feeling angry or disgusted with ourselves for what we are feeling. We fight as if our spirit were the enemy rather than the essence of who we are, attempting to help us manifest into the best of who we can be.

THE ABUSE OF OUR CHILDHOODS DETERMINES WHO WE BECOME AS ADULTS

Whatever we are experiencing, whether it feels positive or negative, joyful or suffering, is determined by whether we are free of or filled with old abusive energies from our childhood. When we are filled with old abusive energies, we are like containers filled with a gas; it doesn't take much for us to overflow or explode if any more is added. When we are free of the old abusive energies, we don't have to avoid how we feel or overreact and explode. Current situations won't touch childhood memories and reactions that are a result of how we were traumatized. We won't have to revert to old forms of rigidity, collapse, or flaccidity as a way of organizing against abuse

when it is re-energized. Therefore, we won't feel victimized beyond the circumstances of the current situation. Free of childhood assaultive energies we are able to support sadness or anger, confusion or powerlessness, rather than act out to get away from these feelings.

Our spirit's job is to move us toward wholeness and, therefore, unfinished, unresolved trauma from childhood is always coming to the foreground to be worked through. Every relationship, every dream, every situation we encounter is the playing field for spirit's work.

Today, when we react to the world as a suffering, tortured victim instead of living in faith and in the light, we are re-enacting the negative bonding of our childhoods. If we are living in the light we have greater perspective of why we feel the way that we do. Living in the light and accepting the darkness in the world allows us to see the beauty as well as the horrors. When our childhood suffering and fears are touched, we can't relate to any current situation with compassion, dignity, and power. We become fixed in our old childhood reactions, stuck in overwhelming anger, despair and grief. When we are cleared of these childhood feelings, we find that in truth, we are not the impotent children we once were. Being able to do this is the life long commitment to the children inside of us and is exercise of true power.

The following personal experience actually occurred as I was writing this paragraph. It illustrates how we can either fight or accept what our spirit is attempting to show us. The path that acceptance provides, will lead us to openness and creativity.

As I sit here, having just written these last three pages, several different thoughts are rumbling around inside of me. I feel myself giving up the old struggle of trying to figure out what to write next. I am letting go of thinking about what I should write and returning to a feeling of oneness. When I feel at one with myself and the universe, what makes sense to write next flows gently and easily out of me. There is no barrier between thought, feeling, and expression. The experience of oneness allows meaning and form to develop out of the vastness of endless possibilities.

In order to come to a simple and clear place inside of me, there are times I need to live through the energy of struggle, pressure, and feelings of frustration and suffering. If these feelings are intense there can be a feeling of agonizing over what to write. This is the struggle produced by not letting go and being with my creative spirit. My struggle occurs as I fight against letting go and attempting to find my creativity all at the same time.

When I can't let go, it is because an old energy of abuse such as fear or the feelings of disintegration gets in the way. Yet, there is something positive for me to see in my struggle. This struggle exemplifies a common human dilemma: how can we support ourselves in the feeling of discomfort and suffering in order to learn why the discomfort and suffering are here, rather than fight with the feelings. If I can stop fighting my experience and learn what the feelings are here to teach me, I can return to the fertile void of endless possibilities.

Although I am writing about what may seem a rather benign situation compared to the horrors that are taking place in the world, the same is true no matter what we are experiencing and how traumatic and difficult a place we find ourselves in. Therefore, whether our response, as in the example above, is to inner emotional distress, a technological problem, or to traumatic local or world events, we need to look into ourselves to understand what the events have triggered in us so that we can return to inner stability and balance.

Fourteen years after what I have written above, we find ourselves in a very different situation in the world where we are dealing with events that began with the bombings of the World Trade Center and the Pentagon. Terrorism was brought to our country and has exploded throughout the world. Our government has invaded Afghanistan and Iraq and we are still at war. The world is at a dangerous crossroad. There are truly frightening life and death events that have more directly touched our lives than ever before.

It is as important today as it always has been, to understand how we can find inner peace and personal power in the midst of the chaos and violence that is in the world. Whether or not we are free of our abusive, childhood energies determines how we react to events and circumstances that are part of our political as well as our personal lives.

The path that re-unites us with a sense of inner balance, to the calm center in ourselves when we are dealing with inner turmoil, is the same path when we are dealing with negative, external local or world events. It is difficult to return to balance when our internal waters are turbulent and muddy. When we are free of our own negative energies we can more easily hold a sense of inner peace that can radiate out into the world.

Peace needs to begin inside of each individual. While living in inner peace we have the greatest possibility of affecting the world in the direction of peace. If we could zoom in to our energy patterns like a close-up camera lens, we could observe that radiating energy of inner peace does impact our relationships and the world in the direction of peace and understanding. The same is true if we are floundering in fear or filled with our own violence and negativity.

HOW TO BRING MEANING TO OUR LIVES: OUR SYMPTOMS ARE GIVING US A MESSAGE

As I have previously stated, we struggle with how to bring love, meaning, satisfaction, and beauty into our lives while we are still affected by the turbulent waters of unresolved childhood trauma; by the negative inner voices that are manifestations of this trauma. At the same time, we are dealing with our everyday struggles of living and the turmoil, trauma, and darkness that are in the world. When we have consciously or accidentally moved through this maze and feel peace and pleasure we then wrestle with how to stay connected to these positive experiences. In my psychotherapy practice, all my clients deal with these issues in one way or another.

How we go about finding balance as we juggle all of these issues is deeply important to our sense of well-being. For example, if we pressure ourselves to feel better than we do, the pressure becomes the way that we perpetuate traumatizing ourselves. This occurs because when we pressure ourselves to be different from the way that we are, the pressure in and of itself creates tension and exacerbates the problem that we are trying to resolve. It is like trying to have someone relax by screaming "Relax!" at them.

As the ever-present pressure to be different creates more tension, in turn, the pressure creates more suffering. Living unconsciously, we perpetuate suffering by remaining connected to the negative, fragmented, dissociative, and violent energies from our childhood and from society. By pressuring ourselves, we are fighting our own spirit and biology.

Our spirit continues to bring pressure to our attention so that we can deal with it in order to take the next step toward enlightenment. Although our spirit may go into hiding and our body develops forms to deal with the negativity, spirit doesn't give up the fight. In fact, the body and energetic forms that we develop are a part of our fight to stay whole in the face of our childhood abuse.

The more mindfully we live the more we are accepting each moment of our lives. Acceptance is the opposite of pressure and, therefore, with acceptance, we nurture our connection to spirit and our inner sense of peace and joy. It is in becoming increasingly conscious that we attain the balance we are looking for. It is in living mindfully that we find the meaning and beauty we seek. Living mindfully carries over to all aspects of our life. It helps us find meaning and beauty in the work that we do and in the relationships we pursue.

Our spirit and our body desiring to remain balanced brings the negative way we treat ourselves to our attention through the development of emotional or physical symptoms. It is like any pain that gets our attention. Our consciousness is being drawn to what we need to deal with to help us return to balance and harmony. It is up to us to "get the message" so that we can deal with it in order to return to a mindful and balanced state. If we don't hear our spirit and body attempting to communicate with us, then we continue on the same old path, with our symptoms often becoming worse, never learning from experience how to move through the obstacle course of internal and external issues that face us. We go around and around in circles, not seeing that the cause of our frustration and unhappiness is of our own doing in how we deal with events, not the events themselves. To break this cycle, we need to see more deeply into ourselves in order to understand the nature and cause of our nonacceptance. It is like untying an invisible rope that binds so that we can move with utmost freedom and flexibility.

The moment-to-moment compassionate acceptance of who we are, how we feel, and how we are living produces self-love, a less tense and more energetic state. With our own acceptance and inner compassion we no longer fight ourselves. Then the energy that has been bound as a part of our internal struggle is released into our body. We feel more vibrant and alive with the increase of energy. Feeling alive and in balance in our body and with our own spirit is what creates meaning. We are now like a finely tuned automobile moving down the road without any stuck places in the engine. Our energy that is now filled with acceptance, and self-love is now available to us to deal with our daily issues: survival, job, relationships, and the external issues of the world, with more aliveness and spirit.

Simply put, aliveness produces meaning, while stasis produces meaninglessness. When we are alive, our heart is able to be touched and we care about many things. When we are stuck, we are filled with a feeling of deadness, malaise, and frustration. If we bring acceptance and compassion to the experience of being stuck and understand its reason for being, then stuck can be the next experience that dissolves and becomes a part of our aliveness. The more alive we feel, the more we have the energy and support to live through the times when old negative energies emerge.

In fact, when the next piece of old abusive energy emerges and begins to obstruct our aliveness, we can be aligned with our spirit by understanding that we now are faced with the opportunity to take another step into appreciation and understanding of how we have been limiting our aliveness. **Each time we hold against the old abusive energies we create a state of impasse, another feeling of being stuck, and this adds to meaninglessness. As we travel on the path of awareness and acceptance, aliveness fills our body again and again and we continue to transform and are moved toward nlightenment.**

BOB: CASE STUDY: LIFE'S MEANING

An example of what I have been discussing can be seen in a first therapy session with a new client. Bob, a rather good looking athletic man in his early thirties, told me that although he had a decent job and was in what seemed to be a caring relationship, nothing had much meaning for him. He felt that he just went through the motions of living, feeling bored with his job and all the women that he had dated. He also didn't derive much satisfaction from the various sports he played. He wondered if he should change his job and break up with his current girlfriend. He thought that perhaps this would help him feel more alive. He felt very frustrated, angry, and disgusted with himself that because he couldn't control his life and his feelings. In fact, anger, frustration, feeling trapped, and experiencing his life as meaningless, were his primary experiences.

Throughout this first session, I focused on how angry and disgusted Bob was with himself and how he was constantly pressuring himself to feel better, rather then caring about himself for the difficulties he was having. I asked Bob to picture himself sitting in the chair across from him. I wondered out loud what it might be like to care about the person he saw, rather than pressuring that person to feel better. Bob argued with me that this change wasn't what he needed and if he accepted the difficult place that he was in he would never get out of it. I commented that he "seemed to be a stranger to love and compassion." He agreed that there had been little warmth in his family as he was growing up.

As the session continued, Bob began to see that he was treating himself in the same uncaring way in which he had always been treated. He tentatively began to acknowledge that compassion was what he needed for the hard time he was having, not pressure to feel better. As a crack developed in the harsh way he dealt with himself, and Bob let in what I was saying, his body relaxed for a moment. As he felt more compassionate toward himself, he continued to relax and he was able to breathe more deeply and feel less pressured. The feeling of meaninglessness Bob had started the session with was no longer present. As he was able to relax, he felt that he was living inside of his body, rather than outside of it. Bob was coming home to himself so that he felt connected to his surroundings and to feeling himself on the ground, rather then floating somewhere in space. His self-acceptance allowed energy to flow through his body, into his legs and feet and into the earth. All of these feelings produced a sense of meaning for Bob.

When Bob felt his feet on the ground, he was living more in the reality of the here and now. **If, like Bob, we are floating in space, we experience the world differently from when we feel the inside of our bodies and are down to earth. The more that Bob, and all of us, live an embodied reality, that is, a reality where we are physically aware of and inside of our body, our surroundings, and our connection to the earth, the easier it will be for him, and for us, to deal with any issues that arise in our lives. This is basic to our feeling of personal power, even with the issues and feelings that we are dealing with in a post 9/11 world.** However, there is much that Bob will have to experience in order to be able to integrate this new compassionate way of treating himself. Old habits that are structured in our bodies return until we work through the various facets of why they are with us in the first place.

CHAPTER THREE

The Earth Is Our Home: Belonging

AS WITH BOB, THERE ARE WAYS EACH OF US HAS LEARNED to block our life force that prevent us from connecting to the feeling of meaning. Without the connection to meaning, these blocks also keep us from feeling satisfied or even moving in the direction of satisfaction. If we fight against the truth of our experiences we put up roadblocks to our heart and our spirit. We are then less able to feel deeply about anything and are more likely to merely go through the motions. If we don't accept each moment of our body's "truth," we nurture our addictions rather than our spirit. In blocking our life force, we cut off our energetic feeling connection to the ground. Grounding on the earth gives us the sense of body stability and security. Only by accepting our feelings do we feel our connection to the earth. To become more conscious and to connect to the earth, we need to live our process - the difficult feelings we have, as well as the joyous ones.

It is the combined energetic connection to the earth, to our heart, and our spirit that provides us with a primary sense of belonging and a connection to reality. When we have our feet on the ground, we feel how we are a part of everything that is alive. We are at one with our own life force and with all sentient and non-sentient beings. What happens in our environment and with other people is no longer outside of our experience. The more that we live with our consciousness inside of our bodies, rather than at its periphery, the more

passionately focused we become regarding everything that is
affecting the environment and the world at large. We then
feel the strands of energy that connect us to the earth and to
one another and see that whatever we do affects the earth and
all its people. Living embodied, our passion contains a quality
of power and of inner peace. In this graceful way of living we
feel the meaning of our lives. We know what it is to feel alive
and to move and live each moment from our energetic connection to ourselves, to spirit, and to the earth.

An example of this is the difference in the way that Bob cared for
himself as he became more fully embodied. We can imagine the
difference Bob felt in the relationship with his girlfriend as lived
with less pressure and stress. Feeling more relaxed, he was now
more satisfied with himself, and, in turn, more satisfied in his relationships. He felt heart for himself in a way that he had never felt
before and, therefore, he had more heart for others. He also began
to consider how much he stressed his body and ignored important
signs of needing to slow down at any given moment. As his body
consciousness grew, he changed the unhealthy way he had been
eating. And as his self-caring increased, he began to see the world
through the eyes of satisfaction, rather than through the eyes of his
old dissatisfaction. Furthermore, Bob began to feel the strands of
energy that connected him to the nature. A loop developed where he
felt that nature was emotionally and energetically nurturing and
supporting him and that he wanted to support and care about nature.

LIVING EMBODIED IN CONNECTION
WITH THE EARTH

As we see with Bob, **there is no limit to the impact on our
lives and our society of our living an embodied reality. The
more fully we are connected to the ground, to the earth, the
more we can allow our emotions to exist and our spirits to
soar.** Then, we can reach the heights of our creative and spiritual
potential. As we feel our feet on the ground, we can allow the feeling
of being alive to fill us, we can follow our dreams, and reach for the

stars. Without this connection to earth, we either hold against letting go, fearing the experience of soaring and the pleasure of feeling alive or our energy rushes away from the ground and we become impulsive and hyperactive. When we hold against letting go or rush above the ground, we are reacting to our old childhood fears in new packages.

Feeling a body connection with the earth allows for the experience of rootedness and supports the experience of having a flexible container for our aliveness. It is similar to how we might have felt when we were children if our parents supported our need to explore our world when we left sight of them to seek new experiences. It would be like playing hide and seek, running into the other room, soon to return to see if our parents were still there, or if we ran and hid, waiting with delight to be found. The more we knew that our parents were there for us to return to or to find us, the further we could allow our explorations to take us. The same is true of being filled with our own life and feeling the earth. The more we feel secure on earth, the safer we feel to reach for the stars. The ability to shift between being practical and then reaching for our dreams is possible when we know in our bones that we have mother earth to come home to.

If we are living away from our connection to the ground, it is because there are feelings of trauma from our childhood that open in us when we were or attempted to become more grounded. We try to distance ourselves from the old childhood trauma because we don't know how to allow these feelings to exist in our bodies. Paradoxically, allowing these feelings to exist transforms them, while resisting their existence exacerbates their intensity and perpetuates their power.

Unable or unwilling to allow for their existence, we disconnect from them and develop various forms to hold them at bay. These forms may be of depersonalization, frozenness, various tension patterns, collapse, formlessness, and depression. They all cause us to live in degrees of denial, furthering our leaving the connection to the ground and to what is real.

To feel our feet on the ground is to know the reality of our childhood. It is to know how we were affected by the energies that surrounded us as we grew up. It is to honor and appreciate that all of our negative and uncomfortable feelings have meaning in terms of how we had to live. Bob, like so many people, had lost his ability to be in contact with his history and therefore, with his spirit and his spirited connection to the earth.

SOCIETY'S PLACE IN SUPPORTING OUR HUMANITY: THE ANSWER IS IN THE ENERGY

As discussed in Chapter One, unfortunately we are living in a culture whose values are deeply split about supporting a genuine respect for the earth. Significant factions of our society, especially those that are often in positions of corporate and governmental power are more focused on manipulating people and the environment for financial and political profit. They see natural resources and people as units of economic growth and profit, or as votes, rather than supporting sustainable growth and the nurturance of our human qualities.

Those who support sustainable growth and choose to nurture humane values are often seen as naïve and as a nuisance to the corporate or the governmental agenda. The way that we have embraced technology also supports our being further removed from our bodies and further removed from human values that respect each other's individual differences. Technology can move us away from our own desire to become more embodied.

Because of societal pressure to build and consume, we easily lose our connection to the ground and to a humanity that supports including our heart and all of our humanness in how we lead our lives. Only in moments of crisis are there general shifts in our society where people care for one another and lead with their hearts. At these times, our consciousness of one another and of the planet expands. When the crisis passes our hearts recede and we are back to living away from any deeper connection to ourselves and to one another. We pull inward and our old, more limited, self-centered way of living takes over. We experienced this in the palpable outpouring of caring and connection after 9/11 and then the slow and steady slide back to "business as usual."

Both familial and societal forces have taught us to ignore, dismiss, or turn against the deep messages that emerge from our spirit that can guide us through our lives. We have learned to value intellect over emotion, and logic and linear thinking over embodiment, imagery and imagination. We have learned to value technology and development over nature and spirit. We have learned to reject what we can learn from our feelings, our body, and our senses and ignore what the earth is trying to tell us as it cries out, in its own way, to be heard.

One could argue the opposite point of view and say that we are living in a time when individual differences have never been stronger. On the surface, the governing values of our society pay lip service to our connection to the earth and to God and to embracing diversity. However, major portions of our population do not possess acceptance for each individual living themselves as a unique person, in touch with their own biology and ideology, while being in touch with the earth and spirit.

We are often considered strange in our self-expression of feelings and emotions. There isn't a supportive ethic for people being real with one another. Some psychotherapy clients complain that therapy is not the real world. I have heard countless numbers of people declare that there is no room for who they really are in their place of employment or among people they meet. If they were to mention to anyone that they were having a difficult time, or that they were feeling sad or angry, they would be seen as strange and counterproductive to the business at hand. "I'm fine" becomes the frequent answer to "how are you," rather than an authentic and complete answer. Although each of us needs to ultimately take responsibility for how we live in the world, and how we choose to express ourselves, it is important to note that the world is often antagonistic to aliveness and authentic expression.

It's important not to reject intellect, logic, technology, and a scientific approach to certain problems. It is equally important to move toward an integration of all that we are. Rejecting any part of ourselves is to leave out parts of the best of who we are. Balance and harmony allows for a fuller life, a life not just based on survival and a focus on accumulating money and power. **As we combine our intelligence with our acceptance of our body, emotions, senses, imagery, and spirit, it leads us to unexpected fields of our humanity and spirituality, as well as opening us to artistic and scientific creativity. As we combine all of who we are, we move toward a sense of completeness and enlightenment as individuals and as a society.**

How can we integrate our intellect and logic in behalf of our emotional and spiritual life? We need to be mindful of whether we use our intellect and our logic and the fruits of technology to distance ourselves from our common humanity or to help us develop our humanity.

There is an energy, a frequency, in everything that we do and in everything that we build and manufacture. The frequency can be either negative or positive. It depends on whether what we do, build or manufacture truly includes a connection to heart and spirit and an appreciation about its impact on the world. There is lasting impact to whatever frequency is added to the world. We are blind if we believe otherwise. We need to be aware whether we are adding to a hostile, negative, and narcissistic frequency where everything is totally self-serving and uses resources that are irreplaceable, or whether we are adding to frequencies that enhance a life of humanity and sustainability for everyone. The frequency that is a result of a heart choice is less dense, more subtle and adds healing to the world. A decision made from heartlessness has a lower frequency and detracts from healing people and the planet.

It is not always clear-cut whether there is a positive or a negative frequency in what we are dealing with. At times, it is the way that we approach an issue that determines the frequency. So many forms of technology can have positive and useful applications when we do not allow ourselves to become dehumanized by them. Yet "computer brain," a condition in which we lose ourselves in the computer and feel spaced and totally lost to any body connection has become rampant in our society. Children and many adults become so lost in computer games that intimacy is becoming a lost art. We are becoming a society where attachment disorders are much more common.

Positive energy is present in pure research and discovery. The exploration of space and the lesser known regions of our planet are exciting uses of both our intellect and technology. However, if exploration leads to the development of every piece of pristine wilderness or vacant lot, we move into a destructive cycle. When technology blankets all that is natural, it prevents us from taking a deep breath, for we need to breathe in open spaces in order to continue to feel free and alive.

Even advances in medical research and the production of new medicines can have a positive or a negative frequency depending on how they are used. We can easily lose ourselves to the hype of pharmaceutical companies and the medical profession and give up our ability discern what our bodies need and to be proactive in our own health. Although allopathic medicines can be very beneficial they can produce debilitating side effects. Therefore, allopathic thinking can add to the quality of our life or further remove us from being in touch with our bodies. We need to learn to dialogue with our body and the symptoms that we develop. This is of critical importance because it is our physical symptoms that are our bodies' way of telling us that emotionally and energetically we are out of balance. Learning to dialogue with our body can bring us emotionally and energetically back into balance and in turn, relieve or remove our physical symptoms.

We can expand the use of our mind, senses, and intuition and explore how our lifestyle and our emotional supports sustain or discard our inner life. Rejecting our supporting our emotional life become an important part of the illnesses that we develop and the healing of these illnesses.

Our lives and our health are also directly impacted by the dehumanizing impact of the proliferation of fast food restaurants, "cookie cutter" shopping malls, and an endless array of the current fads and gadgets. The sprawl of cities, housing that covers the land, roads that seem to grow one shopping mall after another, all deaden our connection to the earth. Even as more malls are built and companies tell us that we must own a new product or a new clothing design so that the quality of our life will be improved, it is so often just another "sales pitch," where products are meant to fill the needs that are really about our emotional emptiness. We live in a "throw away" society where we learn to throw ourselves out as if we are the clothes that are out of fashion.

As a result, many products, designs or assemblages of shops don't possess a real sense of a positive ethic, a positive frequency of caring. In fact, there is a negative frequency of sterility, meaning-lessness, and exploitation in much of our society that supports our spirit being crowded out of our lives. This negative energetic frequency, devoid of spirit, rather than filled with light, therefore adds to the overall trauma and off-centeredness of the world. The negative frequencies of artificiality take us away from a direct experience of ourselves and the earth. What we consume becomes part of us. If businesses, supported by our society, are developing products that possess an energy of sterility, meaninglessness, and exploitation, we bond with this energy, rather than bonding with the energy of light, embodiment, and compassion that feeds our humanity and our spirit.

We are encouraged to consume addictively, which in turn, helps us avoid an inner sense of loneliness, alienation, and meaninglessness. Instead of living fully, we may fool ourselves into believing that we are accumulating exactly what is going to make us happy and fulfilled. Actually, we are living in addiction because we are not taking in what nurtures our emotions, our body, and our spirit. That's the bad news. The good news is that if we give up our addictions, we can begin to deal with the feelings that we have been attempting to avoid. There is a life that is more meaningful than living in addiction.

Having been taught not to cherish what truly nourishes our bodies and souls, we have less energy and vision to care about what feels like it is outside of us. We lose sight that we are one with all. Therefore, in our disregard for ourselves we have more disregard for the earth. As we degrade the home that is our body, we degrade the earth that is our external home.

We pay the price in dirty rivers and forests, unclean air, decreasing ozone protection, dying trees, toxins in our food and drinking water, mounting piles of garbage with no place to go. We also pay the price in a decline of our current state of mental, spiritual, and physical well being. We are directly affected by both the toxins and stress that are disease-producing and the state of mind that moves us away from our own deeper sense of ourselves.

At the same time that we are addicted to material possessions and the "good life," we are really in a downward spiral where we are neglecting our internal call to meaning and true alignment that keeps us healthy. Our technology has outgrown our spirituality. As a result, we are in a race. If we continue in the same direction we are going, it is a race that we cannot win. It is a race about whether we hold onto or give up our humanity and our connection to the earth.

The downward spiral is circular as we live further away from our essential nature and what has deep meaning to our soul. The further we move into the spiral, the need to accumulate and insulate ourselves in order to stay safe against whatever we believe the external assaults will be deepens. We loose sight that we have learned to stuff our feelings, thereby killing our aliveness, and wind up always projecting the killer of our aliveness "out there." Thus, we create and reinforce more and more of a negative frequency in ourselves and in the world. **Because we have been assaulted for our emotions and learned to go underground with them, we don't realize that we have learned to assault ourselves and others for being human. We don't realize that we have become our own victimizers.** Not only is this a dangerous position to take in terms of what it does to our emotional and physical health, we also unknowingly act out our killing, our victimizing, on each other and on the environment.

Our lives express the attitudes with which we have bonded. When our negative energy combines with an attitude that presupposes unlimited natural resources, we end up raping the earth of its bounty, building highways, buildings, and parking lots at an ever-increasing pace. We diminish forests and farm land. We assume an ethic of unlimited growth, rather than sustaining our resources and allowing room for us to expand and breathe.

The exploitation of natural resources becomes the necessary ingredient of an ever-expanding financial balance sheet at the expense of the spirit of our wilderness, clean air and water, and even the ozone that once protectively encircled the earth. As the earth becomes increasingly polluted and covered with cement and garbage, we have less direct access to it. We have less direct access to the healing power that the earth provides to our physical, energetic, and spiritual bodies. Freedom of choice then becomes, "I can have mine at whatever cost to others, I can have a slice of this planet." There is deep underlying hostility and fear in this kind of uncaring competitiveness.

I believe that what goes on is part of an ethic of which we are all a part. We are all in this together. We need to bring consciousness to all our actions and feel how our thoughtlessness affects us and the planet that we live on.

This view was reflected in a letter written by Chief Seattle of the Duwamish tribe of Washington State to President Franklin Pierce in 1854: He wrote: "Whatever befalls the earth befalls the sons of earth. The white man too, shall pass perhaps sooner than other tribes. Continue to contaminate your bed, and you will one night suffocate in your own waste. When the buffalo are all slaughtered, the wild horses all tamed, the secret corners of the forest heavy with the scent of many men, and the view of ripe hills blotted by talking wires, where is the thicket? Where is the eagle? Gone! And what is it to say good-bye to the swift pony and the hunt? It is the end of living and the beginning of survival."[1]

Our society needs the richness and diversity that comes from a connection to the richness and diversity of the earth. Remember the last time that you drove out of the city and immediately felt that you were able to take a deep breath? You might not even have realized that you were holding your breath until the deeper breathing occurred. We need space to breathe. We need a connection to external space in order to feel our own internal space. We need to build into our society a preference for human/land values over corporate expansion and growth. It is now taking longer to drive out of the cities than it did in years past. Buildings extend further into what was once country. I remember when the colloquial definition for *country* was "that place beyond the city where there were farms and few buildings." Now that definition is changing as office buildings, malls, condominiums, and single family homes replace farm land and open spaces, once shared by all. The effect of this conversion of the country into cities and suburbs is that there is now, literally, less room to breathe.

In a speech to the Native Hawaiian Rights Conference held on August 5, 1988, Charles Wilkinson spoke about the need to defend "against the dark, exploitive side of capitalism that grinds under lands and resources and peoples." He went on to say, "It is a belief that this nation and this world are becoming too homogeneous, too gray; that the pressures for sameness are overbearing; and that those forces are destructive for some of the finest qualities of civilization. For to be human is to be creative and to be creative is to search out the differences and distinctness, to make this brief human existence a kaleidoscope of individuality and mystery and color."

As we move away from valuing the land and our connection to it, we move toward valuing intellect over our emotions, senses, intuition, and spirit. We move toward valuing the power of exploitation and accumulation over the power of peace, compassion, and gentleness. Intellect and power without heart is cold, harsh, and calculating. Without softness, power is bullying and cruel. We need to integrate our love for ourselves and the land with a heartfelt power and intellect. The result of this integration would be softness that has power

and assertiveness that has heart. All of who we are is precious. And to be all of who we are we need the integration of all our intellect with our emotions, our senses, our intuition, and our spirit. In this way we won't lose our ability to dream, to feel compassion, and to reach beyond ourselves. When we deepen our inner sense of peace we add to peace in the world.

EXCITED BY A SUNSET, WARMED BY A SMILE: SATISFACTION IS POSSSIBLE

If we continue a downward spiral away from our humanity and our spirit, we learn to sacrifice our vulnerability and our innocence. You might wonder why sacrificing our vulnerability and our innocence is a problem. At first, these qualities may not seem like parts of ourselves that we want to keep. Yet, to meet each day with vulnerability and innocence that is integrated with power and intellect, is to be able to retain qualities of wonder, spontaneity and excitement about the world. Here is our ability to continually live our lives with a sense of newness, to live in "beginner's mind," where we are excited by a sunset, warmed by a smile, and touched by our connection to the elemental forces of nature. It is these qualities that unite us with oneness and universal consciousness. This allows us to experience how we are connected to the river of life. A respectful connection to the land provides us with a meaning that we can carry into whatever else we do in our lives.

To regain more of our spirit, we need to feel that we are stewards of the earth and indebted to it for our life. We need the earth's survival for our own survival. We not only need the food, clean air, and water that the earth provides for us, but we also need a feeling-connection to the earth for our physical, emotional, and spiritual well being. The energetic frequencies of the earth have the same frequency as our heart beat. When we open to earth's energy we move closer to feeling at one with ourselves, at one with all that is alive; we move closer to enlightenment.

The development and continuation of the negative cycle of destroying the earth can be understood as we observe the differences between most native/primitive societies and our own technological/industrial society. Children growing up in traditional native cultures are supported by the ceremonies of the culture to grow from bonding with human mother and family, to bonding with mother earth and the spirit in all living things. The child's passage to adulthood is through bonding with the earth, animals and plants, thereby coming to know of the earth's bounty, power, wisdom, and healing energies. In these cultures there is a profound respect and knowing of the spirit in all living things. Only what is needed for survival is taken or killed, and even this is done with respect and reverence. In this process of bonding with the earth, we are stewards, not owners and conquerors of the land. Life itself becomes a ceremony.

In our Western, technological cultures there are decreasing movements toward bonding with the earth. Growing up is a movement away from human mother and family. We become independent in a way that means we are no longer supposed to need bonding. There is little guidance and connection to bond with nature and revere its purity and spirit. The longer our technological culture exists in ways that exclude a connection to the earth, the further we get from the traditions, and even the memories, of relating to the land as a basic part of each day. We therefore bond with whatever energy is available. In our technocratic world, most of these energies are ungrounded; they are the energies of mind and space, like electrical currents moving through the airwaves, not energies of body and earth.

Bonding is a basic need that is part of all animal and human systems. We are communal beings. As infants, we need protection and heartfelt nurturance for our biological and emotional needs to prosper. Throughout our formative years we need validation, love, and protection for our emotional life, or we will live a deadened existence. We need a bonding connection to nurture our spirit or it will only be present in the function of survival, rather than our spirit being the river that connects us with all life. When we are in touch with this river we know that harming any life is harming ourselves and the quality of all life.

At a very early age children now bond with the unreality of TV and movies, with computer games, cell phones, highly paid athletes, malls and shopping, performance and accumulation. We grow up with our bodies filled with electrical currents and beliefs that further take us away from the ground and the lower half of our bodies. We are reinforced to bond with and live an unhealthy lifestyle in which stress feels natural and connection to our bodies and the earth feels unnatural. We push ourselves beyond what is healthy, so that we have become a society of workaholics and playaholics.

These qualities have so become the cultural norm and we are encouraged to reach, to strive, for them. They become attributes that are revered. We grow up wanting to be like the heroes in our society. And our current heroes are often unfeeling, unreal, metallic, mechanical, authoritative, highly paid, and overly competitive. As we are taken over by these roles, our natural, alive state moves further into the dark recesses of our consciousness, away from nature, away from our primary connection to the earth.

We need to highlight heroic figures of a different mold. We need heroes that move us back into balance. We need heroes of great heart and compassion who continue to grow emotionally and spiritually so that they teach us to expand our consciousness. We need heroes who live a balanced life and feel that can accept everything about themselves. These heroes' lives show us how to allow for the natural, ongoing transformation of life to occur.

We can be shown that all of who we are has meaning and, therefore, that there is a positive aspect to everything that we experience. It is not what we feel that is the problem, it is the way that we live ourselves that determines whether we are in balance or we are acting out. For example, at times, it is essential that we persevere and not give up. At times, it is important to be in our power and stand our ground or to be able to use our intellect and power of reasoning. However, to do this we don't have to eliminate our innocence, vulnerability, open-heartedness, and compassion. It is possible to deal with the difficulties of running a business and remain caring. It is possible to be powerful and assertive and be compassionate. When we unconsciously, compulsively and stereotypically live blinded to the inclusive way of balance we give up our ability to choose and live flexibly, and we then unknowingly follow a path of personal and planetary destruction.

As a young man I remember reading Herman Hesse's *Siddhartha*. I was deeply touched by how passionately and completely Siddhartha lived every part of his life. There was no holding back. He was born to a position of wealth and position. He gave this up to explore the world. After giving up his position of royalty, there were times he lived the life of an ascetic, at other times a very worldly life that was filled with intense sexuality, and still at other times he was again involved with the accumulation of wealth. What struck me was how each part of his life built on the previous and that he expanded his consciousness as he learned from his experiences. The key to his life is that he learned from experiences. The problem for many of us is that we don't learn from our experience. Until we learn from them, the same lessons continue to appear. And when we don't learn from our experiences the lessons only become harder.

Siddhartha lived his life fully, then unformed and let go of the part of his life that had taught him what he needed to know to expand his consciousness. He moved to some inner calling from his spirit. For me, his entire life had a heroic quality to it. He spent the last years of his life in an enlightened state, content to ferry people across a river. He was at one with the river and all of nature. He was at peace, living simply and in tune with the earth, learning life's lessons from the flow of the river and the change of the seasons. He came to understand that at times, the river, like human nature, was rough and choppy, at times it broke through its usual boundaries and flooded the surrounding countryside and at other times it was calm and easy flowing. No matter the river's condition, he learned that it was all a part of the natural order, as is all of human nature. He gave up control to live a life of peace and acceptance.

People who live a life in tune with nature know the simple and profound lessons to be learned from the change of the seasons, the migration of the birds and fish, the birth and death cycle of animals. These lessons are about simply being human and recognizing that part of our humanness is that we are all a part of the river of life and spirit that runs throughout the universe. Feeling the truth in our interconnectedness allows for the feeling of oneness and a humility that makes room for inner peace and power without arrogance and superiority.

The Dalai Lama, in a visit to St. Patrick's Cathedral in New York in 1979 said, "Without inner peace, it is impossible to have world peace." The movement toward inner peace is something that each one of us can commit to. In this way we not only heal ourselves, we add to world peace and the healing of the earth. We often confuse this simple way of living with being naive. In our confusion, we miss the power that is derived from such a commitment to peace.

Thich Nhat Hanh talks about how we are both the wave and the water. As the wave we feel our individuality and that we have a beginning and an end. Yet as the water we are all united, interconnected in a common, never ending energy. We need to feel how both dimensions of existence are true. As the water, we have an impact on every being and are a part of every wave. In turn, as a wave, we are affected by every other being, every other wave.

Living a life dedicated to peace, oneness, and universal consciousness is not a recipe for passivity. The Dalai Lama and Thich Nhat Hanh are both brilliant men of power and integrity who have persevered under very difficult and trying political situations, the Dalai Lama in relation to the Chinese takeover of Tibet, with the continual destruction of Tibetan culture, and Thich Nhat Hanh in relation to the Vietnam war. They have been able to mobilize their power for peace and their brilliance for teaching about our common humanity. They are far from being passive.

Gandhi and Martin Luther King, Jr. are two other people who fit the mold of people leading with their hearts who lived their deep commitment to justice. Their power to lead and sway the course of history came from deep spiritual beliefs. All of these people also demonstrated a deep respect for the earth. And yet they were not without personality struggles.

There are other figures that have lived in the main stream of life and have exemplified a connection to their heart, their life force, and to the earth. They have excelled in their particular field while still allowing for humanness. Albert Einstein, Dag Hammerskjold, Golda Meir, Jimmy Carter, and Melina Mercouri come to mind. They did not live the role of what a scientist, diplomat, Prime Minister, President, or actress-turned-minister of culture should be like. They brought their own brand of aliveness and humanness to the lives they lived. We need to bring the essence that these individuals embodied in their love of life, spirit and the land more into the foreground of our own lives and our culture. Also, business people who have demonstrated compassion for their workers, instead of using them and then casting them aside during difficult times are another model of the inclusion of heart in decision making.

BALANCE

For each of us to move toward a more enlightened state, we need to acknowledge and integrate our soft and nurturing sides with our aggressive and competitive nature. Men and women alike need to explore these issues for themselves.

The problem isn't our aggressiveness and competitiveness. Once again, it is about balance. Robert Bly and Sam Keen are two authors who have written about how men need to be more in touch with their internal "wild man." This is different from the macho man who is insensitive to emotions, kindness and softness. Rather, here is a man who is in touch with his animal nature and who has learned to balance the powerful forces that reside inside of him. They discuss how men need to find their own traditions to return to a more natural state of being.[3] For many years now, women have also been exploring their consciousness and the role models that have meaning for them. From the consciousness raising groups of the 1960's and 1970's to the present day exploration of the Native

American, Goddess, Wise Woman tradition[4] and through psychotherapy, women are trying to find new models with which they can identify so that they can integrate power and receptivity into their lives.

MORE ABOUT BOB: TOUCHING THE EARTH

Returning to Bob, the client I wrote about earlier, we saw that he was continually stressing himself to perform and be the best that he could be within his paradigm of control and accumulation of wealth. What this means for Bob is that he was constantly driving himself, ignoring any messages from his emotions and body to slow down. Although he was athletic and participated in various sports, he approached these activities in the same way as he did the rest of his life; he pushed himself to excel and was angry with himself if he did not reach some standard of excellence that he set for himself. The fact is that his standard of excellence could never be reached because he was constantly "upping the bar" as he improved.

Although striving for excellence in and of itself is not a problem, it becomes one when we can't feel satisfaction in the process. Satisfaction was not part of Bob's life. He approached everything he did as pressure instead of as a way of feeling the gracefulness of his body or to feel himself in relation to the earth. He was bonded with the pressure that he learned in his family, and with all the images of success that are a part of our society.

For Bob to integrate the piece of therapeutic work that we did in our first session, he will need to do more than intellectually understand how he constantly pressures himself. He will need to experience his body and how he uses his body as an instrument to negate all of his senses and feelings. Conversely, he will need to feel that he is a part of nature.

"Stop and smell the roses" has deep meaning in terms of his emotional and physical well being. If Bob does not continue to slow down and soften his rigid body and rigid views so that he can feel himself in relation to the earth, he will continue to split his spirit and his heart from the rest of himself. He will return to living as a robot, dissatisfied, with his life lacking meaning. If Bob continues on a path of awakening, he will need to feel his connection with all that is alive in nature so that he can feel and respect his part of the great mystery of life.

We all need this kind of connection in which we can ground ourselves in the reality that we are a part of the river of life and that this truth runs through every moment of our existence. As with Bob, this awareness will improve the quality of our lives. One way of strengthening this connection is to be aware that all parts of the web of life need our caring stewardship so that they can survive and thrive. I mean this literally! We need to slow down so that we look around and ask the earth to tell us what it needs from us and to feel how much we need our connection with it.

What follows is an experiment that highlights this issue. Close your eyes, relax as much as possible, be aware of your breathing and how you feel emotionally and physically. Allow a spontaneous image of the earth to appear. Welcome the image. Be aware of how much you can allow the image to touch you physically and emotionally. Ask the earth what it needs from you for its continued health and well-being. Allow an answer to come from the image. Then, ask the earth, "What do you have for me?" See if you can take the answers into your heart. Be aware of whatever resistance you may have, allowing the image or the answer to touch you. In the meantime, if you didn't get an image or an answer, ask whatever quality that emerged (like blankness, static, darkness, obsession, contempt), what it is here for and what it is here to teach you.

We are in a vicious cycle. The more that we consume, the more we feel that we need. We have lost all perspective to what is enough. We have covered over our deepest needs with superficial needs. And then being numb, consuming becomes an addiction. Like any addiction, we want to break through the numbness and feel alive. But we have thoroughly identified

with attitudes that perpetuate our addiction. In turn, this numbing, and its results, again quickens the pace away from nature and, therefore, away from what is natural. "Fast" then becomes an ethic to be sought after, rather than part of a biological rhythm that also has the other polarity called "slow" or "easy" which is equally as valuable. In turn, the movement away from what is natural increases the spiral toward technology, financial acquisition, and a negative self-centeredness at the expense of other human values. The negative way that the planet is treated becomes the norm. In effect, thoughtlessness and uncaring have become the norm. This is the way we have learned to treat both the planet and ourselves. We have learned to live in a self and planetary disrespect and self-centeredness. This has now become a part of our identity.

Jeremy Rifkin, in an article entitled, "Time Wars; A New Dimension Shaping Our Future,"[5] discusses this point. "Clearly we have had to pay a heavy price for our efficiency-worshipping society. We have quickened the pace of life only to become less patient. We have become more organized but less spontaneous, less joyful. We are better prepared for the future but less able to enjoy the present and reflect on the past. The efficient society has increased our superficial comforts but has made us alienated, self-absorbed, and manipulative in relation to others."

An important paradox develops in this anti-nature cycle. The flow of our lives quickens with an ever more sophisticated technology in which computer speeds and the amount and flow of information continue to dramatically increase. So does the frantic effort to return to what is natural. It is distressing that our daily lives, the way in which we work and play, has become so frantic. Even in the way that we are encouraged to vacation can become pressure to fill each moment of our time and have "the time of our lives." Ads for products attempt to seduce us by telling us that we will return to the natural glow of youth. Auto ads that are filmed at some remote destination touch our adventurous spirit by showing us that we can climb a mountain because of the ruggedness of a particular car as we drive these cars to the mall. Pharmaceutical companies tout their newest drugs that will help us with social phobias, depression and anxiety, and erectile dysfunction. Besides the possibility of debilitating side effects, there is little or no encouragement to see what it is that we need in a natural way to return to balance.

Our expectations for ourselves, drummed into us from so many different directions, influence us to believe that something is wrong if we don't use a certain product, fail to have a wonderful time, don't look a certain way, or aren't able to live the gusto of life. Here, the allure of the return to nature, to exercise, to a more robust and healthy way of living becomes a part of what is stressful and tension producing, rather than part of a flowing and natural state of being. Stress occurs because we pressure ourselves to fill in every moment of our spare time in order to have a good time. When we feel that we have to fill up all the spaces of our free time, we become less able to simply let go and relax.

Even recreational sports become an exercise in the pursuit of excellence, rather than excellence being balanced with the simple pleasure that is derived from feeling our bodies come alive through movement and inner pulsation. The pleasure of embodiment that comes with practice leads to grace and excellence, while the pursuit of excellence without embodiment leads to stress and tension. When any activity, or the very center of our lives, is lived with the primary motivation being the willful pursuit of excellence, we are organizing our lives so that we are driven and stressed. This can only ultimately lead to emotional and physical breakdown.

Some years ago I was skiing with a friend of mine. He was sharing with me how he was constantly "on himself" about doing better. Every other moment became a moment of how he should improve and refine his technique. At alternate moments, he lectured himself on how he should be relaxing and not be so hard on himself. He wound up in the dilemma of pushing himself to ski better and pushing himself to relax more. Both voices became stress producing and prevented him from enjoying skiing and being "in the moment."

I suggested that as he skied, he try to imagine a supportive parent who was skiing alongside him. No matter how he skied or how he might prod himself, this parent was accepting of who he was and how he was skiing. The parent would be supportive of how he lived each moment. Therefore, even if my friend was angry and frustrated with himself for not skiing better, this parent was totally accepting of his anger and frustration. In essence, no matter what my friend did or how he treated himself, this imaginary parent was giving him the message that he could do no wrong.

When my friend did the experiment, he reported that he began to feel easier with himself. He realized that he wasn't obsessing as much about what or how he was skiing. He also realized that his skiing improved. He had broken the vicious cycle of stressing himself to do better and stressing himself to relax that kept him from becoming more embodied. It certainly was not as simple as my friend declaring to himself that he should "Relax." That is true for all of us. To live unaware of our biological rhythms prevents us from learning in a relaxed manner and affects our enjoyment and performance and our level of stress.

DEEP LISTENING

We have learned to move away from our spirit, our life force, as a way of surviving in our stressful world. We increasingly bond with technology rather than bonding with the earth. We go along with the crowd as a way of being a part of what seems right. Numb to ourselves, we increasingly speed through our lives searching for meaning and satisfaction. Living in this way, we are callous and inconsiderate of ourselves and of the earth. Yet our spirit, our life force, is always pointing the way toward a deeper sense of connection and embodiment.

We can learn how to listen to the messages that our spirit provides for us. We can learn to listen to the messages that the earth provides for us. Our spirit is perfect in the way it can lead us through the darkness in ourselves and the darkness

that is in the world. Our spirit can lead us to experience the beauty and light that is also in ourselves and in the world.

There's a question that I often ask my clients when we need to gain some sense of direction in their therapy. I want to help them access their deeper place of wisdom and knowing in regard to what needs to happen for them to live through their trauma suffering and come to a place of greater aliveness and satisfaction. At first, I lead them through the following relaxation exercise: "Go inside, be aware of your breathing, be aware of any places of tension or ease in your body. Allow whatever you become aware of to simply exist without pushing or pulling yourself in any way. Give yourself permission to relax as much as possible. Ask your spirit or deeper place of wisdom to emerge and ask it what needs to happen right now for your continued growth."

As I do this same experiment in order to have my spirit lead me, this is the answer that I receive. It would be helpful to look more closely at how everything that we do, every way that we live, is an attempt to find inner peace and happiness. At the same time, we need to find ways to live in a world where violence and threat of terrorism, the degradation of the environment through pollution, the loss of open spaces to development, the increasing loss of plant and animal species, political negativity and intolerance, world wide economic suffering, and our personal negativity, unhappiness, and addictions abound. How can we find a place of inner strength in ourselves so that we can see the light and beauty in people and in the world? How can we deal with our own characterological negativity and self-destructiveness, so that we can work for our own inner peace, add to the energy in the world that can produce world peace and not be overwhelmed and dragged down by the darkness?

As was discussed earlier in this chapter, the positive, life-enhancing values that our society espouses are often lip service to the more real underlying attitudes that create an anti-emotional and anti-environmental ethic that we learn to live by. But is the darkness in the world enough to explain our own personal darkness and therefore, how we emotionally suffer? Although we are deeply impacted by society's values and what is going on in the world, in succeeding chapters I will explore how the energy and emotion of our families are even more central in teaching us what to feel and how to cope with our lives. These chapters will explore the details of how it is that we learned to live ourselves in our own unique way. We will explore what all of this has to do with our perfect spirit that has helped us survive.

In Chapter Four we will look at how we have organized ourselves in relation to the trauma and the support that has been present in our lives. We will come to understand how our organization is a direct expression of how we have learned to maximize the flow of energy and aliveness and minimize pain and suffering based on our childhood experiences. Our life force, our spirit, guides us through the cracks of our personal universe so that we can deal with the abusive energies of our childhood while surviving and functioning with as much aliveness as is possible. In this way we will come to appreciate how **everything about our emotional, energetic, and bodily makeup is a solution, not a problem. We will see that we are all heroes in our own lives.**

CHAPTER FOUR

Feelings Are Not Problems, They're Solutions

GROWING UP IN OUR SOCIETY IS SO OFTEN A LESSON in negating much of our inner life and moving away from what is natural and alive in ourselves. Many of our families and our culture have taught us that being brave means being tough and not expressing our sadness or tender feelings; that we are mean and hurtful if we are angry or too powerful; that other people are jealous or upset if we are too excited and happy; that we are being selfish if we express our needs; and that if we are frightened, we really have nothing to be frightened about or that we should not show our fears because that is a sign of weakness. **We are taught to deny our fears rather than learn to live through them and sort out what is truly dangerous. Generally, we are taught not to feel and then not to express our feelings if we know what they are. In our families and in society at large there is an emphasis on looking good that replaces being real.**

Actually, our life force always produces the exact feeling necessary for us to continue to grow, allow more of our aliveness to come forth, and to help us return to a state of inner balance. When we are emotionally or physically assaulted, we feel angry. It is our life force's way of providing the energy to set a boundary. When we lose something or someone that has meaning to us, we feel grief. It is the way that we have of honoring what has had meaning to us and to begin to say good-bye.

When our family environment is too hostile for us to stay balanced, then our life force produces the perfect defense. For example, if we feel angry for being assaulted and then our anger is assaulted, we feel sad. And then if our sadness is assaulted, our life force may produce spite as a way of helping us feel some sense of power and integrity in a situation where someone is attempting to control all of our emotions. If, in turn, each emotional expression is met with abuse, than we finally develop some form of rigidity or collapse to defend against the feeling of the abuse. **We become heroes in our own life. We find whatever way we can to survive and prosper given the energy that we are met with in our formative years.**

Emotions are simply expressions of our inner being. They are expressions of our spirit, our life force. Emotions are neither good nor bad. Usually, they are neither comfortable nor uncomfortable. If, as children, our emotions are met with acceptance, we learn to accept the feelings that flow inside of us. Then we grow up feeling positively about ourselves. If our emotions are met with rejection, we learn to reject our internal experiences and we grow up feeling negatively about ourselves. As children, we internalize the particular set of negative and positive energies with which we are met.

Imagine, how as children, we reached out to our parents in order to feel reassured of our connection with them. We simply needed to feel safe. We came toward them with open arms and asked, "Do you still love me?" Or we came toward our parents with some other expression of our vulnerability, need, and dependence. Now, imagine that our parents felt that our need, vulnerability, our dependence, was the cause of their feeling burdened and, therefore, they believed it was our need that was the problem. As a result of their belief, they met our need, with some form of abuse such as disgust, humiliation, violence, abandonment, craziness.

Whether their feelings were obvious or hidden, we felt them just the same. Children are sensitive to the subtleties of energy, and we knew deep inside of ourselves that our need and our reaching caused our parents to be upset. For example, imagine that our parents' negative response came from their attitude that we should grow up to be brave, strong, and independent. They believed that independence meant never feeling dependent. They wanted to toughen us up to deal with a tough world. They merely wanted to wean us from feeling dependent. At the core of this belief is their negative reaction to dependence. They saw dependence as an experience that should be grown out of, rather than to be supported as a part of a range of human experiences, along with independence. Over time, we learned not to reach. As children we learned that not only is there is something wrong with our reaching, we also learned that there is something wrong with our need, our vulnerability, and our dependence. Therefore, over time, we learned to not make room for our need, vulnerability, and our dependence.

The truth is that basic needs for love, understanding, connection, support, and touch are a part of life. In order to be loved and to ward off our parent's abuse, we had to block need out of our awareness and become overly hard and independent or we moved in the opposite direction and became depressed. Either way how we organized our emotions was a result of the impact of our parent's energy and defensive structure.

However, our basic needs will not go away. They will always be a part of us. When assaulted, and when we have to stuff our needs, they will find expression in some indirect manner. Hidden, our needs might drive us for perfection and seeking of attention or they may cause us to be over solicitous of others, hoping that this will ultimately provide satisfaction. This indirect expression of needs is never really satisfying.

We can't absorb what we need when we are contending with an underlying message that there is something wrong with us if we have needs. There are two reasons for this. One is that when we need to defend against the underlying abusive energy our defense prevents us from absorbing positive energy. The second is that if our needs begin to surface, whatever the original abusive energy was that we absorbed (disgust, humiliation, violence, etc.) will begin to emerge.

However we learned to organize ourselves in relation to our childhood abuse, we will grow up associating need and abuse. It will affect how we feel about our own needs as adults and how we will reach for what we need. Rather than having a simple channel between feeling and expression, we now have to contend with the feelings of the abuse that surround our needs. Our early childhood emotional learning also effects how we feel toward other people having needs. As with fear, we associate our own and another's needs as a sign of weakness, rather than as an expression of aliveness.

If we look deeply into the dynamics of energy and emotion, no emotion, in and of itself, including need, feels bad, negative, or uncomfortable. What make our emotions difficult to live with are the negative abusive energies and beliefs that we've internalized from our childhood experience that now surrounds our emotions. We defend against our emotions to distance ourselves from the negative energy that we now associate with the emotion itself. The negative energy becomes so fused with the emotion that we grow up unable to differentiate between the two.

The internalized energy from our childhood is the basis for how we form our belief systems. The energies that have become fused with our emotions formulate our view of ourselves and of the world. Positive energies form positive beliefs, negative energies form negative beliefs. The messages that we have received on the wings of abuse also form how we feel about our emotions. We embody our internalized lessons about emotions. Our responses to these lessons become what we think of and experience as our identity, that is, how we know ourselves.

We also organize our bodies in a variety of ways to defend against the negative energies. We tighten our shoulders to not feel angry, or tighten our stomachs to not cry. We pull up from our pelvic floor to not feel sexual abuse or we freeze our muscles and dissociate to not feel the violence from our childhood.

Think of someone you know who has a hard and rigid body. His or her body tells the story of their childhood. It tells the story of how they learned to organize themselves in a hard and rigid way in relation to their emotions because of the hardness of the abuse that came toward them. It speaks to the hard and rigid views that they will have about themselves and about life. Whether their awareness is close to the surface or locked deep inside, this person will not like him or herself or others who threaten their beliefs.

Continuing to look deeply, we see that it is not only the internalized negative energies that make us feel bad about our emotions. The avoidance of these old negative energies also produces uncomfortable feelings in relation to our emotions. In forming our belief system and our body structure we are attempting to avoid the distress that we associate with the emotions our childhood experiences branded as negative. In this attempt to avoid certain feelings, we move our bodies away from a centered, flowing position into one that is more defensive and ultimately, more unsatisfying.

For example, as children, we literally might try to make ourselves smaller to get away from the humiliation and disgust that we are met with when expressing our needs. We could do this by dipping our neck and shoulders and tightening our pelvis, as a spontaneous body response to disgust and humiliation. In effect, we would be compressing ourselves in order to find protection from the negative feeling that disgust and humiliation produce in us. Compression is the body's natural way of defending itself against this kind of energetic and emotional assault. The compression and tension now have their own set of uncomfortable feelings. As a result of the compression, a barrier has been erected that impedes the flow of energy and the expression of simple emotion: pleasure, need, anger, and sadness. The only place of power left for us is in spite, spiteful thoughts or actions, since we can no longer support our formed, alive emotions.

I want to reemphasize that it is either the energy in the negative messages with which we bonded that causes our emotions to feel negative or uncomfortable, or it is the feelings created by our defensive structure that produce their own particular set of uncomfortable feelings. It is not the emotion itself that feels bad.

We learn how to respond to our own emotions as we internalize the way significant people relate to our being alive. That is, when our parents truly welcome our existence, we grow up welcoming the moment-to-moment formation of our life force and the various emotional forms that it takes. We welcome our inner motility, the flow of energy and fluids through our body. We welcome our outer mobility, the movement through space that provides us with the feeling of being in the world.

Virginia Satir once said that "feelings are never problems. It is the way we feel about the way we feel that is the problem."[1] She believed that the feelings about our feelings are learned responses. In effect, we are programmed and molded to live the way we do in relation to our emotions. Just as Pavlov's dogs learned to respond to certain stimuli in specific and planned ways, so too, have we learned to respond to our own inner life in ways that negate the depth, the very essence, of who we are. Most of us are not taught to support and learn from how we feel. We are taught to control, fight, and turn against ourselves.

Since emotions are part of our life force, they should be treated with great respect. Trying to rid ourselves of our emotions or holding onto or against them limits our aliveness. It limits our inner motility and our outer mobility. We need to treat our internal processes as one would treat a beautiful and delicate butterfly, enjoying its beauty and movement and allowing for its freedom. Not allowing the butterfly to fly either by holding onto to it or clipping its wings is to deeply limit the grace that is part of the essence of the butterfly. The butterfly struggles until it is freed or gives up and dies. Like the butterfly, not allowing the full existence of the flow of our emotions, we struggle as long as we can against a stronger opponent and then a graceful part of us dies. We have learned not to appreciate our emotions as a beautiful part of our life and in doing so a part of us dies, creating tension and stress in our bodies.

To reverse this negative process, we are better served by learning how to dialogue with our emotions, by noticing the areas of tension, collapse, flaccidity, or spaciness that hide our emotions or to learn how to welcome those emotions that we ordinarily reject or condemn. We also often reject the body states that hide our emotions.

Instead of rejecting the tension or collapse, etc., we need to learn to ask in a caring way why it is here. We then need to breathe mindfully and make room in ourselves so that we can listen for a response. We can ask the same question of all our feelings.

Imagine that a butterfly has landed on the palm of your hand. What happens to the butterfly if you try to close your hand and keep it with you? And what happens to your energy and muscles if you constantly keep your hand closed? Tension and stress are produced by the opposing forces of our spirit moving to be free and the suppression of this freedom. The two forces come together as opposing armies, neither giving any ground. With limited awareness, we may not have any other choice than to live with the negative lessons from childhood that formed our way of living. In order to soften our structure so that change can take place, we need to deepen our awareness of how we are specifically organized against our emotions. This transformational process begins by understanding and appreciating the form our emotions and our body have taken.

LEAVING OUR BODY: THE SEARCH FOR SAFETY

As children, our spontaneous, automatic, biological response to emotional or physical assaults like rejection, humiliation, violence, hatred, abandonment, craziness, incest, spankings, our parent's chronic suffering and depression, etc. was to organize our bodies into a defensive, protective stance away from a centered and flowing position. The feelings of shock or depression, tension, flaccidity, collapse, depersonalization, fragmentation that these assaults created in us were too traumatic to live with over a long period of time. We automatically gave up our being aligned and moved out of the center of our life and spirit, out of the center of our bodies, in order to survive. But even though we developed defenses, our bodies still retained the memory of the abuse.

At the same time, we still needed to feel connected to our parents. In order to balance our protective stance with keeping the connection with our parents, we often lost the conscious memory of why we organized defensively in the first place. Our life force played a protective trick on us by hiding the full impact of what had happened. It was often too much for us to bear that the people that we trusted most in our lives were the ones who abused us. To continue this balancing act that allowed us to survive childhood abuse we turned against ourselves, often in the same way that we were assaulted. We identified with the aggressor. We internalized the energy and the voice of the victimizer.

This way of coping is our body's, our spirit's, perfect way of surviving. It is the very essence of our body and our spirit doing their jobs in a perfect, orderly, and efficient manner. We all leave the center of our bodies when the feelings in them become too difficult bear. Our legacy from childhood, as a result of this process, is a variety of uncomfortable, distressing, and negative feelings that we have at different levels of consciousness.

We left our bodies in order to find a safe place. To understand fully why this was necessary it is important to know the connection between our physical bodies and emotional process. Basically, there is no difference between the two. All of our thoughts, images, and emotions have their functional expressions in our bodies. There isn't anything that we do, think, or feel that doesn't involve our bodies. We feel our emotions in our bodies. Pleasure, sadness, anger, and need are all body experiences. In fact, our emotions are energy and body forms. To block our emotions is to block our body feelings and sensations. Therefore, to block our emotions is to have a body that is blocked. Whether we are aware of the basic unity of our existence or not, the body's connection with every part of who we are is still happening and affecting how we live. **We are our bodies. Our bodies are a direct and immediate expression of who we are.**

The example I used earlier, in which our need for reassurance was met with humiliation and disgust, provides us with a clearer view of this process. The disgust that we internalized is present as an energetic force within us. The disgust forms our beliefs about our needs and, therefore, affects the way we think about and live with our needs. That is, it will affect whether we think that needs are disgusting, and then, in turn, whether we are disgusted with our own needs and disgusted with the feeling of need when it is felt or expressed in other people.

How we learn to organize our bodies against the feeling of need affects our physical well-being. As indicated above, we may collapse and compress ourselves away from the feeling of disgust and humiliation in order to get away from that feeling. The collapse will effect the natural placement of our inner organs for they too become compressed. So too, will the distribution of blood, oxygen, and other nutrients be impacted, as even our blood vessels can compress under the weight of how we had to cope with the abuse.

Stanley Keleman writes about how continual patterns of emotional distress cause our internal tubes, layers, and pouches to arrange themselves in various forms, depending on the nature of the assault. One of the forms that our body can arrange itself into is a dense and collapsed structure. Here, "the pouches may telescope into each other so that the neck shortens, the waist disappears, the chest collapses, the head or belly swells. Under these conditions the tissue no longer supports waves of pulsation; thinking, feeling, action and uprightness are affected."[2] This is one example of how our learned body organizations create specific emotional sets. Various childhood assaults create different body organizations and therefore, different ways of experiencing and living with our emotions. Alexander Lowen and Stanley Keleman, as well as other writers, have written extensively about how childhood assaults creates specific body structures.

Our physical health also is affected by how we learned to defensively organize our bodies in relation to emotional and physical abuse. Various stomach and intestinal disorders are produced later in life because of our viscera having become compressed from a process that began as a way of defending ourselves.

Another example of how our health is impacted by how we learned to live as children has to do with how we may tighten our backs in an attitude of bravery, living as if we actually don't need anything. We develop a rigid, inflexible stance in our lives. This stance of denial becomes structured in our bodies so that it becomes a part of who we are and how we live in the world. We then become frightened of relaxing. We confuse collapse with the letting go and letting down that is essential to maintaining a healthy emotional and physical balance. We need to be able to balance our ability to organize ourselves in order persevere; to complete a task and move toward a goal, and our ability to let go into a state of rest where we may become temporarily unformed. Without this ability to balance between being organized and unorganized, between being formed and unformed, we meet the stresses of life with a constant and inflexible stance of bravery that becomes structured in our back and therefore, our back muscles become less resilient and flexible. We have called on the stance of rigid bravery one time to many. We wonder why simply bending over may cause our back to spasm. It was simply the result of the proverbial last straw.

Unlike our formal education, where we spend only part of each weekday in school and then have weekends, vacations, and summers off, we all have been taught every day of our lives how to live in our bodies. We have learned this within the intimacy of our families, set within the context of our society. Our parents have had the most profound impact on our development. As, children, they are the first people we bond with and we remain deeply connected to them in terms of our everyday needs and survival. Yet, society has its own profound impact on how we have learned to organize our bodies. We are constantly exposed to an array of influences that affect the way that we learn to live our lives. We absorb messages from relatives, friends, friends' families, teachers, and clergy, from television, movies, newspapers, books, and magazines. Whether directly or indirectly, we are constantly being bombarded by a constant stream of energetic, sensory messages about how we should look, feel, and act.

With all of this input and demand for the "shelf space" in our psyches, we live our bodies the way we do because it is the way that our life force balances its biological need to minimize pain and maximize pleasure. For so many people, survival, not satisfaction, is often the basis for how we have learned to live. Satisfaction will always be sacrificed if our need for safety and survival is more immediate. As children, our instinctive search for safety and survival provided us the emotional and body structure that allowed for the greatest amount of satisfaction that was possible within each situation. Whether our bodies took on various forms of rigidity or flaccidity, depersonalization or fragmentation, these were the body forms that helped us defend ourselves and remain as integrated as we could, given the abuse that came our way.

As adults, we continue holding onto the particular defensive structure that we developed as children even though the childhood abuse is no longer a part of our lives. We loathe letting go of familiar structures. We fight our own life force and spirit. Therefore, we remain in the same survival vs. satisfaction balance and battle.

Our life force always seeks ways to survive whatever situation it is presented with, however destructive it may be. The tenaciousness of the human spirit is beautiful to behold. And given the perfection of our spirit, unless as adults we fight our spirit, we automatically sacrifice only the exact amount of satisfaction needed to survive. This process of finding a balance between satisfaction and survival, between minimizing felt pain and maximizing pleasure, begins in fetal development. **The way we live all our energies, all our emerging emotions, even how we begin to organize our muscles, is absolutely efficient in terms of what we need to do to find this balance of survival and pleasure.** If there is a shock to our infant system, there will be a spontaneous contraction of our body in a very simple and efficient way in order to get away from the source of the shock and the feeling that shock creates in our bodies. This is an absolutely efficient process. Our bodies react with the precise amount of contraction needed to survive the amount of assault to our system. When the assault has passed, our entire system reopens, and this too is very efficient, clear, and a simple release of the shock and its resultant tension. If the shock is a single, not overly traumatic incident, after a time the body memory of the assault will fade. This sequence of events is apparent in an infant's startled response to a loud, abrupt noise, and then his/her relaxation after the noise is gone.

But suppose that abuse that keeps us in a constant state of shock is a chronic feature of our childhood. Then in the same simple and efficient manner, we learn to form our bodies based on what we have to do to survive such repeated abuse. With prolonged exposure to these assaults, such as physical abuse, or emotional rejection, humiliation, contempt, unreality, cruelty, abandonment, or craziness, our bodies do not lose the memories of the abuse. Therefore, our bodies are habitually organized to cope with the trauma. Whether or not the trauma is still present, we keep living our bodies, emotions, and energy in the same protective, defensive manner.

Through the years, the way that we have organized our bodies becomes the basic way that we know ourselves, a manner of being in the world so familiar it becomes second nature, our identity. A pattern has been set into our emotional DNA, and we are slaves to the rules that have become structured into this system. Later in life, even though this defensive way of being may not provide us with the greatest amount of satisfaction, we know no other way of being or are reluctant to change. At this point, change feels like giving up our identity. We experience our identity as the essence of who we are rather than as how we formed in order to protect ourselves. We are frightened of giving into the flow and the stream of life, into our spontaneous, organismic processes. We are frightened of giving up to our own life force, our own spirit. We are frightened that we will lose our hard won control and be left with nothing to hold onto.

Whatever struggles we may now have that prevent us from letting go of our old structure and transforming our lives so that we can feel more alive and satisfied are only signs that we did exactly what we needed to do as children in order to survive. In terms of the way that we learned to survive, we are living perfectly. As adults, we lose sight of the fact that the war is over.

The way that we learned to form our bodies as children is based on the impact of all of the experiences we have lived—every assault we have suffered, and every beautiful and supportive connection we have had. Our bodies carry the memories of these experiences. These are not intellectual, easily verbalized, or always pictorial memories. They are memories in all our muscles and in every tissue and cell of our body. They are experiential, energetic, and emotional memories that begin at conception and continue post-natally and are therefore, often pre- or nonverbal.

These childhood memories are brought forth toward consciousness by our life force in the orderly and efficient manner that is needed in order to help us return to a balanced, centered state. They are often released as body and emotional feelings, rather than as clear and distinct childhood memories. We need to learn to understand the language of our body and emotions so that we can receive the messages that are being sent to us.

An example of this is when we feel a new area of tension. The tension is our body's way of holding against a childhood experience that is rising toward consciousness but that was too difficult to feel and to integrate when we were younger. Perhaps it is some old grief about how we were abused. Or perhaps the feeling of the abuse itself is emerging. In our body's way of communicating with us it is telling us that we are once again holding against the experience of the childhood emotion and the memory of the abuse. The tension is our body's way of reminding us of the childhood feelings and events. It is our life force's way of offering us a chance to reconnect to how we learned to tense our muscles not to feel and to forget and deny what was happening to us. To learn to read the code is an opportunity to allow for the old emotional memory to return so that we no longer have to tense and hold against it. We then can return to a more balanced and centered body state and be on the path that leads to integration and expanded consciousness.

We need to learn to accept and live through the unfolding of the experiences of how we were treated as children. When we are able to live within the perspective that our uncomfortable, distressing, off-centered experiences, our tension and pain, are all the impact of our holding against childhood experiences, we realize the differences between the old realities of our childhood and current reality. We then realize how our childhood realities bleed through into our present reality.

As children, we were less powerful than we are as adults to fend off our parents when they were being assaultive. As adults, each time we bring compassion to our emotions and body experiences we are building a new support system, we are accumulating power. When we support ourselves with compassion we are also supporting our inner abused child who did not receive compassion.

A positive cycle develops. The more that we are able to support our inner child, the less we need to live in "role layer," and therefore, the more closeness we can allow with other people and, in turn, the more we can feel loved, supported, and nurtured. Part of the cycle becomes a giving up of old defensive structures born of our childhood experiences. When we no longer have to rigidly hold onto the emotional structures and body armor that we developed as children, our defenses against abuse soften and we can return to more balanced and harmonious state of emotional and physical well-being.

RESISTENCE

However, much of the time, we do not live our process this neatly. When the old forces of repression begin to weaken or break down, we often struggle not to feel what is opening in us, or we complain and condemn ourselves for whatever begins to percolate inside of us. All that we may be aware of is that the experiences feel horrible, and we may have some sense that we have been coping with these horrible feelings all our lives. We just want them to go away. We have no room to ask them what they are here for. Whatever the nature of our struggle, until we are able to be kind with ourselves, the fight keeps us away from being closer to our heart and our center.

Chronic complaining is an example of such a fight. When we reject our feelings and continue to complain about our distress we block out other people's concern. This is often opposite to what we truly desire. As we reject ourselves, we also are rejecting other people's support. This style of constant complaint becomes a way of life. It's becomes the way we say hello and reach for understanding. Unfortunately, it becomes the way life is drained of any pleasure. Other people feel drained when they are in contact with people who constantly complain and defeating other's concerns. There is no exchange of caring and energy.

Constantly complaining, we live unconscious to the fact that our life force is presenting us with the next experience that we need to accept and to integrate so that we can move toward wholeness. Chronic complaining is an expression of living our feelings as if we are still the child victim. We do not understand that our feelings are being presented to us by our life force so we can see and deal with what happened to us children. In effect, we are jamming the transmission from our spirit with our chronic complaints. If we stop complaining and accept the feelings that arise in us, we can begin to feel how we need to re-parent ourselves in a different and more caring way than the way that we were originally parented.

I am not suggesting that complaining is always counter-productive to aliveness. If we complain as a way of sharing our distress and then can soften so that we hear and "take in" people's caring and concern, this will bring us closer to our center and to other people and alleviate the distress that we have been feeling. However, if we chronically complain and feel that taking in understanding and compassion is tantamount to submission, we remain stuck in suffering. We remain stuck in a body structure that is organized into compression in order not to submit to the feelings of abuse that are stored in our body that created the compression in the first place.

As children we were victims of the abusive energies that came at us from grown ups. We needed our caregivers to provide for our survival and well being. However, as adults, to continue living as if we are still victims is to perpetuate the old assaultive energies that are stored in our bodies. We keep them in the dark, rather than allowing light to shine on them. In this way we perpetuate our old identity and prevent ourselves from accumulating the power to breathe mindfully, to bring appreciation to our feelings, and to feel supported by others. Instead, we hold our breath and feel that no one understands as we endlessly complain about how we feel.

The same is true of all defensive structures that are now our resistance to change. Whether it be frozenness that defends against feelings of terror and annihilation, collapse as a defense against deprivation and abandonment, shifting our center of gravity to the upper part of our body to defend against unreality and craziness, or withholding as a resistance to feeling how we were rejected, all structures that were organized to help us survive childhood abuse become a way that prevents us from feeling more alive in ourselves and intimate in our relationships.

To live mindfully and to have compassion for our feelings is be powerful in our own behalf. To endlessly complain, or to stay frozen, collapsed, in an upward displacement, or withholding about our feelings is to live with the old sense of helplessness, as if we were still children, wanting someone to come along and save us, yet never allowing anyone to really touch us. Building a body that is supported by self-appreciation, and allowing ourselves to be touched emotionally by others, allows us to relive our childhood experiences in a way that creates the kind of parenting that we needed but didn't receive as children.

When we stand in the center of whatever it is that we feel, we are clearing out and then filling in the holes in our personality that were created by the childhood abuse and our defenses against the abuse. We are cleaning out the old assaultive energies and the feelings of emptiness, deprivation, alienation, and meaninglessness that are the byproducts of having been assaulted. We are then filling in the cleared out spaces with appreciation, caring, respect, mindfulness, and dignity. In reliving our experiences in this way, we return to the center of our beings. This is the process of transformation that leads to satisfaction and meaning that becomes our path toward enlightenment.

THE CONNECTION BETWEEN INTIMACY
AND OUR BODY RELEASING OLD TRAUMA:
LIVING THROUGH DEATH LAYER

As we un-form our defensive structures and our bodies soften and relax, old repressed energies have the opportunity to emerge into consciousness. A natural process unfolds. As we open to ourselves, we are also opening to the next piece of un-integrated energy. For example, letting go of our defensive way of constantly staying busy and believing that we always need to have something "constructive to do" can energize old victimizing energies that create agitation. Or we may feel that we always need to be in intimate contact with someone or we fall into a pit of emptiness and aloneness. For example, if the latter is the case, then unfinished business from our childhood arises when a person chooses to temporarily "take some space" after we have had intimate contact with them. This experience can either be a simple matter or one in which an array of emotions are activated.

Remember a time when you felt a deep, loving connection with a friend, lover, or spouse. Then imagine that after this loving contact they withdrew to do something that didn't involve you even though you wanted them to remain open and in contact with you. If you didn't have the support within yourself to hold the open hearted connection to the person and be able to return to your own inner connection, you might have felt angry, frantic, depressed, collapsed, longing, abandoned, agitated, lost, humiliated, desperate or crazy.

Without support for your own process, these are times when it can be difficult to easily come back to yourself or to reach out to a friend for support so you can return to a more centered place in yourself. Instead, you might spend your time complaining to friends about your situation, not being able to emotionally separate so that you can feel full being alone or with friends. Or perhaps, in order not to feel these experiences, you might find yourself fighting with the other person, blaming them for their withdrawal, believing that what they did was wrong or bad.

This kind of fight that is full of blame and underlying desperation is what we call an *impasse fight*. That is, the underlying purpose of the fight is to avoid having to come home to ourselves in a deeper way. If what awaits us when we give up the fight are the distressing feelings of depression, loss, longing, abandonment, rejection, annihilation, craziness, etc., we can't let go of the other person. We resist the feelings that are contained in what is called Death Layer.

"Death Layer" is the layer of experience where feelings of childhood trauma reside that we believe we are unable to tolerate. It feels as if we will die if we take another step into the experience. In the Death Layer experience we reexperience emotional, physical, and energetic abuse as both the introjected abuser and the child who was the victim of the abuse. For example, if our care giver's energy and actions originate from acting out cruelty, hate, humiliation, abandonment, depression, rejection, craziness, deprivation, unreality, seduction, invasion, devouring, incest and/or sodomy, etc., it leaves its mark.

In effect, as children there was a spontaneous, organismic movement in us that created the perfect internal organization that helped us survive with as much integrity, power, and pleasure as possible. It was beyond our ability as vulnerable children to live in the rawness of the impact of abuse. This was especially true when our protest to being assaulted did not stop the abuse.

These body memories that emerge not only reflect what was done to us, but also how we felt about being abused (our fear, anger, sadness, etc.). The memories also contain the cellular experiences of how we physically and emotionally reacted to the assault. That is, how we may have tightened our muscles, spaced out, collapsed, become unreal, etc., in order to defend ourselves.

The body and emotional memories also hold the old feelings of powerlessness, helplessness, and despair, as well as our sadness and anger at the injustice, and our fear that our aliveness was tampered with and could be again. Emptiness, deprivation, alienation, and meaninglessness that are by-products of having been assaulted, are also present. All of the moments where our muscles remain chronically tense or we are living in isolation, deadness, collapse, or the ickiness that we don't have words for, the unnamed something we've lived with and hated all our lives, or the experience of flatness, blankness, and spaciness, all have specific meaning in terms of how we lived and survived our childhood and may open under the intensity of intimacy.

If this is what is waiting for us, we can appreciate why we wouldn't want to return home to ourselves by being gracious with the other person for moving away. We can also begin to appreciate why we might argue with them, rather than accept their taking space. It feels safer to fight than to feel what's waiting inside of us. Since we may be disconnected from the truth that these feelings have anything to do with our childhood, we might feel angry and frustrated with ourselves and/or blaming of the other person. Perhaps we feel spiteful and full of revenge. Unable to factor in that spite and revenge was the only place of power that we felt as children, we can easily feel justified that spite and revenge are all about the present situation.

Just like we are back in our childhood reality, we believe that spite and revenge are now our only power and our only protest. We wind up punishing the person who has just backed away from us when they return. In this way, we would be treating ourselves and the other person in the same way we were treated when we were assaulted as children. In effect, we are being like both the victimized and spiteful child who has no control over being left, as well as the punishing parent.

In intimacy our emotions and our body opens. In the example of our partner withdrawing, we can be thrown into the Death Layer experience because we have opened beyond the place where our usual defensive structure has organized us away from Death Layer.

Because of the avoidance of the Death Layer feelings, or our non-acceptance of these feelings if we are aware of them, we are prevented from naturally coming home to ourselves when the other person withdraws. In a sense, we are stuck outside of ourselves feeling as if we desperately need the other person for our survival.

In reality, it is our connection to our own life force and the ground that we need. **Living through the Death Layer experiences is how we get there. There is always aliveness beyond Death Layer.**

However, if we have no understanding and support to live with and through these feelings, then fighting, complaining, or just being stuck becomes safer. As the other person withdraws, we can blame ourselves or them for our feelings rather then understand that the Death Layer feelings that are being touched actually are from our childhood.

To re-emphasize: the emotional and physical uncomfortable, distressing, stressful, painful, frightening feelings we experience are the result of old childhood assaultive energies that we have been holding against. We can often believe that if we can have perfect, expansive contact with someone else, we can avoid these feelings forever. However, in relationships where there is deep contact, it is the very nature of the intimate contact that allows us to open more to ourselves. Then, when the other person moves away we are left with our own process. At these times we need support and appreciation to contain what we are feeling in order to come home to ourselves. Blame and addictions distract us from the task at hand.

We need a frame of reference that provides understanding that these feelings are messages from our life force informing us about what we need to deal with next to have more of ourselves. As we build in our internal supports to live into each feeling that opens in us, we can more easily separate from the old negative, childhood bonding energy to live through the Death Layer feelings that have been touched. We can then return home to our center and to our spirit.

Supporting ourselves through the Death Layer experiences is necessary for our continued growth and integration. As we work in therapy to identify and work with the feelings that are opening in us as the old abuse from childhood (Death Layer), we are building support to live through these feelings. We are gathering support so that sharing how we feel with a friend becomes about taking in a connection for the Death Layer experiences, rather than merely complaining about how we are feeling. Without the therapeutic interventions, we most often flounder in the feelings or continue to resist them.

We all need a sense of community to help us through the difficult times in our lives. The way that we use our community support is also important. If we share as a way of making contact, then the sharing becomes a way of supporting ourselves through the feelings. So much of the time discussions with friends focus on how the other person we are upset with should be different. We end up blaming, looking for justification for how we feel, rather than gathering support to live through our own feelings.

When we know that the experiences we are having are Death Layer feelings, then we are also more able to "live into" the experiences and find a quiet place inside of ourselves to come home to. Either way can help us live through the Death Layer feelings so that we can return to our center and the renewed feeling of aliveness that is waiting for us there.

Feeling more centered and embodied we are more available for contact without blame or spite when there is an opportunity for contact with the original person. When both people in a relationship live in this way there is a simple flow between contact and withdrawal.

Let's look even more closely at the meaning of these uncomfortable, Death Layer feelings. As we open our hearts and our body to someone else, a body memory of support or abuse will be released. This body memory will reflect either how we were supported in childhood in flowing with the natural rhythmic movements of life or victimized for our simple needs for contact and withdrawal. What at first might seem like "just a bad feeling" actually has many facets to it.

As we have seen, it is common to live our feelings and reactions to everyday events, as when someone withdraws after having been intimate, without any awareness of what is actually going on with our deeper process. It is important to understand that so often as children, we had to separate from the conscious memories of abuse. As Kurt Vonnegut has written so eloquently in *Slapstick*, "The museums of children's minds automatically empty themselves in times of utmost horror to protect the children from eternal grief."[3] It is unfortunate that, as children, we were emotionally and/or physically victimized. We absorbed the assaultive energies, and now, as adults, we either live fused in the victim-victimizer energy, or we are free; both ways of living deeply impacts our relationships, one positively, the other negatively.

If we can't move freely between contact and withdrawal, it is because we are fused in the old, negative energies of our childhood. When we are not fused in these old, negative energies, we are free to live our lives clearly and simply from our own centers. Then, we are not burdened by our histories that we otherwise carry around with us in all the muscles and sinew of our bodies.

APPRECIATING AND UNDERSTANDING THE EFFICIENCY OF PROCESS

No matter what we may be experiencing, there is an organismic reason for the particular experience. What we are experiencing is never a sign of bad or wrong, worthlessness or stupidity. The unpleasant, at times traumatic, feelings are always current reality, touching past emotional/body memories in the unfolding process. The orderly and efficient unfolding of our body memories carries us through a cycle of victim and victimizer, impasse, death layer, and aliveness. Each experience is worthy of appreciation and understanding no matter how unpleasant it is. The significance of appreciating and understanding each experience cannot be overemphasized. How we feel is never a sign that something is wrong with us; it is a sign that something wrong was done to us and that we are now reliving that experience. The fact that we are reliving the experience is a sign that we "work

right," that our bodies are attending to a "sore spot," an old wound that needs attention in order to heal so that we can achieve a deeper sense of balance and inner peace.

CASE STUDY, DEBRA:
"I CAN'T STOP BEING ANGRY"

An example of how we "work right," how our life force presents us with what we need to deal with so that we can come to center, can be seen in a session with Debra. Debra came into my office and told me that she wanted to feel more satisfied in herself. Unlike many clients, she was not looking for the external aspects of her life to be different. Rather, she felt that she couldn't allow herself to feel pleasure about the good things that were going on in her life. She was aware that she was distancing herself from what was positive about her life.

I asked her to be aware of her voice and how she was talking to me as she told me about her concerns. She was aware that her voice was tight and thin, and that she was talking very fast. I was aware of how high strung and tense she was. She reported how desperate she felt regarding compulsively saying "no" all the time, even to the people that she loved. Her immediate response to people asking her for anything, especially her ten year old daughter, was an emphatic no. She felt that she had no control over feeling hard, angry, and disconnected from her body. The way that she was emotionally and physically organized in her body prevented experiences from being pleasurable and satisfying.

What emerged as the session progressed was Debra's awareness that she felt shame if she began to soften and relax. She was fused with humiliation in a way that she believed there was something basically wrong with her. During the session she became aware that the internal messages that produced the shame were the same humiliating messages that she received as a child from her mother. As a child, Debra felt hopeless about doing anything to get her mother to stop humiliating her.

Debra felt that there was something basically wrong and bad

about herself as she had fused with the childhood messages of humiliation from her mother. At the same time, her father had been very seductive with her, always wanting her to be bright and alive. He had no support for the range of emotions that occur in children. His range was happiness or nothing.

It was safer for her to harden and keep her energy in the upper half of her body and say "no" to the people that she cared about. This was safer than to soften, and allow her energy to drop in her body and to open her heart and feel the old humiliation and seduction that surrounded it. Since she had internalized feelings of how hopeless it was as a child to stop the way that her parents treated her, she still believed that it was hopeless to find a different way of being. Despite feeling hopeless, she wanted to give therapy a try.

The way Debra tensed her body in order not to feel the depth of the humiliation, seductive energy, and hopelessness, created Debra's particular set of body and emotional experiences. This was the underlying basis for the specific tension pattern that caused her to be so high strung. It was as if she were being stretched in two directions. In fact, she was. Her mother had been pulling her in one direction, her father in the other. She was constantly attempting to cope with 1) the underlying feelings of worthlessness caused by the humiliation, 2) the sexual charge caused by constant seduction by her father, 3) feeling crazy as a result of being torn in two directions, and 4) the hopelessness of not being able to stop either of her parents.

Furthermore, this constant emotional, energetic, and bodily tension pattern caused Debra to organize her energy in her head and the upper part of her body. The impact of the abuse was a major assault to her groundedness. Her parents couldn't tolerate her being fully alive, embodied, and grounded.

She complied and became the child her parent's had wanted; always looking bright and happy and full of energy for her father, while at the same time, being emotionally distant, non-existent and not liking herself for her mother. As her therapy progressed, we understood the other abusive forces in her childhood that added to her upward displacement of energy.

**Remember, every body sensation and emotional experi-
ence makes sense, however formed and clear or unformed and
muddled. The fact that Debra felt the way she did was not a
sign that something was wrong with her. It was a sign that
something wrong (abusive) was done to her and that as a
child, she was helpless to do anything about it. She had learned
to victimize herself in the same way she had been victimized.**

She remained a victim of the humiliation, seduction, craziness,
and hopelessness. She was stuck in these energies and the holding
pattern that had been set in place not to feel these energies. Until she
is able to gather enough support to live through the underlying feelings that she is guarding against, being stuck is Debra's safe place.

She saved herself from the hatred that was in her mother's humiliation the best way she knew how. She saved herself from her father's
seduction by saying "No" on the inside, while looking as if she was
saying "Yes" on the outside. Her constant look of brightness and
happiness was a façade. Her holding pattern was the 'No," the protest
that she could not openly have as a child with her parents.
Unfortunately, the "No" was now so structured in her body and
psyche that it compulsively emerged with everyone whom she was
close to. As an adult, if she continues to emotionally beat herself
for how she is living, she abuses herself through self-humiliation,
internal seduction, and by driving herself crazy, in the same way
that these energies came at her as a child.

Once again, it is not true that something is wrong with her, or that
she deserves to be humiliated, seduced, and driven crazy. Actually,
she deserves appreciation and love for how she was treated as a
child, and that she had to find a way to go along with her parents in
order to survive. She deserves appreciation and love for her defensive structure that created her compulsive "No." How her body and
emotions are organized is a sign of the heroics that she needed to
survive. It is also an indication that her body and life force were
working to save her from the abusive forces in her childhood.

As therapy progressed, Debra was able to take in understanding
and appreciation for how she had to form around the assaults of her

childhood. She was able to soften and open her heart more. In this way, she also felt more in possession of her anger, rather then her anger possessing her. Therefore, there was a diminution of her compulsively saying "No" to her daughter and other people that she loved. When she was angry, her anger was now a passionate anger that came from her heart, rather than a defensive anger that indirectly expressed her childhood frustrations. She had been angry and punishing of the wrong people as she held them out of her heart. Being able to soften and open her heart more and possess the power that comes from her passionate anger about her childhood, gave her the ability to feel the positive things that were happening in her life. It also helped her gain perspective about her childhood that led to being separate from it and therefore, ultimately, less angry.

BONDING AND EMBODIMENT

How we care about ourselves as adults is based on the emotional and energetic climate that was provided for us when we were children. We bond with and internalize whatever energies were available to us. If love and support were present for us to take in during our formative years, we now have this as the emotional and energetic substance that we use to parent ourselves. If abuse, i.e., the energy of humiliation, invasion, negativity, rejection, abandonment, unreality, seduction, cruelty, hatred, incest, craziness, etc., were what was available during those early years, then this is the self-parenting energy that we return to, especially in times of stress. In effect, we become our own worst enemy, for we have become our own victimizers.

With negative bonding, we learn to hate or feel disgusted and frustrated with how we feel and live, or we continue to seduce ourselves out of our own perception of reality, or we invade and undermine everything that we feel or want. We abuse ourselves for not feeling stronger, clearer, and more alive. We have learned to reject or abandon ourselves when we most need a loving and compassionate connection. During these times of self-victimizing, it is the negativity that we have internalized during the bonding process that emerges as we start to feel more alive. This occurs because our aliveness is fused with the childhood assault energy. As our aliveness opens the feelings/energies of the assaults are also energized.

There is a life force in all of us that is always moving us to grow toward greater aliveness, completion, and spirit. Even through the negative bonding energies, our life force still has a part in directing us. It certainly has been our ally in helping us survive whatever trauma has been a part of our lives. Given the right circumstances, our life force can shine through like a long dormant bulb springing forth into life.

Our life force has been present from the moment of conception. From the single fertilized cell, as egg and sperm joined, our life and growth began. From the moment of conception, no matter how our parents felt about having us, we continuously moved toward our birth. As a growing embryo and then as an infant and growing child it was our birthright to live in safety and comfort.

At the deepest level of our biological, animal nature, our spirit is doing whatever is necessary for us to be in balance and to maintain our internal stability; at first to cry, scream or fuss if we were hungry or in other forms of distress. We made sounds of contentment when all was well and later reached out for love, understanding and touch, or withdrew in order to be quiet with our own thoughts and feelings, or when the contact felt uncomfortable.

Our needs for acceptance, understanding, and individuation took form as we grew. At the same time, at the deepest level of our biological, animal nature, we bonded with our parents in our dynamic process of staying alive and growing. We took on many of our parents' characteristics; we imitated the way they spoke, the way they walked, developed similar facial expressions and other body mannerisms. We were energetic and emotional templates absorbing the totality of their energy and emotions. Energetically, we became "chips off the old block."

We needed them for our survival and satisfaction. And we continued needing them to protect, love, and nurture us as we grew. Unknowingly, we paid dearly for our fragile state by internalizing so much of who they were and how they treated us. We paid dearly, because we internalized their negativity, hostility, and their lack of support toward us as much as we internalized whatever love, encouragement and support was available from them.

To some degree we could protect ourselves, but only to the limit of our dependent, vulnerable system. Instinctively, we knew when we were in danger so that we could protect ourselves. A sudden sharp, loud noise when we were an infant was perceived as an attack. The intensity is more than our vulnerable system can tolerate. We spontaneously shrink and become smaller in the face of being assaulted. This is our way of defending against attack. We automatically move away from the source of the assaultive sound in order to protect our core. The greater the intensity and the longer the duration of the attack, the more likely it is that our natural defense system would be permanently violated. The body and emotional pattern of shrinking, that tension pattern, would be set in place as a permanent fixture of our being. We would have needed outside protection to stop the noise so that we would have room to expand and feel alive again.

The same is true of the assaultive energies that come from our parents. Parents that are emotionally and/or physically violent have the same impact on the child as does that sudden and then constant loud noise. It causes the infant to shrink, to become frozen.

The kind of protection and safety that we needed to recover from the assault was an open hearted, energetic bond with our parents. **We needed parents who would fight for our right to live an alive and vibrant existence. This would have meant setting a boundary for us against the assaultive energy when we were unable to do this for ourselves. Feeling our parent's open hearted protection is tantamount to absorbing safety.** We would then have been able to feel grounded in their stronger energetic and physical field. It would allow us to remain in balance, opening or closing, moving toward contact or withdrawal, all within our own biological and emotional rhythm.

We would bond with the supportive connection, and therefore we would have been able to know our needs for support. The positive bond would become imprinted into our system, rather than having to shrink and feel that shrinking is the form of protection that is available to us. With protection and the feeling of safety, we could have remained in balance. Positive bonding enhances every aspect of life.

It would certainly have been wonderful if we could have gotten all the loving, supportive, and protective connections that we needed to help us feel secure and remain fully embodied. None of us did. Although this is what we needed, it does not follow that our parents were always free of acting out their negativity, that they always cherished and wanted us, that they were happy with their own existence and were free of the burdens and stresses of life. Therefore, it does not follow that they always felt supportive and loving of us while we were inutero, infancy, or childhood. Quite the contrary, all of our parents were human, possessing both positive and negative qualities. All people are a combination of light and dark and, therefore, all parents act out to varying digress.

As our parents deal with the pressures of life they are attempting to find love and meaning in their lives. At the same time they are coping with the energy of their own childhood abuse that would cause them to live away from their centers. Parents may have their own underlying feelings of sadness, anger, frustration, and bitterness at how they had to compromise and not have the lives that they might have dreamed about as children or as young adults. Other parents learn to look and act as if everything is perfect, yet they do this by disconnecting from what is real inside of them. To look perfect and disconnect from a deeper sense of reality is also assaultive to us. The nature of this kind of abuse is to teach us to turn against our own humanness. In this way, we are taught that everything is about form, rather than substance.

We bonded with all of the various off-centered currents within our parents. This created a conflict between our emotional, spiritual, and biological need for a safe home and the truth that the only home we had required us to defend ourselves in some form or another against our parents. The negative legacy from our parents is that all of their unresolved and unformed negative energy and emotions were transmitted to us.

The transmission of our parents' energies began while we were still in utero. There is convincing research that suggests that we are affected by our parents' emotions, both conscious and unconscious, prior to birth.[4] The bonding process continues to be complicated after we are born when our parents' feelings toward us were negative. Our parents did not create a problem for us when they were able to contain their anger in a flexible manner and share with us in a clear, simple, non-blaming manner that they were angry or when they told us that there was something that we did that they didn't like. To have treated us in this way teaches us how to respect ourselves and other people. It was their disowned, and therefore, acted out negativity that created a problem for us.

Bonding with our parents is the basis for how we parent ourselves. Negative self parenting has it roots in those moments that our aliveness triggered the assault energy our parents internalized from their parents. Then the very expression of our aliveness would be met with the assaultive energy that was touched in them. These were times that our parents believed that we were victimizing them rather their knowing that their feelings were based on their own internalized negative childhood energies. During these times our parents felt justified in abusing us. They might have believed that they were saving their lives or their sanity. They might have believed that how they felt was simply their anger. However, blame contains cruelty and violence and therefore, blame comes at us as an energy of destruction.

The energy of destruction is exactly what it sounds like. This is an energy, a feeling, that our parents want to destroy us. It can have many different emotional and energetic expressions. These energies are all disowned in that our parent's justify their feelings. They can come at us in an overly hard, rigid, irresponsible way, as an outright assault, control, and bullying manner that many parents practice. There can be a harshness that is the energy of smashing, knifing, murderousness, or annihilation. Uncentered anger can also be fused with the energy and belief of the importance of punishment and revenge toward the child as being essential. All of these beliefs and energetic qualities are conveyed to us and internalized by us as children.

Parents' disowned negativity also can be diffuse, like a fog that passes through all openings and gets into our bodies and emotions. Here the negativity is being denied and hidden at the same time that it emanates from our parents' bodies. A simple example of this is a parent acting in some unreal, pleasant way, but denying that he or she is angry and feels destructive. This parent doesn't clearly share that they are angry. In fact, they might always look happy as they tell the child that he or she is only being helpful and doing whatever it is for the child's own good.

These negative energies are assaultive to our life and growth. Without having experienced an open-hearted connection with our parents, their chronically closed heart in and of itself is assaultive. We then have to protect ourselves from the same person we are bonded with as our protector and nurturer.

One of my partners at Hartford Family Institute wrote: "One of the ways we keep children unprotected is by not acknowledging how we, as parents, can be the greatest adversaries our children will encounter. Because of the depth of connection and absolute need children have for parents, everything that we, as parents, do touches our children at the deepest places of their existence. We, therefore, have the power to wound our children more deeply than anyone else in the world. To openly acknowledge this with heart and help our children build their power to defend themselves in an open way against us, is to provide them with the resources they will need as they mature, separate from us and move out into the world. This acknowledgment of the adversarial aspect of parent-child relationships should be a custom. The entire pretense that is lived about love, with the denial of hate, violence, and negativity has a crippling effect on a child's inner power and resources. Having to blind ourselves to the power parents have to hurt our children translates into having to live a constant state of defensiveness."[5]

As children we were in an organismic state of conflict because of our parents' victimizing energy. We wanted to move freely and openly toward our parents for love, protection, and for nurturance, and to share our own feelings of love, excitement, and distress. However, when our parents didn't have a way of containing their negativity, we needed to withdraw and close ourselves in order to feel some sense of protection from their assaultive energy. A deep split is produced within us when we identify our parents with abuse rather than safety and nurturance.

The degree to which our parents and the energy of 'home' were assaultive to our aliveness is the degree to which there was an internal movement to get away from being at home in our bodies. The more assaultive the energy in our childhood was, the more frantic we want to get out of our bodies. At the same time we still need love. We need nurturance even more because the assault to our aliveness cuts us off from the center of our life force, and therefore, the center of our own supports and our internal sense of meaning. Without a sense of being deeply embodied we loose the connection to what has meaning for us. We become more dependent on other people to help us create meaning in our lives.

A vicious cycle develops. We all are born being dependent. When abused, we defend ourselves by contracting against the assaultive energies which moves us away from the center of our aliveness. When our dependence is met and we feel nurtured, we are able to feel what has meaning for us since we are more in tune with the core of who we are. Being abused, we loose a deeper connection to our core and, therefore, we loose a connection to meaning. Then, in turn, as we are disconnected from our center we become more internally formless and are more likely to bond with the unreal, overly competitive, aggressive, mechanical aspects of our society. Labile on the inside, we can become rigid on the outside in order to function.

We grow up with the memories of our childhood. If the memories are not vivid in our awareness, they are memories in our body: as a muscle memory, as tissue memory. Because of the way we retain our childhood as body memories, to internally return home, which means to return to our own center, to our heart, to a deeper, embodied state of satisfaction, is to re-experience the energies of our childhood assaults. What a paradox! When we begin to open to ourselves, at first what we may experience is an uncomfortable feeling full of distress and agitation, rather then the pleasure of feeling alive.

Therefore, to open more deeply to ourselves is often to experience the old assaultive energies that we absorbed from our parents. To open may be to re-experience such old feelings as unreality, craziness, abandonment, cruelty, contempt, smashing, seduction, incest etc. Also, we come up against all the internalized societal messages about how to be. The more formless the assaults were when they were delivered, the more our experience of the assaults will be wrapped in the experience of formlessness. And if we don't have support to feel the clear energies of the assault, we will take another step away from our center and feel vague and formless body moods, such as helplessness, despair, collapse, flatness, isolation, spaciness, or perhaps just a vague and persistent feeling that nothing is right.

We need safety to embody our experiences. At the same time we feel the need to get away from ourselves in order to feel safe. For each of us, to various degrees, home as an actual physical and emotional place was unsafe; and therefore, home as the experience of a fully embodied state also becomes unsafe. To the degree that we internalized the lack of safety in our childhood homes, we do not go into the world, away from home, feeling safe. We do not enter the world fully embodied.

DEFENSIVE STRUCTURES: HOW WE LEARN TO PROCESS INFORMATION

Because no child can actively live in the feelings produced by this conflict, a number of defensive systems develop. In the extreme form, our need to block out our parent's assaultive energies leads to emotional blindness and paranoia. In the less extreme case we block out the awareness or expression of our needs and live a life of emotional stoicism. Or we may over identify with our needs. Here, we are intolerant of other peoples' needs. We live as if other people having need take something away from us. It is difficult for us to feel satisfied.

Another possibility is that we become rebellious and act out. We live our life in opposition to our parents. In this way rebellion becomes the continuing connection to our parents. Living in opposition, rather from our own centers, is not freedom.

Without having been supported into a full and safe energetic connection to our bodies, we feel unsafe. The more unsafe we feel in our bodies, the more we feel a frantic need to search for safety outside of our bodies. Then, in turn, we feel a need to get away from the frantic feeling. So we tense, or collapse, become flaccid or dissociate, all in order not to feel unsafe and our need for safety. Yet, returning to our emotions is exactly what needs to happen for us to come home to our body.

Instead, we have been cut off from our emotions and our senses and we perpetuate this pattern. Since the path toward feelings has a detour sign around it, we are unable to feel a way out. What's left for us is to *think* a way out. We go over and over in our thoughts how to be safe, how to feel some sense of power and integrity in ourselves; and conversely how to escape feeling powerless, hopeless, and other assaultive energies. We go around and around with these thoughts; sometimes clearly, at other times very muddled.

The more tense, collapsed, flaccid, or spaced we become because of the impact of the abuse and as a way of finding safety, the faster all of this goes on inside of us. Our thoughts then move past our mind's eye as a never changing kaleidoscope not clear enough to hold onto or slow enough to stop and see. Our thoughts become our support. The more unsafe we feel the more we either spin in our thinking or lose the ability to think and reason clearly at all. We hold onto our particular thought pattern, when giving it up would open us to memories and feelings stored in our bodies. Our thoughts become something we hold onto, because there wasn't the support of a caring parent to hold onto. It doesn't matter whether we feel that this is effective or not. It doesn't matter whether there is pain or frustration associated with this way of functioning. What matters is that in relative terms, deep inside of us, we believe that this is the safest place there is for us when we need to feel safe by getting away from the experiences that are held in our bodies. This was the safest way of being organized for us as children. This old truth is now structured into our bodies and psyches.

All of this can happen either in our awareness or occur so quickly and formlessly that we only experience it as constant noises or voices that go on in our heads. If we are even more removed from the reality of our bodies, because the reality of our childhood was too devastating to live, then our obsessions also become further removed from their source. That is, our obsessions may no longer be about how we were abused as children. Rather, our minds are filled with distracting thoughts so as not to remember the abuse. We then obsess about the weather, our job, relationships, money, perhaps, how the world is filled with violence and that people are always out to get you, or what to buy and what to wear. We may obsess about our weight and all the ways we aren't like the perfect model that society has set up for us to emulate. Any and all decisions may become major problems to be endlessly pondered and deliberated, with no possibility for failure overlooked. Any decision becomes a commitment that takes us a step closer to ourselves. Commitment means landing and making contact with ourselves. This will touch the energy of our childhood assaults. It feels safer to believe that there is no safe place in the world than to revisit the utter helplessness of our childhood. In being unable to live with and through the reality that our childhood was not safe, we perpetuate living frightened, frantic, and numb.

I want to reemphasize that whatever we are experiencing is exactly what we should be experiencing. In reality, our bodies and emotions are perfect expressions of our history. We are living our lives based on the degree of support we have for our aliveness. Therefore, how we live is always based on having found the safest place in ourselves at any given

**moment. This is always true. No matter how we are living at
any moment it is the safest place we have found.**

Besides our obsessivness, being addicted to alcohol or drugs,
being a workaholic or compulsively needing constant sexual activity,
being in physical pain based on extreme muscle tension, or being in
a psychotic hallucinatory state, all represent different ways that we
are attempting to find safety. The severity of these activities and
emotional states are our coding the degree of that we feel unsafe.
Being filled with our child victimizing energies we are both acting out
these negative energies through our addictions and expressing our
need for safety at the same time.

We always live the best way we know how. The various ways
that we learn to cope with our childhood abuse goes on. Living
emotionally in suffering or danger can also be the safest place we
know how to live. To give up suffering and chronic complaining or
danger, and therefore, live outside of the identity of being a victim
or needing a constant adrenal high, might mean that we have to
feel the real devastation of our childhood. In this case, living the
life of a martyr or living on the edge of life and death is safer.

In terms of living the life of a martyr, we can recall the earlier
discussion about constantly complaining. We may believe that we are
always being caring and doing everything to make others happy. In
this scenario, we believe that we are never cared about enough to
alleviate our misery. We believe that we are always giving more
than we receive. Suffering and torture are our constant companions,
yet we believe it is the way that other people treat us that is the
problem. What we are unaware of is that the suffering and torture is
the childhood energy of abuse that we grew up in. We are filled with
this old suffering and torture and continue to act it out, believing that
it is always about the current situation. This belief is our distorted
sense of safety. Until we have support to revisit the truth of our
childhood, it is safer to continue to believe our present life is what
causes the suffering and torture.

On the other end of a polarity from suffering is someone who has
to live the adrenal rush of living with danger. Someone involved in

extreme sports is an example of living danger as their safest place. Not to be involved in constantly pushing ourselves to the limit can open the experience of restlessness, boredom, despair or humiliation that we are being less than we can be. When being pushed and challenged is filled with contempt and shaming it mirrors abusive, negative parenting. Being driven with this energy, rather than being encouraged with love, creates an underlying sense of depression that we organize against by risking our life in the exploration of a new challenge. Then, extreme sports become an addiction that is fueled by the internal pressure to remain distant from the old victimizing energies.

This doesn't mean that we never challenge ourselves. There are times when we have enough support that we can give up comfort for the aliveness and excitement that can come from a new challenge. We give up the known, because we have the support to seek deeper levels of aliveness, instead of living an old level of comfort. There is an internal restlessness that calls us to move on. Our spirit, our life force, is calling us, and we are following the call. Not to go on at this point feels like dying, and in fact, not to follow the call at this point is to take a step toward an emotional numbness, a piece of emotional dying. At that moment the challenge is safer than the emotional and energetic death. The more that we are on speaking terms with our inner, emotional process, the more that we have a sense of when we are living our lives out of defensiveness and when we are living and following our life force.

We need to grow and move in order to feel alive. We need to balance moving with rest and quiet. We need this organismic balance. Our life force, our spirit, is constantly pointing us in the direction of enlightenment. The path to enlightenment needs to include our body. Balancing and tuning our body aligns our frequencies with the beat of the earth. We need to embody our life force and appreciate our emotional and physical experiences. Only then can we give up certain body states and move to higher planes of existence.

Remember, no matter what we are feeling and how we are living, whether it feels satisfying or not, whether it is pleas-

urable or frustrating, energizing or full of tension, we are always living the safest way that we know how to live. Because we are all products of our childhood experiences, any way that our life force has helped us organize ourselves is a sign that we "work" correctly and that all of our experiences are worthy of love and understanding. We all need validation for all the aspects of our humanness. We need appreciation and support for who we have become. Whatever the nature of our support, it is at the center of how we live and form ourselves. In the next chapter we will look into the nature of support.

CHAPTER FIVE

Supports and How They Got Bad Press

Our deepest fear is not that we are inadequate. Our deepest fear is that we are powerful beyond measure. It is our light, not our darkness that most frightens us. We ask ourselves, Who am I to be brilliant, gorgeous, talented, fabulous? Actually, who are you not to be? You are a child of God. Your playing small does not serve the world. There is nothing enlightened about shrinking so that other people won't feel insecure around you. We are all meant to shine, as children do. We were born to make manifest the glory of God that is within us. It is not just in some of us; it is in everyone. And as we let our own light shine, we unconsciously give other people permission to do the same. As we are liberated from our own fear, our presence automatically liberates others.
—Marianne Williamson[1]

WE ARE HEROES IN OUR OWN LIVES

WE ARE HEROES IN OUR OWN LIVES. NO MATTER HOW WE struggle, we have found creative and heroic ways of supporting ourselves and surviving. Supports are everything that we do to survive. Supports are how we maintain ourselves in the world, cope with our inner emotional and physical processes, how we sustain ourselves in relationships, deal with conflict, how we cope with daily living and try to transcend our daily lives and expand beyond our everyday existence.

Everything that we do, every way that we have learned to live, is a support. To the degree that we received caring for each moment of the forming or unforming of our aliveness as we grew up, to that same degree we can support ourselves with caring. And caring supports lead to feeling alive, compassionate with ourselves and others, and possessing a sense of well- being. To the degree that we were assaulted for our aliveness, our supports take on a totally different tone. Abuse creates more of a survival mode of living. We have to defend ourselves against the abuse and then our defenses, our resistance to aliveness, become our supports. Although our defensive supports help us survive, at the same time, they limit our aliveness as adults. They were our allies to begin with, and now, as adults, these supports have taken over and lead the show. Therefore, they lead to a darker and less alive existence. This is why I call them defensive supports.

An example of a caring support is as simple as self-love and compassion for how we feel. When we can hold ourselves in the energy of love for who we are and what we do, we experience a feeling of support. If both our conscious and deeper body memories are mostly of positive and validating experiences, we grow up with a positive sense of ourselves. This positive feeling forms a base of positive support. We feel good in our bodies, our emotions do not feel alien to us, and we possess a positive inner attitude regarding our own aliveness. In this way, our energetic, body, and emotional memories are support for our aliveness. The positive, internalized memories help us move in the direction of authenticity and aliveness. These internalized memories are support for our growth and aliveness being natural and wonderful parts of our existence, rather than something that we have to defend against. Here, we have not learned to be self-destructive and to get in the way of our own life force.

An example of negative, defensive support is spite, various forms of tension or formlessness, depression etc. When we look more closely at spite we observe that we tighten our bodies, withhold caring and understanding, and blame others for how we feel. Spite is based on feeling as if our survival is at stake and we believe that revenge and wanting to punish, rather than the feeling of being open to life, is what will save us. We justify how we feel as a way of setting a boundary and saying no. Our withholding contains the hidden expressions of our negative and hostile feelings. Constricting ourselves, we decrease energy flow and our sense of well being. When we are in spite we have less warmth and compassion and the result is that we suffer more.

Inner conflict and suffering are a part of life. We deal with the conflict based on our supports. Remember that our supports were either set in place to survive childhood abuse or based on positive, loving energies or some combination of love and abuse. Often times, the struggle and the nature of our suffering as adults are the result of a lack of being positively supported as children. Our suffering and struggle occurs because we have learned to reject certain aspects of ourselves. This rejection is how we repeat the old abuse and stay connected to our childhood.

Deepening our discussion about dependence that we began earlier can show us that self-disgust for our dependent feelings are an example of repeating the old abuse. The *disgust* is the problem, not the dependence. Without disgust, dependence can be a simple experience to feel and to form. Often, feeling and expressing "I feel dependent and I need love" will transform the feeling of dependence to one of satisfaction. It is the disgust that prevents us from feeling and forming our need in a clear, simple, and grounded manner. We have learned to defensively support ourselves by rejecting our dependence. Now disgust reinforces dissatisfaction and stands in the way of our absorbing love.

We need loving support to live through and transform the feelings of disgust. **When we grew up with love we have enough inner support to experience unpleasant feelings and find the aliveness that is buried underneath.** If we lovingly support ourselves through the disgust, we are simply left with our dependent feelings, which we can then form; like asking for a hug or for understanding or sharing with someone: "I feel dependent and I need love."

HOW MUCH SUPPORT DO YOU HAVE?

How much internal support do you have for your life at this moment? Do you have enough to live without having to manipulate your emotions and hold your body in some rigid or collapsed form? Do you have enough support to breathe fully, so that each breath fills you with the feeling of being alive? Do you have enough support to spend time alone and feel full of yourself? Do you have enough support to feel what it is that you need and then reach out in a simple and clear manner to someone if what you need is a connection with another person? Do you have to chronically tighten some part of your body and act braver and fuller then you actually feel? Do you have to deny that you are angry, sad, frightened, or in need? Can you allow yourself to balance the powerful adult in you, with the child's feelings of vulnerability? Can you allow pleasure to surge through your body, or are you more apt to try to control these feelings? Do you have support to say no to something that you really don't want to do, and still feel a connection to yourself and the person you're saying no to? Do you have to harden or break yourself into passivity when it comes to setting a simple boundary? Do you feel guilty that you are being selfish, when you do something for yourself? Does opening your heart depend on someone else being open first, or do you possess your own heart feelings? And finally, do you feel that it is all right to need support, or is the need for support a sign of weakness for you? I ask all of you and myself these questions. It is meant to help us focus on how we are able or unable to support our own feelings and expressions of aliveness. Even if we are not able to support the depth of our aliveness, and the path of integration and enlightenment has no meaning, we still need support.

HOW SUPPORTS GOT BAD PRESS

It is a fascinating and distressing dilemma that the very nature of needing support is seen as a problem. Even though being supported into life, supported for every breath and for every step we take, should be our birthright, we have been separated from this birthright by the abuse in our childhoods. We often feel humiliated if we truly need support. This stems from the belief that to need support is a sign of weakness and, therefore, there is something wrong with us if we feel dependent. This belief isn't true.

What *is* true is that when feelings of dependence emerge they are present to help us return to a deeper, more balanced state within ourselves. The statement "I need support" is recognition of the reality of our dependent feelings. It is recognition that we are not all-powerful gods and goddesses. It is recognition that we are simply human, and that being human, there are times when we need help. There are times when we want to share our needs. To do this is to integrate the feeling of dependence that we have kept hidden.

The truth is that the denial of the need for support is a sign of an underlying fear. It is the fear of falling into the feeling of weakness that is in us because we weren't supported in the naturally dependent state of our childhoods. It feels safer to live as if something is wrong with us because we need and want support rather than to recognize that it takes courage to live through the abusive energies of our childhood to acknowledge our feelings of need. For example, if we were hated for our needs, hatred now surrounds our needs. We would have to reexperience the old hatred in order to free the aliveness that is in the pure experience of need.

Being independent is an important part of our lives. Independence in and of itself is not a problem, in fact, it helps us to persevere and to be successful. The problem develops when independence becomes a rigid response to all situations and does not make room for other parts of our emotional life. An ascetic, tenacious, willful, persevering spirit is not the be all and end all of our lives. In this way of living there is a denial of other parts of our humanness which also deserve to be respected. There is something twisted and backwards in growing up feeling that the need for support is an assault on independence, rather than a way to reach independence. We are being so influenced by these negative beliefs about dependence that the very nature of support is misunderstood and, as the subtitle of this chapter declares, has gotten bad press.

This rigid form of independence prevents us from navigating our inner emotional landscape and the landscape that is necessary for intimacy. These negative messages of independence include denial of support, rejection of emotion, and shame about vulnerability and dependence. We shrink away from what is real inside of us and, therefore, the negative messages do not support freedom to live emotional processes in a way that leads to health, satisfaction, wholeness and intimacy.

As we attempt to live by these principles, we wind up being stuck on one side of a polarity between dependence and independence. When we are unable to live flexibly we most often wind up on the road of unreality, pressure, and an illusionary independence, an independence that is a role, rather than one that comes from the depth of who we are. As has been expressed earlier, we need to balance letting down and letting go with being able to be focused, organized, and strong.

As children, we are dependent and need our dependence to be valued in order for us to reach independence. As adults, we now need to support our unmet childhood feelings of dependence that still live in us so that we can reach true independence. This helps us to let go and let down, in order to recharge our emotional/energetic batteries. There are times when we draw on our reserves of strength to see us through some difficult situation. It is natural to then feel vulnerable, dependent, and in need of support afterwards. Like being tired after a race, there needs to be a time to rest.

Whether there are people whom we trust and who are available to us when we feel dependent is only part of the story. The other part is that we need to honor our own feelings of dependence, our own need for support. Acceptance allows for a connection to the reality of what we are feeling, rather than fighting what we feel. Like removing a boulder in a stream that creates turbulence, acceptance of need allows for the stream to flow freely. Compassionate understanding, where we acknowledge our need for support, in and of itself, is healing. We are being good parents to ourselves rather than the negative introjected parents who taught us to fight our feelings.

Building self-support makes it easier for us to share our needs with others in a way that allows them to be present, supportive, and caring. When we feel accepting of our own needs we share them without being demanding, defeating, or desperate. Therefore, people have room to respond to us more openly. We can have the best of both worlds when we develop a balance between sharing as a way of reaching for support from others while supporting ourselves with self-acceptance.

SUPPORT FOR OUR ALIVENESS

It is not only in the difficult times and the difficult feelings in our life that we need support. We also need caring support when we feel balanced and alive. At these times, the feeling of caring support would be like an inner voice or body sense validating and reinforcing our good feeling. Although everyone wants to feel relaxed and alive, it is so easy to feel undeserving of relaxed, pleasurable moments. How many times do we all felt guilty if we're not working or doing something we consider "constructive"? The pressured feeling that we should always be doing something is the lack of support for feeling we can let down and relax.

To break this pattern, we need to bring loving support to the feelings of pressure and guilt. This will return us to simple, relaxed, and pleasurable moments. Love is like a broom sweeping away the pressure and guilt.

As we gather support to live mindfully, to live into each moment of our experience, we begin to separate from our own internal assault energies and feel more independent and alive. As less energy is involved with continuing cycles of self abuse, a new cycle develops where we have more energy to accept present day happiness and deal with our difficulties.

GRIEF AND SUPPORT

If we have support for our internal process we are better able to cope with the daily problems of living and the catastrophes that can be a part of life. An example of the importance of support in our lives is how we deal with grief when someone we love has died. With the experience of support as a part of our being, in time, we will live in and through the grief to the renewal of separateness and aliveness that is waiting for us. Grieving takes time. It is necessary: Grief is the way that our body and spirit has of acknowledging the connection that we had with the person who died, a way of saying good-bye and allowing aliveness to exist once again, in our bodies. It is our way of honoring the person's life and our connection with him or her.

Our body and our spirit know that we need to grieve as long as the process is alive in us. We cannot rush our separation process. We cannot rush the unfolding of our life. To push ourselves to finish our grief is an assault to our aliveness. In fact, it is actually the assault of non-acceptance that perpetuates the grief longer then it might otherwise be with us. If we push ourselves to be finished with our grief, we lock it in our muscles. We therefore don't allow the grief to take its natural course and allow new aliveness to flow through our bodies. If we try to stop our grieving it will remain locked inside, and any time we open to ourselves, like a seed waiting for the right conditions to blossom, the grief will be waiting to be allowed expression.

If we can appreciate our grief, rather then assaulting ourselves for the feeling, we eventually come to our underlying strength and inner reserve. This is the power that emerges because we accept and nurture ourselves. As we give up feeling like a victim and accept that we often don't have control over how life is going to turn out, we find peace within our grief.

Sometimes we live our grief by measuring ourselves against how we believe other people would feel and react in such situations. If our measure consists of unreal images of stoicism, success, and happiness that are presented to us in our society, we will fall short of reaching that standard. To live based on external images, instead of accepting our own uniqueness, is to turn against ourselves. We then alienate ourselves even more from the source of our life, strength, and spirit.

Without positive feelings of support for our grief we live surrounded by the old negative assault energies of how we were treated when we were sad or in grief or how we experienced our parents deal with their own grief. These negative feelings and belief systems will block us from feeling our grief. In this case, we will defensively support ourselves by not feeling our grief. Instead, we will tense our bodies, or rationalize and deny the impact of grief. We may pressure ourselves to be prematurely finished with our grief. If we cut off our grief too soon, believing we will never be rid the grief, it results in a constant state of hopelessness and despair. Without support for our grief, whatever else we do creates a movement away from aliveness and authenticity. Paradoxically, the decreased aliveness now becomes the way we defensively support ourselves because we are afraid to feel what is locked in our bodies.

In this state of decreased aliveness, every defense is a support. When we mask our real feeling, the mask becomes our support when we don't have support for deeper and fuller states of aliveness. Instead of living from our core we now live in "a role" of how we should feel and act.

ROLE LAYER AS SUPPORT

In this light, consider the trend in our society to teach children not to feel. We are taught to be less alive and to join society's standard of valuing controlling power, money, technology, consumption, and production rather then valuing being real, open-hearted, and mindful. It is difficult for parents to be separate from these standards and therefore, they often reinforce this overall cultural ethic. If this is the energy that is available both in our families and in society, it is natural for it to become a part of us.

The result of this bonding is that we move away from aliveness into some emotional/energetic role. To live in a role is to live in a level of unreality, rather than living creative lives that flow from our own center and authenticity. Our role may involve being a hard worker, a striver for perfection, or behaving in a dutiful and caring manner. Our role may also be one of rebelliousness and uncaring, seductive, suffering or of being intellectual and all powerful. Whatever role we live, it is meant to defensively support us in the world when we do not have the support and encouragement to feel and live who we really are. We live in a layer that surrounds our core, *a role layer*, and thus, unreality becomes our support.

IMPASSE AND PSYCHOSIS AS SUPPORT

Feeling stuck, unable to move, constantly in impasse, can be a support. If we unconsciously believe that we are going to "die" if we experience old childhood trauma, than remaining stuck, being in impasse, becomes a relative place of safety. It protected us from the old belief that we would die. The dilemma with this form of safety is that without experiencing the old childhood trauma we stay removed from feeling alive, creative, spiritual, and integrated. As Don Juan said as he spoke to Carlos Castenada, to feel whole and free we must recapitulate and face every aspect of our lives. Feeling frustrated and angry with ourselves for being stuck doesn't help us move, in fact, it reinforces impasse. We need love and understanding for our stuckness in order to come back to life. When we, in turn, support ourselves by bringing love to our stuckness, we allow it to transform to aliveness.

The same is true of psychotic states. By psychotic I am referring to the state of being where it is difficult to have any sense of reality. The psychosis is a way of living in an emotional layer of death energy. In psychosis, we are overwhelmed by the intensity of the victimizing energies that are stored in our bodies. We are unable to allow ourselves to know that the victimizing energies are expressions of what actually occurred in our childhood. The childhood victimizing was so incredibly intense that it broke all abilities to hold a boundary and any sense of body integrity. A psychotic episode produces a coding about the abuse. For example, hallucinations that someone is constantly stalking us are code for the stalking that actually happened in our childhood. Therefore, in psychosis, the psychotic state is a support if forming more centered and grounded aliveness brings with it the clear emotional and body memories of the childhood abuse that literally threatened our lives.

Many unsettling and unpleasant experiences in our daily lives have a supportive aspect to them. Isolation is a support when coming out of it means feeling the actual abuse that caused us to be isolated in the first place. Living in fear or terror is a support if having personal power means feeling how we were terrorized for displaying any sign of life. Every way we have learned to block aliveness is a support we developed as a way of surviving when there wasn't someone to meet us with heart and understanding.

If our supports are everything we have learned in order to survive, then the roles and emotional and social games we play become our supports. We also support ourselves with all our ways of detaching, spacing out, blanking, tightening and stressing our bodies, collapsing, or being stubborn and spiteful. In addition, all the ways that we use emotions as defenses are supports, e.g., being angry in order not to feel a deeper place of sadness, hurt, or need. All of these defenses, in the unique way that each of us uses them, make up the defensive support system we developed as children in order to survive.

BUILDING LIFE-AFFIRMING SUPPORTS

A foundation of Body Centered Gestalt Therapy is to help people bring understanding and compassion to whatever they experience. We want to help each person understand and support themselves with self-love no matter what layer they are living in; role layer, impasse, death layer, aliveness, or pure spirit.

The moment we are good parents to ourselves, supporting ourselves with kindness and compassion for our present experience, appreciating our uniqueness and our common humanity, is the moment that transformation occurs. We don't have to try to rid ourselves of any part of who we are. In fact, we can begin to feel how every part of who we are, including

our negative, self-destructive parts have meaning in terms of how we have been abused as children. These parts have even been our ally and have prevented us from feeling the abuse even more deeply.

The ability to reclaim our aliveness and live in tune with our life force is based on whether we can support the feeling of each experience as it forms inside of us. When we don't block or manipulate each internal experience, we possess the depth of our life force.

To bring caring support to our sadness, our needs, our anger, our fear, and our pleasure allows us to experience sadness without suffering, need without desperation, anger without the desire to punish or blame, fear with discrimination, and pleasure with the ability to share or live quiet peaceful moments by ourselves. When we accept each experience as having meaning, we can then possess the warmth, softness, and sense of direction that comes from our needs, the power that comes from the feeling of anger, the positive critical judgment that fear can provide us, and the joy that pleasure brings.

When we control our feelings we create tension. Our life force always wants to be free. Controlling our feelings is like building a rigid container that encases our life force, rather than creating a flexible container that can breathe. It is a container that can't breathe and won't allow for simple expression. Imagine water in a confined space under pressure to expand. It will take an opposing pressure or a rigid container to keep the energy confined. A dam does this kind of job. If the water pressure increases behind the dam there has to be an increase in the outside pressure to contain the water or some of the water has to be released. Without this release the dam will spring a leak and rupture. In a dam there is always extreme pressure between the dam and the water. This pressure is a point of tension. That is why there is a way of releasing water when the water builds up beyond the ability of the dam to hold it back.

The same is true of how we live in relation to our emotions, whether we allow release for them or dam them up. Both the way that we pressure ourselves, and the tension that is a result of the pressure, have become ways that we defensively support ourselves. We may feel that the pressure is too much to tolerate and yet, we can't give it up. We don't have the support to soften into our body and allow the expression or release of our emotions.

When we don't have enough support to experience the reasons that we built the dam of our emotions in the first place, we disconnect from what we are experiencing. Then, we often live as if our feelings simply do not exist. We continue to replicate our childhood defensive structure and abuse ourselves the way that we were abused. In effect, the disconnection becomes the way that we support ourselves when we haven't integrated a kinder and more heartfelt way of dealing with ourselves. Once again, we are caught in a vicious cycle of unending abuse that began in childhood.

In summation, in order to cope with the negative ways we were treated as children we creatively learned to treat ourselves in the same ways that we were treated. We are then allies with the abusers. Both our parents and the introjected abuse now hate the same person - us. We continue a negative connection to our parents and a bad connection feels better than no connection at all. We continue to abandon and reject ourselves, treat ourselves with self-contempt and self-hatred, be passive or rigid, etc. We negate our aliveness in order to preserve an even deeper place of spirit in ourselves, in order to keep some form of inner emotional and body integrity intact. Our body will automatically organize itself in order to survive abuse. For example, we contract our body to protect our core from the attack. This is a way of having some sense of power and body integrity in a situation that we were powerless to do anything about. As children, prior to being abused, our openness was a natural state to be in. With chronic abuse, living defensively became our natural alternative.

CHAPTER SIX

Supports As Our Identity

WE'VE EXAMINED THE WAYS WE FORMED THE VERY ESSENCE of who we are based on the emotional/energetic environment of our childhood. We've seen that we do whatever is necessary to survive and to support ourselves in as balanced a state of being as possible. We've learned that to varying degrees, we needed to survive family and societal energies that were unfriendly and uncaring for our aliveness. We now understand that ideal bonding from birth would be living in a completely positive symbiosis with our parents.

Positive symbiosis occurs if our parents fully welcome us into the world and allow for our needs as well as their own. In positive symbiosis, they balance attending to us when we are infants, while at the same time, respecting themselves. This doesn't mean that parents can always satisfy their own needs while taking care of us. At times, their satisfaction may come from honoring and accepting their and their partner's feelings of need rather than actually getting their needs met. If their needs conflict with ours, they can appreciate the dilemma and respect their own existence as well as ours. In perfect bonding, our parents understand that we must first be dependent. As we grow, they are also sensitive to our steps into separateness and independence. They understand and accept that dependence and independence is a process of repeated movements from contact to separateness that needs their support.

At birth, if we could speak and be conscious of our own growth process we might say to our parents, "*I can't differentiate between you and me. I can't support myself. I am totally dependent and I need to be in a positive symbiotic state with you. I must remain attached to your supports for now. If you can love me and accept who I am, I will grow beyond this stage of development and then naturally develop supports that are just right for my age. Thus throughout my childhood, if given the proper conditions, I will move from symbiosis to self-support."*

What actually occurs, since no parents provide this perfect environment, are degrees of negative symbiosis. In its most extreme form, negative symbiosis begins in utero or at birth with deadly parental messages. Here, as fetuses and/or as infants, our parents' energy of hate enters every cell of our being. The center of our parent's feeling toward us is, "I don't support your existence. I won't support your claim to life. I hate you. I wish you were dead." This message is present as a part of every interaction. I am not referring to the occasional time our parents feel angry and hateful toward us. I am referring to those of us who had parents who consistently hated us. The bonding process insures that we absorb the energetic and emotional message of hate into our core.

Again, if we put words to our preverbal experience they would be: *"I am surrounded by the energy of hate. I know nothing else. Since I am in a totally symbiotic state, I don't know the difference between what is coming at me and what is inside of me. Hate is who I am. My existence is worthless and not deserving of support."*

Hatred that can't be lived as a contained, embodied experience is called disowned hate. Disowned hatred has a much different energetic quality than does the energy of embodied hatred. Disowned hatred has either an energetic vibration of harshness and coldness or searing heat. In the harshness and coldness or the heat there is an energetic form of justification, blame, cruelty, smashing, knifing, or some other hostile way of emotionally destroying the object of the hate.

In negative symbiosis all warmth and caring are withdrawn and withheld. We, as adults, can live hatred by acting it out or as a grounded and centered experience. Living hatred from center means that we are containing the hatred. It is then a feeling and an expression of aliveness rather than being like solar flares destructively shooting out of our bodies or of icy coldness. Any feeling, contained and centered, possesses light and promotes intimacy. Because of this, it does not enter our child's energy field as negative and destructive. Acting out disowned hatred means that it is uncontained and filled with darkness. It penetrates our child's energy field and destroys intimacy. Acting out the hatred bonds our children in destruction. This is the origin of self-hatred.

Conversely, the energetic qualities of love are expansiveness, inclusiveness, and warmth. Love contains qualities of acceptance, understanding, light and space, rather than darkness and density that are the energies of disowned hatred. Whether we express disowned hatred or love, it was the air that we breathed as children and becomes the air our children breathe.

If, as children, we bonded with the hatred, our preverbal experience is, *"I hate myself, I wish I were dead."* As was discussed earlier, we saved ourselves by joining our parents' hatred and forming ourselves in relation to the hatred. Self-hatred becomes our defensive support. It remains the bonding energy that binds us to our parents. Consistent internalized hatred leads to the feeling of suicide, that is, the experience of *"I hate myself for being alive and I want to die."* Now, *"I want to die"* is the bonding energy with our parents. Feeling that we want to die is both the impact of the assault as well as a form of power; the way that we support ourselves rather then coming into life again and feeling the depth of how we were hated. This feeling of suicide is an expression of the statement, *"I would rather die than have to continue putting up with this abuse."*

As adults, if we have support to live through the death layer feeling of suicide we open to our underlying aliveness. Without support for the feeling of suicide, we have to block our aliveness because it stirs up the suicidal feeling and we live the best way we can with our aliveness locked inside of us. Having bonded with the feeling of death, it certainly makes sense that we would have a layer of depression, hopelessness and worthlessness in us. What also makes sense is that depression, hopelessness, and worthlessness are supportive, because they save us from feeling the underlying suicidal impulses when we don't have enough support to breathe through them instead of committing suicide. Without support and understanding for why the feelings are there in the first place, we might believe that the only alternative is to either kill ourselves, remain depressed, or organize above it all and live in a role of unreality. Whatever way we choose, we have completely bonded with the parental message that we shouldn't be alive.

The way through this dilemma may seem paradoxical. Instead of fighting against the darkness, we need a new kind of support to live into and through our depression, hopelessness and worthlessness. We need support to feel the underlying feeling of suicide, and to support each experience as it emerges into our awareness. By living through the experiences, we travel back through what we've created as protection, back through the old assaults, to find the aliveness that we had to bury. Accepting and supporting the feelings that emerge allows us to follow the path toward wholeness that our spirit has set for us.

If our life was surrounded by hatred from our parents then when we are parents, the old hatred is what will be touched by our child's aliveness. If as parents we don't have a way of supporting our feelings of hatred we will indiscriminately act out these feelings toward our children just like our parents did to us.

A FURTHER UNDERMINING OF OUR POWER: THE ASSAULT TO OUR "NO"

If our parents accept our basic existence, a less virulent form of negative symbiosis may develop during other stages of childhood. We may learn that "*Mom or Dad support my existence to some extent, (e.g., they love babies), but one or both of them can't tolerate me now that I'm beginning to become more independent. I feel undermined in my need to say 'No'. I can feel that they don't have an open-hearted appreciation for the formation of my boundaries as I experiment with exploring the world, by saying 'No.'*" As with the example of hatred, the more chronic and intense our parents intolerance of our "No" is, the greater the negative bonding will be.

Experiment: Imagine you grew up being stopped every time you said "No." Examples of this are constant anger or criticism directed against your experimenting with saying

"No", or being labeled selfish if you say "No." See if you can remember how your parents stopped your "No." Feel how you would learn, or did learn, that something was wrong with forming a boundary, protesting, or disagreeing with the grown-ups. Ask an image to emerge that will show you how you supported yourself when your "No" was assaulted.

Although we may grow up still being able to form a "No," it has lost the quality of an easy, simple, full-hearted "No." Instead, we may have learned to form our "No" through toughness, stubbornness, spitefulness, defeating, rebelliousness, passivity, depression, and sabotage. We learn any number of ways to express ourselves other than with a simple and clear "No" that both respects our needs as well as acknowledging the existence and needs of the other person.

The energy of disowned hatred surrounds our existence, we automatically bond with our caretakers' energy and grow up with this energy fused to our aliveness. Emotionally, energetically, and intellectually, we have formed a way of viewing the world through this assault energy that we will carry into adulthood. When we were children, our view that the world is hostile was based on reality. As adults, it is a view of the world that is not totally accurate and is based on living as if we are still children who always have to remain bonded with our parents, and then we project their energies everywhere. We believe that we constantly have to defend ourselves against their negative energies. Living with the belief system that all people are like the people that we grew up with, limits our perspective, flexibility, and spontaneity. In effect, a negative illusion about the world was created in childhood, and we carry it with us wherever we go and with whomever we meet because we have not worked the introjected abuse out of our bodies. Our negative illusion becomes a part of how we support ourselves. It becomes a piece of paranoia that becomes structured into our system.

In the situation where we are learning to say "No," we see the creation of the "No" illusion. Here is the basis of it: *"If I dare to say a simple, full-hearted "No" directly to anyone, I will have to feel the fear and the negativity of how I was treated as a child when I said "No" to my parents."* The power of this negative myth lies in the fact that it becomes a part of our unconscious identity. We generalize and project the negative bonding that we internalized from our parents to the way we see and live in the world. A student in our training program shared how she swings between placating others and being overly harsh as a way of saying "No." She either has a hard boundary or no boundary at all. In her psyche, everyone becomes the potential abuser if she comes from the center of her real desire to have a simple boundary.

This is so important to understand. If we can't have an embodied "No," we never have access to a full, open-hearted "Yes" for ourselves or for other people. Without our "No" we unconsciously feel unprotected so we can't open or have a "Yes." In other words, if we can't hold people out, we can't let them in. Without our protest we had to give up a piece of our hearts and passion to survive, and now we withhold a piece of our hearts and passion as protest. We are no longer able to live our bodies, our energy, and our emotions in a full-hearted way. The negative messages we have taken in regarding our protest are so much a part of our identity, our belief system that we often don't realize that these messages prevent us from feeling more alive.

We also need to be clear about how we project our lack of power to set boundaries and to claim our aliveness, onto other people. Once again, having support for our "No" provides us with the power that we need to stand our ground and to be in the world alive and full of ourselves. For example, other people may not want us to say "No" to them. If we use this as the reason for once again giving up our "No," we are living as if we were still powerless children in our families. Ultimately, it is our lack of inner support for ourselves, not the other person's insistence, that prevents us from having our "No" and stepping into the world.

We are responsible for how we say "No" and for how we set our boundaries. It is not another person's responsibility to provide us with total support and acceptance. That is what we needed, and didn't get, as children. Furthermore, we need to recognize that saying an embodied, centered "No" is not an assault to other people. In fact, not having the support for a clear and simple "No" is why we usually victimize people with unclear, passive and formless "No's," or overly formed, hard, and hostile "No's." Once again, to emphasize the main theme of how every way that we live is a form of support, living with formless or hardened "No's" is how we learned to support ourselves. The way that we learned to support ourselves needs to be appreciated and nurtured in order to begin a process of transforming the form of our "No."

To have an empowered "No" gives us the ability to feel our own uniqueness and individuality as well as how we are all a part of a shared humanity. Within this paradigm of power, we understand that how we live does affect others. However, allowing for our sensitivity toward others does not mean having to be insensitive to our own needs and to "give ourselves away."

Having the ability to say "No" to what we don't want or need, can also help us feel more connected to what we do want and need. We then have a greater ability to discriminate which needs lead us toward further embodiment and which ones are addictive and lead us away from our aliveness.

A simple experiment can further our understanding of the importance of an embodied "No." Try on the sentence, "No, I don't want this." Allow a feeling of something that you don't want to emerge. Don't push! Allow the experience of what you don't want to open inside of you. Now, again, say the sentence, "No, I don't want this," so that it feels like you are stating a simple truth. Take a breath! Don't hold onto this "No" in a way that it will harden or become meaningless. Now ask the question, "What is it that I do want?" The need or desire in this case is the polarity of the "No." Having support to feel and say "No" provides us with the feeling of power that enables us to go after what we need and say "No" to what we don't want or need. The "No" helps us form a container for our needs. That is, a simple and clear "No" provides us with boundaries that help us determine our likes and dislikes. As our preferences and needs become clearer to us, free from the energy of the old assaults, we are more able to have and contain the experience of need in our bodies.

NEEDS AND 'NO'

We often try to avoid the feeling of need because it opens us to the old feeling of how we were treated when we did feel our needs in our childhoods. As we learn to support ourselves through these old assaults, we learn that the feeling of need can help us develop a sense of direction in our life. If we can ask ourselves the question "What is it that I need?" and then allow ourselves to feel the answer, we become clear regarding the direction to go in order to feel satisfied and return to a balanced state. Allowing ourselves to stay aware of our needs is like a gyroscope. Often, just having the awareness of our needs themselves can help us feel more centered. Awareness moves us more into our center, while defending against experience keeps us defensive and uncentered.

Again, imagine yourself saying "No." Allow the "No" to be firm, but not angry; quiet, but not passive. Practice it a few times. See how it feels. See if you can allow the "No" to radiate fully through your body. Then add to the experiment, "No I don't need this, I need this." Experiment with different forms of "No." Imagine that someone is supporting your ability to say "No," someone who cares that you have a boundary and that you can form what it is that you need. How does having someone who supports the formation of a "No" feel? Are you more familiar with the feeling of not taking in support than with allowing yourself to feel supported? Do you feel accepting or rejecting of the support?

UNDERMINING OR RECLAIMING OUR POWER: WE HAVE A CHOICE TO SAY YES OR NO TO OUR ANGER

Being able to embody our "No" is directly related to how we embody our anger. However, anger is a very misunderstood emotion. On the one hand, we are easily frightened by anger's potential to be destructive and to hurt others. On the other hand, we may be frightened of the emergence of someone else's anger if we were to express our own. We may fear abandonment or rejection. Or perhaps we may feel that anger does not fit our image of being a loving person. Despite these fears and beliefs, we may be angry a great deal of the time, never clearly forming our anger and taking responsibility for it. Instead, we may blame ourselves or everyone else for how we feel. In this way, we may feel righteous and justified in our anger or believe that something is wrong with us for how we feel.

How simply we can support our "No" directly relates to how we experience and express our anger. The easier it is for us to say "No," the simpler our feeling and expression of anger becomes. **That is, the easier it is for us to say "No" the more we possess our anger. The more we possess our anger, the easier it is for us to say "No."**

When we can support the feeling of anger in our bodies, our anger feels natural to us. Without access to a simple "No," anger is often used defensively either in an overly aggressive or an overly withholding manner. Either direction is a movement into defensive support. This occurs when we don't have positive support for our power, boundaries, open-heartedness, sexuality, vulnerability and needs. When our anger is defensive we are defending against feeling the childhood abuse that is stored in our body.

The more positive support we have, we only become angry when we are being assaulted. With increasing self-possession and inner security, even this anger begins to shift. And when our own boundaries are clear, we are able to differentiate between when someone is simply saying "No" to us as a boundary or when someone is saying "No" to us from abusive energies. We can feel more secure and grounded in our perception of what is taking place in our relationships.

As we gain in self-possession, it feels more natural to be open and share the truth of our being. We don't feel as defensive, frightened, or humiliated about ourselves. Therefore, as we feel more powerful, we don't feel angry in advance of someone disapproving of us. If someone doesn't approve of how we feel, it is more likely that we will still feel secure. In the case of our reaching from need, we don't have to automatically believe that someone's "No" is as an assault.

Virginia Satir[1] wrote about five styles of communication that we employ in order to deal with underlying feelings of inadequacy. Two of the styles she called "the placater" and "the blamer." We are a "the placater" when we blame all our problems on ourselves. We feel that everything is our own fault and that if we only could improve ourselves, our life and relationships would be better. We are a part of "the blamers" when we feel that all our problems are someone else's fault. Then we believe that if only the other person would change their ways, our own life would be different and we would feel better.[2] When we are in either of these two communication styles we do not recognize that **anger is a feeling to be experienced and lived, not one that needs to be blamed on oneself or someone else.**

Satir was referring to two styles of "being," neither of which include support for anger. The person who is always angry and blaming has as little support for his/her anger as has the person who is passive and placating. As Satir said, both are defending against underlying feelings of inadequacy. They are both also defending against feeling the underlying assaults from their childhood.

In discussing how to support our anger in our bodies it is easy to have the impression that there is a right and a wrong way to express our anger or all of our emotions. I am very aware of this danger while I work with people in therapy. Working in therapy and becoming more conscious can be used as a new way to victimize ourselves by being self-critical of the way that we expressing ourselves. We can be negatively self-critical for not being more alive, more expressive, more aware, more open-hearted, or for acting out. I am not judging good or bad, right or wrong. I am always focused on which way of living provides more of a feeling of aliveness, clarity, centered-ness, and well being. As I already have written, we need support for whatever we are experiencing. And because we

are all human, there are many times that we feel and express ourselves based on our early childhood experiences and supports. That needs to be understood and accepted.

CASE STUDIES
CARL: VIOLENCE, BLAME, AND REVENGE

Two clients I have worked with illustrate different forms of dealing with anger. The first client, Carl, was always angry. He was in his mid-thirties when he entered therapy. Carl is of medium height, and his body is lean and taut. He looks hard and driven. He came into therapy when his wife told him that she wanted a divorce. Carl angrily talked non-stop about how devastated he felt. He told me that he had been crying uncontrollably for the last few weeks and that his crying was his wife's fault. So too, were all his upset feelings. He couldn't understand why she wanted to leave him since he had given his wife everything she ever wanted financially and he had always placed her interests before his own. The example he shared with me was that if she wanted to do something that he didn't, he would go along with his wife and give up his own interests.

He noted that one of his wife's complaints, throughout their marriage, was how angry and abusive she felt that he was. He agreed with this for a moment and then went on about how enraged he was with her, as if he hadn't made the prior statement about having been abusive. I was hard-pressed to get a word in during this session. If I suggested that Carl stop for a moment and begin to understand something about himself, he became furious with me. His anger had a hostile, cutting edge to it, as if he could kill anyone who got in his way.

Carl could not support his feelings of anger. He was continually exploding in a negative, hostile, and cruel manner. He felt that his explosive rages were justified. I understood that if he stopped discharging his anger by constantly blaming others and attempted to contain himself he would not be able to tolerate the build up of energy in his hard and tight body. He felt that he would literally explode and fly apart if he tried to contain and feel any of his anger.

At first, when I tried to talk to Carl about his anger, even as he was in the midst of an explosion, he would deny that he was angry. Rather than simply feel and acknowledge his anger, he would attack and blame his wife or employees or the general stupidity and ineptitude in the world, all the while, denying anger. There was no sense that he had the ability to possess and take responsibility for any of his own emotions. He was totally at the mercy of an inner storm that was continually erupting.

For Carl to stop blaming his wife and the rest of the world for how he felt, he had to soften and live through feelings of how, as a child, he had been humiliated for his needs, invaded and smashed around any sign of life, and driven crazy for trying to stand up for himself. Uncontained hostility was rampant in his family. Every family member was always enraged at something or someone. The way to be part of his family was to join them in their explosiveness.

The purpose of all of the negativity in Carl and in his family was to explode away from feeling helpless and impotent. Carl's anger was also an expression of his wanting revenge for all the hurt he had suffered. His denying his own needs and then being angry that he wasn't satisfied was a distorted way of attempting to express need. He never felt any peace and satisfaction. As a child, he lived in a no-win situation where it didn't matter how he behaved or how he felt, anger was the only form of emotional expression. He was truly helpless to extricate himself from this constant hostile field and as a result, he felt trapped.

Both as a child and as an adult Carl felt that he would be a "fool" to soften and share what he needed. His anger was not only a defense against all of these feelings, it was also a distorted way of trying to get people to be soft with him so they would love him. In this way Carl's anger was meant to tenderize people, as someone would tenderize a tough piece of meat by pounding it. He could not fathom that he was an integral part of co-creating the hostile environment that his wife now wanted to leave. He hadn't a clue that his wife and others hardened around him as a result of his continual uncontained rages.

My work with Carl was not meant to stop him from feeling angry. It was to help him take in support for how angry he felt. He was already able to justify his anger to the precision of a Supreme Court brief. The support that I'm referring to was not meant to add to his harsh, hard, righteous, and justified way of being. Carl needed support that understood and appreciated that his anger made sense, albeit the sense it made was in terms of the abuse that he had suffered as a child. He needed to appreciate that his anger and his hardness had saved his life. He needed to develop compassion for himself becasue he couldn't have tolerated being vulnerable and innocent in the face of his family's hostility. It was only through appreciating how his hostility had been his bonding with his family and had become an ally in order to help him survive that Carl could begin to develop a softer and more contained way of being. Carl also needed to see that at the same time his rage protected him, it sealed him off from intimacy. To understand this was the path that led to being able to soften and thereby lessen his angry charge.

I spent a great deal of time in Carl's therapy sharing my appreciation for how much he needed his anger. I also told him that I realized from the way he presented himself that he had never had any support as a child for his sadness and pain. We talked about how his childhood was like living in a hurricane of negativity. He shared with me that if he ever told people in his family that he felt hurt or sad they would be brutally contemptuous, change the subject as if what he was saying didn't make any sense, or overwhelm him with their own pain and sadness. I continued to emphasize my realization that Carl needed his anger, and how much it had helped him survive. I told him that until he could appreciate how much he needed to be angry, he could never have any heart for himself and the predicament that he was in. If he couldn't have any heart for himself, he would never be able to live through his underlying hurt and sadness about what was going on between he and his wife. Without being able to experience his anger and the basis for it, he was doomed to a life of unhappiness and isolation.

BILL: ADAPDIBILITY PREVENTS AUTHENTICITY

A polarity to Carl's constant rage can be seen in Bill. He was in his late thirties. He was overweight, and there was a passive quality to the way he looked. Everything that he said had a tone of obsequiousness, depression, and defeat to it. Bill entered therapy because he felt that he wasn't getting anywhere in his life and was generally unhappy. When I asked him about whether he ever felt or expressed anger, he told me that once in a while he might feel angry. He was quick to add that he believed that if he ever expressed his anger, people would surely leave him. As I questioned him about this belief he always had an example of why it was too dangerous to be angry. Along with his fear of expression, Bill told me that if he could only find the real reason he was angry, everything would be all right. He felt that his anger was an overreaction, and that it was always from his childhood. He never felt that he had a right to be angry, no matter how abusive people were toward him and he always found an excuse for other people's actions.

Although Bill's body and emotional structure was so completely different from Carl's, he too was unable to support his anger. They both needed support for containing their anger and its expression. The course of therapy with Bill was very different from my work with Carl. Without his anger, Bill lived like a giant marshmallow, easily pushed, prodded, and poked by other people.

At first, I worked with Bill to help him appreciate and support how frightened he was of feeling and expressing his anger. As a result of his fear, Bill lived in a continual state of formlessness. For him to form his anger (as opposed to Carl, who needed to soften to feel and contain his anger) he would need to feel how deeply he had been emotionally and physically assaulted as a child. Abuse could come when he least expected it, so Bill learned to expect it all the time. No matter how good he was at anything, his parents were smashing and contemptuous, telling Bill that he was not good enough. This was very unfortunate, for Bill was very talented in many areas. As a result of the intensity and the nature of the abuse that he received, he believed that he wasn't good enough at anything.

He, therefore, never felt satisfied or accomplished no matter what he achieved. He was terrified of succeeding beyond a certain point, for that would mean emerging from formless collapse and suffering. Forming himself would re-energize the feelings, messages, and memories of his childhood abuse.

Bill was jumping out of his chair with enthusiasm for everything that I said. Each session seemed like a minor miracle had been accomplished, yet, nothing really changed in his life. I began to understand that everything Bill said and did was an attempt to save his life. He was a master at adaptation. This included the way that he approached therapy sessions. He believed he would be safe if he made me feel that I was a wonderful therapist. He was doing his therapy for me, learning to adapt to what he believed that I wanted him to feel, rather than using therapy to understand himself and grow. Adapting and hiding what was real was exactly how Bill had learned to deal with being blown out of his center, and the resultant formlessness and lability. No matter what I said, or how I supported and expressed understanding, nothing changed. Bill would always return to his endless self-blame and find reasons to defeat everything that might make a difference in his life.

As I continued working with Bill, I wanted to help him understand how he was supporting himself by saying "No" to himself and saying "Yes" to other people. His anger was always directed inward, and he was unable to possess any of it in order to feel assertive and powerful. I focused on how he had spent every moment of his childhood saving his life and that he still lived as if this was necessary. I wanted to help him see that this way of supporting himself deadened his life and kept him formless. I realized that the only way that therapy was going to be successful for Bill was to help him become aware of whether he had any commitment to his life or if maintaining the status quo as a way of remaining safe was his only priority. If this were so, he would continue killing any experience that might lead him toward more aliveness and satisfaction.

OUR COMMITMENT TO LIFE

A few general comments about our commitment or lack of commitment to our life are in order here. If we are committed to resolving where we are stuck in our lives, therapy is about becoming aware of the all the ways that we have learned to support ourselves in order to maximize pleasure and minimize pain. Therapy can then focus on both our positive and defensive supports and how these supports have helped us deal with the mix of pleasure and trauma. In order to continue growing and deepening our connection to ways of forming that enhance our life, we need to especially deepen our understanding and appreciation for our defensive supports that we developed as children.

If we don't have a commitment to live through the old assault energies so that we can come to a deeper place of aliveness, we are supporting ourselves by endless self-blame, like Bill, or we blame others for our difficulties, like Carl. By living in these ways, we defeat compassion and positive efforts made in our behalf. We were defeated as children and now we carry this defeating legacy with us. It becomes relatively safe to defeat caring and support and, thereby, remain stuck in suffering and torture, endlessly complaining about our lot in life. This *is* the crucial point that needs to be dealt with if therapy is ever to be successful.

BACK TO BILL

Bill's adaptive and defeating structure became the essential point in his therapy. If these issues were not directly dealt with, then therapy could only continue in "unreality" with Bill pretending that he was motivated to grow. Reality was that at a very deep level, Bill was committed to adapting instead of moving and feeling more alive. He had become an expert at this way of being. Because of the way he learned to survive, i.e., looking as if he was agreeing with people, while in reality he was withholding his life, therapy became a process of continually recycling through the same issues. Living like this, Bill remained in the old energy of suffering and torture and the hopelessness that accompanies feeling that these experiences will never end. If there is no commitment for life, no real growth takes place.

Without the issue of commitment being addressed, both Carl and Bill would remain stuck in endlessly blaming themselves, the therapist, or other people in their lives, as a way of avoiding feeling what actually happened to them as children. They would remain stuck in unformed revenge their entire lives. This would perpetuate the pattern of trying to save their lives from old childhood assaults, while perpetuating the same vengeful, withholding manner that they had learned from their parents. They would continue to want to punish others and themselves more than they would want to reach a deeper feeling of aliveness and authenticity.

A dilemma in therapy is that there are times when we don't have a commitment to our life. This is because abuse broke our spirit. When our spirit has been broken, the spark of life that is necessary to help us live through the energy of the old assaults is hidden in the feeling of brokenness. Without that spark, which connects us to our life force, it is extremely difficult to rekindle a desire to support ourselves through our brokenness. Rather than reliving these feelings that are essential in helping us return to our spirits, we try to pull people into our misery, instead of using the connection with others to support our existence. We want to be magically saved rather than taking in support so that we can re-experience the old abusive energies and come into a new and more satisfying form of aliveness.

In some basic way, this was true of Bill. There was a place of deep, hidden spite where he swore that he would never form again, and therefore, never be broken again, or, certainly, never again feel how he was broken as a child. As I confronted and supported the reality of Bill's lack of commitment to his life, he eventually was willing to live into and support this awareness. He began to live through the feelings of how his spirit had been broken and how angry and spiteful he really felt. At this point there was hope that he could begin to grow and his life could change.

It is worth emphasizing and re-emphasizing that the moment

we are able to support the reality of how we have had to live is the moment that there is a positive shift in how we treat ourselves. Awareness is transformative.

For Bill to see the reality of how he had learned not to form was to understand that he found safety by living in suffering, hidden spite, and revenge. As he began to appreciate and support this reality, he took his first steps toward caring about himself, rather than living with his ongoing diet of self-torture that he was used to. If I had overlooked Bill's adaptive structure and his underlying revenge, I would have fused with Bill's earlier enthusiasm about how "wonderful" therapy was and not seen that his spirit was missing. I would have believed that he really wanted help and ultimately felt frustrated and defeated, more committed to Bill's life than he was. Bill would then be treating me in the same way that he had been treated as a child. He would have become the victimizer in the guise of a victim. His spite, revenge, and endless suffering would remain hidden, acted out by not really taking me in and using our connection to remain stuck, instead of for his growth.

What I've written in regard to Carl's and Bill's therapy is a summary of what transpired over a number of sessions. I did not lecture them about what they needed to do to get their life in order. Whatever I said was framed to help both of them validate in their bodies and in their minds my understanding of their process. It was important that they experienced whether what I said felt like their truth. To experience their truths, they needed to feel truth in their bodies. That is, they needed to experience the truth of how they learned to organize their bodies in order to survive the assaults of their childhood, and how this organization affected the way they currently lived their emotional and relational life.

Every moment that Carl and Bill couldn't slow down and appreciate how they had learned to survive abuse was another moment of holding onto the abuse that was still stored in their bodies. Their continued ways of living bonded with their parents' negative energy (where there was a lack of appreciation, compassion, and support for their needs, sadness, anger or pleasure) was a movement away from their hearts and their spirits. As children, if they openly protested the lack of acceptance, the abuse would intensify. Carl had developed a form of continually protest, while Bill lived split between a hidden protest and an outward acquiescence. These defensive structures developed because as children, if they openly protested the abuse, the abuse would intensify. There was no way to have an open accepted "No" in their childhoods.

CHAPTER SEVEN

Reclaiming Our Aliveness: Support With Heart

WE CAN LEARN A GREAT DEAL FROM UNDERSTANDING Carl's and Bill's ways of coping with childhood abuse. The way they dealt with their anger as adults was based on all of the negative energies that they bonded with as children and how they had learned to defend themselves against these energies. The first step in growing beyond our old negative bonding energies is to appreciate that how we live *is* based on these negative energies and the supports that we developed in relation to these energies. Secondly, we need to gain positive supports for our deeper and clearer "No's" and our deeper and clearer "Yeses." Without appreciating how we had to survive by giving up our clear and simple "No," trying to learn to be more assertive or open hearted becomes a mechanical exercise. We would be trying to push ourselves beyond our current level of support and that just doesn't work. It is our connection to our own spirit and life force that is primary in assuring that our growth is based on aliveness, not on pushing ourselves to be something, and someone, we are not.

Becoming fuller and more alive involves a transition from the old survival mechanisms that encapsulates and limits our aliveness to new supports that enhance and welcome our aliveness. To do this is to move through a transition from having to live in "role layer" and manipulate our own aliveness in order to stay protected and feel safe. The power of the negative myth's hold on us — that we always have to live in the same way that we always have lived — can be broken as we feel the truth of what happened to us as children.

As we open our eyes to our history we don't have to remain bonded in the energies of abuse. Our energies, freed from this old prison, can form in new supportive ways where wholeness and connection become a part of our lives. We are now free to bond with a more alive feeling of safety and protection. This results in our possessing and living with more flexibility and power, even if we are met with a similar energy as was present in our childhoods. Just because someone is now emotionally abusive doesn't mean we have to freeze or collapse or abandon ourselves as a way of living through the experience. We have more ability to stand our ground with heart and power.

The movement toward increased aliveness, the path to enlightenment, occurs through each moment of self-acceptance, through each moment that we are able to support ourselves in the reality of our internal process. To do this is to live every moment of our feelings with acceptance, awareness and support. To experience the reality of our anger, sadness, needs, joy, and fear, and all the unformed and unclear emotions that reside in us, is to bring our energies together, rather than to divide them and further alienate parts of ourselves. To live in this way is to support each breath of our existence, love ourselves no matter what we feel, and to learn to balance the expression and containment of our emotions. Although we can't change our process, we can change how we live our process.

THE POWER OF LOVE

Our heart is the central ingredient in the support of our aliveness. Energetically, our heart can radiate that wonderful feeling of "I love you" through our entire being. The power of love allows for the feeling that anything is possible. At that moment everything feels right. And to have heart for ourselves is to feel fully alive and experience ourselves as a part of all life. For life to have its deepest meaning, we must have support for a connection to our heart. The meaning of life as Joseph Campbell has observed, is the rapturous feeling of being alive at any moment.

We are preoccupied with the concerns of the heart. Allowed to, our hearts produce warmth, comfort, and passion, and without heart, life becomes only a series of disconnected or disembodied experiences. Without heart for ourselves, we are more often surrounded by feelings of emptiness, meaninglessness, and isolation, while lacking in the support to understand where these feelings came from and to live through them. Instead of living on a path of heart, we live a path of hard-heartedness, the projection of heartlessness, longing for love, and the fear of love. We remain alienated in a world that supports alienation.

When we are passionate and full of heart about something or someone, life becomes a continuous flow of experiences with meaning. Having a full and meaningful life is the connection of heart to all that we do and feel. Whether we are looking toward God and longing to experience our oneness with the universe, or whether we are looking toward the earth and where we are going to take our next step, a connection to our heart allows for meaning and in fact, leads us toward God and the ground.

The path to the center of our life force is the path of heart and the path to enlightenment. This path must be the theme in the story of therapy or we remain disconnected. Without a connection to our heart, we are in a defensive structure and, therefore, remain frozen, labile, collapsed, overly rigid or overly passive, blaming, super intellectual, self-castigating, or any number of other ways we have learned to form in order to survive in the world. If we believe that we have complete understanding of our problems and for the issues that we have to live without our heart, our information is just that, information, that can't be effectively digested and used. It is like having the computer hardware without the necessary software to process the information. With only the hardware, we remain helpless as we pile up more and more data. With a connection to our hearts we now have the software that allows for processing to occur.

We are all survivors of how our hearts have been treated. If we received love and support, our hearts flourished. If the balance was weighted toward chronic abuse, then we are survivors of all the humiliations, losses, abandonments, rejections, cruelties, and craziness that we suffered in our childhoods. We have all been touched with enough of these assaults to cause us to live distant from our hearts. Yet for many there is a desire for more: to improve the quality of our existence, to feel more alive, to have better relationships, and to recapture a place of spontaneity and pleasure that we once knew or dreamed of as children.

To recapture our heart-body connections is to get to know and support the inner child with all its emotions, excitements, inquisitiveness, traumas, assaults, confusions, and uncertainties. If we are to support our heart, and therefore, our life force, we have to be aware of our childhood and its effects on how we learned to live our body, our emotions, our thoughts, and our relationships. Until we learn to accept the deep body knowing of how we had to live as children in order to protect our hearts, we can't fully accept who we are as adults, nor can we allow ourselves to enter into the reforming process that leads to further growth and aliveness. To move toward the acceptance of our inner child is to open to the energy of the negative parenting we bonded with and replace it with positive parenting. We thereby replace the negative myths that we carry with us from our childhoods with positive energy, with open heartedness and compassion for ourselves.

An experiment may help you understand more about how you protect yourself. Locate a place of tension in your body. Now alternately, exaggerate and relax the tension pattern a few times. Imagine you can work with the tension as you would with a gear, opening and closing a notch at a time. As you become more able to open and close, be aware of the emotional statement that the tension pattern is expressing. You might allow an image to emerge from the tension. Ask the tension pattern or the image the emerged what it is here for and if it has a message for you. Perhaps you will be aware of an expression that says "Don't hurt me" or "Don't touch me," or some expression of fear, anger, spite or defiance. These are only a few possibilities. Allow yourself to experience the unique expression that your tension pattern represents. As you experience the under-lying expression, imagine that you are being surrounded with love. What happens to the tension?

In the example of Debra, in Chapter Four, we see that chronic tension is an expression of some underlying emotion that we are not able to freely possess. Therefore, we have had to lock the expression in our muscles. Until we have support to feel and be able to express the feeling, we are not fully in possession of our own emotions and our own bodies. The tension is there, and we can't do anything about it. We need to understand and appreciate why the tension is there in the first place, and support the awareness in our bodies, not just in our minds. If we don't do this, we will continue to be slaves to a past that created the need to support ourselves with tension in the first place. In effect, we will be supporting ourselves with our tension and continuing the negative self-parenting that we learned as children. We continue to say no to our aliveness, the tension expressing the message that we cannot feel or speak. Debra said no with her tension. She therefore did not possess the alive-ness that would be there when she was actually able to verbalize her "No." When Debra was able to say "No" with heart, it increased her aliveness. The same is true for everyone.

Our tension serves an important function in this way. It is our ally, our support. It is also an expression of the negative parenting we received. Once we are able to begin to support in our bodies the reality of how we had to live as children, we are more able to allow a place for the positive emotional and energetic forces that can guide our lives. Instead of having a rigid or dense structure that holds against our energy, or a flaccid and under energized structure that won't allow for energy to build, we are making room for the flowing of our energy to develop new and creative forms. Our lives can become a continuous creation of new forms to deal with each situation as it arises, rather then meeting each situation in a stereotypic way.

Allowing the energetic forces that are contained in our bodies to flow naturally so that they are able to form, unform and reform freely ultimately provides us with the connection to our childlike qualities of spontaneity, innocence, and open-heartedness. When we integrate these qualities with our adult abilities to conceptualize, discriminate, and contain, we more deeply understand the simple truths of life and can live ourselves as process and experience rather than remaining fixed in a role.

There are times that it is in our own best interest to express ourselves in a forthright manner. There are also times that it is in our own best interest to contain our expression and hold onto our thoughts and feelings. To have the flexibility to live with either containing ourselves or being expressive as each situation unfolds, is to not be stuck in only one way of being and, therefore, not being chronically impulsive or chronically withholding. Having this flexibility, we can contain our feelings at times in order to allow for the full, ripe expression when the time is right. Then, we can express ourselves with fullness and eloquence. Having the support to experience and move from this integration is the basis for the rapturous feeling of being alive. It also enables us to live through the stressful times in our lives with more sense of direction and purpose.

Supporting our own process with heart also produces support and heart for the earth. In effect, the more deeply we care about ourselves, the more we are caring for the natural formation of all life. When we live within the natural flow of each expansion and contraction in us, it does not feel good when someone or something tries to limit our feelings of aliveness. We instinctively recognize that, if we don't say no to the limits that are being imposed on us, we have to split, break, or numb ourselves from what is real and alive in us in order to survive.

So it is when someone tries to limit the natural flow in nature. Instinctively, it doesn't feel good. It doesn't feel right. Because it goes against some natural order, it is an assault. And that is so often the way that we experience another shopping center, another road in the wilderness, another off shore oil rig, another non-biodegradable plastic cup; they are all assaults on nature, they are all assaults on our spirit and life force. The feeling of this being an assault may not occur on a fully conscious level. We may only be dimly aware that something doesn't feel good or right. And we may once again push our discomfort aside for the seeming convenience that is being provided for us.

In the next chapter, Exploring Our Past: Our Personal Archeology, we will look further at what stops us from simply supporting ourselves for each moment of our aliveness. Our exploration will continue into the darkness of our beings that we little understand and often try to avoid. We will explore that part of the darkness that is an accumulation of old assault energies, the part that is connected to archetypal fears, and the part has to do with the mystery and magic of life.

CHAPTER EIGHT

Exploring the Past: Our Personal Archeology

ENTERING THE DARKNESS

Spiritual Warrior
Life offers us the opportunity to become a spiritual warrior
A warrior is one who bravely goes into those dark areas within
themselves to ferret out the Truth of their being.
It takes great courage, stamina and endurance to become a
spiritual warrior.
The path is narrow, the terrain rough and rocky.
You will walk alone: through the dark caves,
up those steep climbs
and through the dense thick forest.
You will meet your dark side.
The faces of fear, deceit, and sadness all await your arrival.
No one can take this journey but you.
There comes a time, in each of our lives, when we are given the
choice to follow this path.
Should we decide to embark on this journey,
we can never turn back...
Our lives are changed forever.
On this journey, there are many different places
we can choose to slip into and hide.
But the path goes on.
The spiritual warrior stays the course,
wounded at times, exhausted and out of energy.

Many times, the Warrior will struggle back
on their feet to take only a few steps
before falling again.
Rested, they forge on, continuing the treacherous path.
The journey continues. The Spiritual Warrior stays the course.
Weakened, but never broken.
One day, the battle, loneliness and desperate fights are over.
The sun breaks through the clouds;
the birds sing their sweet melodies.
There is a change in the energy. A deep change within the self.
The Warrior has fought the courageous fight.
The battle of the dark night of the soul is won.
New energy now fills the Warrior.
A new path is now laid before them.
A gentler path filled with the inner-knowing
of one who has personal empowerment.
With their personal battle won, they are filled with joy.
A new awareness that they are one with
the Spirit beams as they go forth to
show others the way.
They are not permitted to walk the path for others.
They can only love, guide and be a living example
of the Truth of their being.
Author unknown

AN ARCHEOLOGICAL DIG

Webster defines *archeology* as the "scientific study of the life and culture of ancient peoples, as by excavation of ancient cities, relics, artifacts, etc." In this chapter I take poetic license and use the word to refer to the study of our personal life and culture through the exploration of our past. As with any archaeological dig, we carefully and respectfully uncover the past, piece by piece, as one would sift through the ruins of an ancient civilization. By doing this, we slowly uncover shards, relics, and artifacts of emotional pottery that have remained hidden and buried in shadow or darkness since childhood.

We may enter chambers that have been sealed for many years by chronic muscle tension, collapse or lability, by frozen walls and doors that have become rusted with age. We may enter rooms that we cannot initially find because they appear unformed, having been surrounded with protective layers of denial, fog, and blankness. We have to work our way through the surface layers of justification, blame or self-blame, denial, confusion, unconsciousness, distractions, and intellectualizations to the life and core of our existence.

As we find either pieces of emotional artifact and pottery or sealed and hidden chambers, we are looking to remove our emotional cobwebs and bring understanding and compassion to the areas that are blocked. We want to relax chronically tense muscles in order to allow more light and air into these sealed chambers of our body and psyche. We are looking to increase our respiration so that the flame of our aliveness can burn brighter. We are searching for the roots of how we had to separate from our hearts, our power, our joy, our gracefulness or whatever aspects of our being that it weren't safe to live openly and fully, so that we can reclaim these aspects of ourselves. We are looking to bring together the pieces of artifacts and explore the hidden chambers to help us understand why we had to leave parts of who we are back in the culture of our childhoods so that we can feel more whole. We do this in order to know the effect of how we have had to live our lives partially shrouded in darkness or shadow. Hiding from our darkness and keeping parts of ourselves in shadow, we are unable to accept and be nourished by these parts.

Our "dig" allows us to become more accustomed to the dark, unknown parts of ourselves and to get to know them. In effect, we are making more room for the darkness that is a part of us. We are making room for acceptance to replace criticism, for love to counter judgment. As we bring pieces of ourselves into the light, we can see them more clearly. Allowing light to shine on what had been previously shrouded in degrees of darkness allows for more emotional, energetic and bodily definition. This, in turn, leads us to the possession of all the qualities of our aliveness. Also, seeing ourselves in a clearer light leads us to a deeper understanding of how our defensive qualities have been our ally.

We can discover aspects of our darkness that are wonderful and miraculous, parts of the magic and mystery of life. Making room for our darkness opens the hidden channels and rooms in us that allow us to come to the very center, the essence, of who we are.

The more deeply involved we become with actually embodying this archaeological dig, the greater our understanding becomes of how each of us has been affected by growing up in the personal culture of our family, and the shared culture of our larger society. As in any archaeological dig, the more we explore, the more we can uncover. This leads to a deepening understanding of ourselves.

It is one thing to have a passing or intellectual understanding that we have been affected by various family and societal qualities. In this more cursory understanding we might appreciate that the personal family culture has its own unique sights, sounds, smells, tastes, textures, attitudes, rules, and modes of living. We might also appreciate that each family may share some similar aspects with other family cultures. For example, each family can have both shared and unique attitudes, rules, religions, and modes of behavior. At this level of understanding, we can see that each of us is a product of the blend of our own unique culture, i.e., a product of the specific family in which we grew up. We are also influenced by certain values of our society; school, religion, friends, basic media messages, etc. Personal cultures interact with social cultures, each impacting the other, producing our uniqueness.

If we choose to continue pursuing our understanding of how we have been affected by both our personal family culture and the shared culture of our larger society a step further, we can go beyond a simple appreciation of recalled sights, smells, tastes, attitudes, rules, and modes of behavior. The next step is to emotionally and energetically feel and appreciate how our personal culture has a deep and lasting effect on the formation of *every* aspect of our being. Throughout our discussion this theme emerges again and again; every aspect of our existence is molded by the energies that we have absorbed as children, first and foremost the energies in our families and then by the energies in our broader society. We are taught what to value and what to devalue. We are taught how to think, feel, and express our power and sexuality. We are taught how to live with, and express or not express, the feelings in our heart. We are taught which feelings and thoughts are acceptable, what to believe in, and how to experience and relate to ourselves, other people, and the world. We have been imprinted with the emotional forms that our lives should take. Even if the outer forms that our lives take look different from our parents' lives and different from the social culture that we grew up in, our internal lives have been molded to follow a specific pattern.

Now, if we further expand our understanding of how we have been affected by both the personal family culture and the shared culture of our larger society, we will experience that the impact of how we were raised goes beyond affecting us at an intellectual and emotional level. The teachings are so deeply rooted into us that we have also being trained how to hold and organize our bodies, how to live our muscles, how one organ lies in relation to another, and how our body energy should respond to external and internal stimuli.[1] [2] I am referring to the fact that there is an emotional transfer of information handed down from generation to generation. I liken this to DNA and call it Emotional DNA. Our way of dealing with our emotions, handed down through generations, directly impacts our cellular, chemical, hormonal, and neural connections. Our personal culture, within the context of our society at large, structures us as totally as any civilization structures housing, food, and water supply.

The philosopher George Santayana once wrote, "Those who cannot remember the past are condemned to repeat it."[3] To explore our past in greater detail so that we don't continually repeat it, makes room for us to understand ourselves more completely. To blindly repeat the past by continuing to live in some old stereotypic manner means that we are still bound by the abusive energies of our childhood. Not being condemned to repeat our past enables us to live fuller and more satisfying lives as adults. Connecting the pieces of our psyche and body process is an exciting journey although at times, it is a difficult and painful challenge. Like any archaeological dig, there can be hard work and frustration in the exploration, and deep pleasure and satisfaction in the "find." It is a challenge worth pursuing in order to bring our personal histories into balance, so that we are not continually making up for our past or denying its impact on us.

CASE STUDY
DAVID: NO WOMAN FIT THE BILL

Let us move from the conceptual to the practical. David, a client of mine, told me that he wanted to understand more about his relationships with women. Wanting satisfaction and dealing with problems in relationships are a central part of most people's lives. David reported to me that he ended relationships because he felt dissatisfied. He was beginning to wonder what part he played in his dissatisfaction. In the past he had always felt that the relationships didn't work out because he was simply involved with the wrong woman. David was not at a loss to find women to go out with. He would begin each relationship feeling excited and hopeful that the new person would be the woman of his dreams. After three to six months, when the initial glow was over, he would leave feeling that still another woman was not the one for him.

As we explored his feelings, David told me that short-term relationships felt safer. There was a period of time with each woman when he felt emotionally available. Soon, something shifted, and he would feel trapped. He had recently ended a relationship, even though he cared for the woman and had often felt that they could have a good life together. When he ended the relationship, it seemed like the right thing to do. However, during the ensuing months, he felt very depressed and confused about why he had ended it even though it had felt very satisfying.

As we talked about the similarities between why he had ended this and other relationships, he began to see that as soon as a woman reached out to him from her needs, he withdrew. He would always feel that her reaching was the beginning of his being used and manipulated. It turned out that David might even withdraw before a woman needed something from him because of his fear of his own needs. The way this worked in David was that as the relationship became deeper and more meaningful, his own needs would begin to surface. He had learned to support himself by withdrawing from his needs. As he withdrew from his needs, he was unable to respond to the woman's needs because her needs touched and energized his. Living in denial of his own needs he could neither have an open heart for her when she needed something from him, set a simple boundary where he could tell her that he didn't have what she needed, or tell her the he too, needed something.

He felt too trapped to say "Yes" and too guilty to say "No." Instead, a woman's needs became a sign for David that she was not perfect, that he'd be manipulated and, therefore, that he'd better end the relationship. He then moved on to look for the "perfect" relation-ship, always feeling frustrated. David was continually frustrated because he was unaware that he was acting out of resistance to his own needs. He projected his fear onto all the women he dated. The trapped feeling was created by how trapped his own needs were inside of himself, not by the woman's needs. Not knowing this, he was constantly projecting that the woman in his life would trap him.

He needed to see how the fear of being trapped was based on how he had been trapped as a child. It turned out that his mother was the trapper. David's fear, anger, and entrapment were created by a manipulative and invasive mother. He lived as if it was safer to continually end relationships than to explore his childhood. He could hold onto a false image of his mother rather than know how his aliveness touched his mother's manipulative and devouring energy. As a child, David was deeply used and manipulated when he was open-hearted, and smashed by his mother when he said "No." Therefore, he was frightened to both open his heart and to set a simple boundary in the face of someone else's need. How David dealt with his present reality was then deeply affected by how he had buried the memories of his old childhood trauma.

The more that early trauma resides in the denial of our beings, the more we, like David, are likely to deal with old fears by using behaviors meant to control and hide the fear. Not only are we burying our fears, but in the process we deny where they really comes from. As David and I further explored why he had ended the relationship, he realized how frightened he had always been and the real basis for his fear.

There could be people in David's life who have trapping and manipulative energy. We all can have this kind of energy surface in us at times. However, whether he deals with this reality by exploring how his childhood trauma is being touched or by denying the impact of his childhood and living like a victim in today's reality alters and co-creates the negative outcome of his relationships. A simple inter-action where David could either feel caring for the woman's insecurity or have a simple "No" for her need, might lead to a clearer and more intimate relationship. Instead, David has to close his heart to all women and to himself. After the initial glow of a relationship allows for a deeper level of personal and relational process, what is unresolved in David begins to surface. He interacts from the under-lying sense of powerlessness and fear from his childhood that he had to deny in order to survive.

By being unconscious of his process, David lives in a closed loop in which he does not learn from his own experiences. This is true for all of us who still live present reality in old stereotypic ways. When we have our energies and emotions divided between old and present reality, we are unable to come together. If we work through old trauma, we can interact in ways that allows us to deal with conflict and feel satisfied, rather than avoid conflict and have to leave.

To unconsciously live as though we were still in an "old reality" prevents us from coming together and bringing full and heartfelt meaning to our present existence. His "dig" will help David under-stand more about all of this. Referring back to our exploration of supports, David can then begin to appreciate his feeling trapped in the context of his childhood experiences. This can lead him to re-experience the old trauma and free him to form himself and his relationship with greater fullness, meaning, and satisfaction.

STUCK IN OUR TENSION

Another way that living as though the past was happening now is that we develop chronic muscle tension. This results from how we physically hold against feeling the impact of the assaultive energy of our childhood. Denial of emotions prevents us from fully relaxing our bodies when someone cares for us. We remain stuck in a limited range of physical and emotional feelings and expression. In David's case, he was always frightened of telling a woman that he loved her. Instead, when he would begin to feel open-hearted, he would automatically tighten his chest, stomach, and back, as he had learned to do as a child to protect himself from being invaded. In the face of abuse, this had become his way of holding back both his need for love and his own heart-felt feelings. David's chronic tension was created by how he defended himself against the assaultive energy of his childhood. His chronically tense muscles now store the memory and emotions of those events. David's tension kept him fixed in a pattern of perception about caring and support. Specifically, after he felt very close with a woman, he would begin to feel her caring and support as if he were being manipulated and smashed. In reality, her caring was energizing the earlier trauma. As his muscles began to open in relation to the woman's caring and support, they would release the old feelings that David had internalized as a child, when caring and support was a "set up" for David to be controlled by being smashed and manipulated. As a result, he would incorrectly judge that a woman's caring or support was meant to smash him, trap him, and take away his independence.

Rather than being able to react to events in a simple manner, David lived each experience still surrounded by the energy of his childhood assaults. Life, therefore, became confused and complicated because David unknowingly was trying to juggle two realities at the same time. In order to protect himself, he felt that he needed to control intimacy rather then allow it to happen. His judgement of the situation was further skewed by other details of how he was treated as a child. For example, after the honeymoon period of the relationship was over, he felt contemptuous or disgusted with what was being offered to him, because the ways in which he was controlled in the past had elements of contempt in them.

When David did feel someone's caring, his chronic tension prevented him from softening and allowing the caring into his heart. To allow someone's caring and support to touch him would be very nurturing. If he could breathe the caring energy into where he had been assaulted, he would also reinforce a connection to his own life force. However, because of the underlying childhood trauma that still resides in the darkness, and David's resistance to entering that darkness and feeling the reality of how he had been treated as a child, he continually recreated the old reality in each of his current relationships. To the degree that David, or any of us, don't soften enough to let someone's caring fully touch us because we believe that we will be assaulted if we open to our deeper feelings, we live in degrees of dissatisfaction.

Whatever else David does in his life to feel satisfied, if he is unaware of how his old reality affects him, he will always have a layer of dissatisfaction and depression that remains a part of him. David does what so many people do as a result of this dilemma. He drives himself in his work and in his play as a way of trying to find satisfaction. At the same time, David's drivenness reinforces and perpetuates the avoidance of his underlying dissatisfaction and depression.

For David, and for all of us, being more enlightened doesn't happen in the past. Nor does it happen in the future. It only occurs in the present. Yet, when we are blocked from fully living the present moment, we need to uncover how and why we remain blocked in order to become more conscious. Only then can we stop struggling with being blocked and being held in darkness and enter a pure moment of awareness. In this aware state, we can fully breathe and be one with our experience. Each moment of acceptance of the darkness is like taking a bellows to the spark of life. Each succeeding moment of awareness allows the spark to continue to burn brighter. We need to enter the darkness to become more enlightened. Then we can bring light into the darkness and live a life filled with consciousness.

A BASE CAMP FOR ENTERING THE DARKNESS

It can be helpful for us to have a frame of reference of what the darkness is composed of before embarking on our "dig." There are three aspects to the darkness.

The first is composed of all the feelings that we have had to keep hidden from ourselves, or that we have some awareness of, but have been unable to accept. These are the feelings that we don't have support to feel and/or express because we are still fused in the negative energies of our childhoods.

The second are all the qualities of the darkness that have to do with our primitive and existential fears of being human. Here are archetypal fears about being alone in the universe. In some basic and primitive inner place we are alone. No one can live our experiences for us. The unending vastness of the universe is dark and to a degree unknowable. Yet there is a paradox about this second element of the darkness, which has to do with...

The third—the magical, mysterious, and mystical parts of life. The paradox is that as we are able enter our existential aloneness we move toward a universal consciousness where we are not alone-where we are a part of all that exists in the universe.

It is ultimately enlivening and exciting to center ourselves in a feeling of darkness, rather than pull away from the darkness and therefore, divide our energies. To bring awareness and acceptance to any of the feelings in the darkness offers us a fuller connection to ourselves and a sense of belonging and oneness to the humanity of all people, to the earth, to the universe, and to universal consciousness. When we are surrounded with awareness and acceptance, we become reconnected to our primary sense of magic, wonder and spontaneity. To avoid experiencing any aspect of our darkness is to perpetuate our defensive structure that reinforces our connection to the old abusive realities that we have internalized from our childhood.

As we treat these "finds" from the darkness with gentleness and caring, we begin to experience how every part of us was, and is, valuable and necessary. Like a perfect ecology, we find out how each part of who we are has a place and a reason for being. As we bring understanding and appreciation to who we are and why we feel and have lived the way we have, we piece together alienated parts of ourselves, thereby feeling more whole. In doing so, we get to know about all the life that is taking place in the darkness that we have been unable to fully know or experience before.

We will discover long-hidden chambers of our being that, once opened, help us feel fuller emotionally and more relaxed physically. Fitting together pieces of our puzzle, we gather these findings so that they speak to us of the whys of personal behaviors, attitudes, relationships, spiritual connections, and world views, as well as a deeper understanding of our individual body organization.

I want to emphasize that this process does not simply provide an intellectual understanding of who we are in the world. It provides us with an in-depth awareness, an intimate understanding of who we are on every level of our existence—from the way that we function in the world and in relationships, to the way that we live in our bodies, the way that we live with our emotions, the way that we live our spirituality, and the way that we live and treat the planet. Through the discoveries from our "dig," we increasingly understand and appreciate how we fit together into a beautiful mosaic, seeing more clearly how each and every aspect of who we are and how we live is interrelated. In this way we are releasing old trauma and thereby, becoming more conscious and enlightened.

MORE OF MY PERSONAL STORY

As I wrote in Chapter One, learning about how frightened I was became the doorway to my aliveness. The more I was able to support and tolerate feeling my fear, the more I began to understand that holding against fear prevented me from relaxing into my body and feeling more pleasure. There was a layer of darkness that contained feelings of emptiness that always had been with me.

I believed that if I could only be in a relationship with a loving woman that I would have everything that I wanted and needed and be rid of these feelings. I didn't realize at the time that my feelings of emptiness and deprivation had to do with my learned response of withholding my life from myself and others. I believed that my aliveness and good feelings were dependent on a loving relationship, rather than in my ability to unlock the withholding that prevented me from experiencing the depth of my aliveness. I had learned to stubbornly deny the impact of my childhood, and its relationship to the distant way that I treated people. As I pieced together the shards of how I had been emotionally abused as a child and as I opened spaces in me that had been locked as a result of my needing to withhold, I could appreciate and let go of my withholding. This allowed me to breath more deeply, feel more alive, and enter and sustain a relationship.

Each connection I made regarding how I had learned to live my emotions and organize my body, as a way of surviving my childhood, allowed me to take more responsibility for my own happiness, fortunes, and misfortunes. The more I accepted how my past affected me, the less I had to project how I felt and how I lived onto my lack of a relationship with a woman. I had blamed my loneliness, depression, and isolation on not being in an intimate relationship. I believed that if I could find the right woman, my loneliness, depression, and isolation would dissolve. This was not true. I began to understand that the way I had been living actually prevented me from having the relationship that I had sought. Old suffering began to transform and make room for happiness. Even though I couldn't control external circumstances and will someone to love me, I could be responsible for my own happiness and then meet people from happiness, rather than suffering.

Greater personal responsibility came as I understood that I had always felt insecure and collapsed, that I had always been a walking history of my childhood. The loneliness, isolation, and depression were the legacy that I had brought with me into my adult life. It was the truth of how deeply I had been affected by the violence and craziness of my family. The more I felt the truth of where my feelings came from, the more my loneliness, isolation, and depression lifted. I then began to have the kind of relationships I had always wanted.

My body no longer had to hide my feelings by remaining both rigid and collapsed. I no longer had to have a low grade sense of depression as a result of the rigidity and collapse. As I became friendlier with my body, I could feel how any physical illness that I developed was caused by withholding my aliveness, stressing my body, and depriving myself of nurturance. I gained appreciation for the relationship between my isolation and my cynicism toward spirituality. As long as I was isolated from my heart and my life force, spirituality and a connection to my own inner truths remained distant. I felt cynical toward what I couldn't personally experience.

Finally, I began to experience the relationship between all of these aspects of who I was and my disconnection from nature. As I began to heal these aspects of rigidity and collapse in my body and psyche and my heart opened, I found that I felt more of a sense of oneness with all people and the earth. I cared about what happened to people and to our planet.

In working with many people over the course of my career, I have found that what happened with me is not unique. I have seen that my experiences are part of a shared humanity and quite typical of what occurs as people grow and change based on their acceptance and appreciation of each moment of existence.

EXPLORING THE DARKNESS

I want to return to the discussion of the three aspects of the darkness. First, let's look more closely at the part of the darkness that consists of feelings that we have had to keep hidden from ourselves or that we have felt unable to share. The darkness consists of any experience or emotion that we treat as an alien part of who we are. Anything we don't want to see or know about ourselves is a part of the darkness. The unfinished grief that we don't know how to deal with, or treat as if it does not exist, becomes a part of the darkness. Also, what we've blocked out or denied about the impact of how we were abused as children becomes a part of the darkness.

An example of this is when we have to deny that we were assaulted as children, and then we live as if everything about our childhood was "just fine." Or we live as if the trauma that we remember really didn't have much impact. We live as if we are above and beyond the trauma, and energetically we are. To live in denial means that our consciousness is disembodied and resides above our physical body.

It takes energy away from our aliveness to live in denial of what was real. The life energy is employed for suppression or repression of our emotions and the perpetuation of our disembodied state. The organization of our energy in this defensive way literally produces less room in our bodies and therefore, more darkness. There is less room because we have organized our muscles in a more rigid, dense, collapsed, or flaccid manner. There is less room in our body because we live disembodied. We now live defensively in relation to our life force.

If we deny that abuse was a part of our childhood, then we also deny the reason for all our emotional reactions to that abuse. For example, anger is a natural response to being abused. If we had to organize ourselves against our anger because being angry would only bring more abuse, we may then feel that our anger was the problem instead of the abuse and that we have to relegate it to a dark chamber of our being. If turning against our anger was our only alternative, than we lost the positive function of being or feeling angry. In the present we might still feel that allowing room for angry feelings can only lead us to being abused or to being frustrated because no one will understand us. We shy away from containing and accepting our anger because it would then lead us to reliving old hurts that we believe can never heal. We have no experience that anger is the raw material for a positive feeling of power, the ability to say "No," and the raw material for having a boundary. We have no sense that anger can be contained and expressed in a way that is not destructive. Without building in supports for our anger, we continue living the feeling of anger in ways that are never satisfying. We have re-created the abuse to ourselves by destroying our own anger as a safety measure, but what we don't see is that we have bonded to the destruction coming at us and joined with it.

To varying degrees, people are stuck in darkness. There are some people who live in total darkness regarding their emotions and their understanding of themselves. Others of us live degrees of darkness: dark at times and clear at others, or shades of gray. There are the times that we may live in the shadows of our experiences. We may feel foggy and vague, unsure of where our center is. Or we may have some sense of our deeper aliveness and understand that the difficulties in our life, our dissatisfactions and unhappiness, are a part of unfinished emotional places. Our life force wants to guide us through the darkness, but it is stuck in the shadows of our existence, waiting for us to have enough support to make the journey.

If we are unable to intimately accept our history and bring it into balance in our present life, then a layer of negativity remains in our personality. This negativity consists of different forms of unexpressed and unaccepted anger that has turned into withholding, protest, spite, revenge, cruelty, meanness etc. How we relate to our negativity determines whether these feelings remain part of the darkness or not. To fully accept and appreciate our negativity brings it into the light. To hide from it, and to be disgusted and contemptuous of it, creates further darkness. Let us imagine feeling guilty or ashamed of feeling negative, and, therefore, being disgusted or contemptuous each time the negativity rises to the surface of our awareness. Treating the negativity with negativity further exacerbates the creation of darkness.

To emphasize this point, **we create darkness when we are contemptuous and critical of, or disgusted with, any aspect of ourselves and, therefore, forcibly try to get rid of the feeling or experience. We create darkness when we are frightened of our feelings and either obsess about the fear, also trying to rid ourselves of it, rather than live into the fear. Our life force is always trying to move us toward freedom and expression. We can't force parts of who we are out of existence. To try to do that is to create opposing forces inside us, which in turn creates tension, feelings of nonexistence, confusion, and distortions of our simple experiences. Emotions, and their**

accompanying body experiences, are part of our life force that can be hidden, but not eradicated.

Here is an experiment you can try in order to personalize how opposing forces work within us. Imagine that you feel tired and need to rest. Then imagine that there is some old message you have internalized that tells you that you shouldn't have to rest. The message may be that you should always be able to be active and productive. Picture your simple need for rest being met by an opposing force of impatience, contempt or disgust, that you are not being active enough.

The simple emotional and body message that we need to rest is a message from our life force. If we don't allow for the tiredness and instead follow the old abusive message, then we drive ourselves into constant activity. If this becomes the usual way that we treat ourselves, then eventually, the two opposing forces of aliveness and unformed negativity will lead to some form of a breakdown.

We may become workaholics and playaholics as we are led by the messages to be constantly productive. There will also be a layer of confusion in us as we reject our natural biological rhythms. Like Pig Pen, the cartoon character in Peanuts who is constantly living with a cloud of dirt around him, we live with our emotional cloud of conflicting signals. And like Pig Pen, who never washes, if we don't follow what our life force tells us that we need, we become darker and feel darker because of it.

NEGATIVITY AS A PART OF THE DARKNESS

As we sift through our attitudes, emotions, and body experiences that are a part of our personal archeological dig, we will come upon unformed negativity that we have been afraid to feel or even know about. Or we come upon negativity that we do feel but have never been able to put into perspective and live with comfortably. **Negativity is the childhood abuse that we have internalized and that has become locked in our muscles.** Our negativity is also composed of the distorted form of all of our unsupported emotions. All abuse is aimed at children's light and since the pure emotions of pleasure, need, anger, hurt, and sadness make up our light, we shut them off to be safe. As these repressed emotions back up in our system, they become unformed and change to more negative experiences including spite, cruelty, contempt, disgust, punishment, revenge, rage, murderousness, hate, incestuousness/rape, lust, jealousy, etc. When this occurs, we all have a difficult time making room for these negative experiences. We can't feel and/or share these feelings in a simple way and accept them as a part of our humanness.

As we remain stuck in these negative feelings, they also become part of the external manner in which we relate to others. The problems in our external lives are always a reflection of what is internally unresolved in us. The struggles we have with other people are manifestations of the struggles we have with ourselves. When we stop the inner struggle, we stop struggling with other people.

These unformed feelings that back up in us can range from Carl's hostility and violence that then is acted out on other people, to Bill's passivity and acquiescence that became his style of acting out, to Debra's constant anger with her daughter, or to my withholding. As with Carl, negativity can be expressed as a blast that feels as if he is smashing us, or as the experience of being knifed. Or the negativity can be expressed more covertly, as with Bill, who lives in passive aggressive ways seemingly acquiescing to other's needs yet always unconscious that his "messing up" and "forgetting" things in relation to others is his form of anger. Negativity can also be expressed in other ways such as someone's martyred complaining that they are never treated with the same caring and consideration that they provide or by someone acting out helplessness in order to be taken care of.

Although the negative feelings we have were originally meant to be directed at the victimizers in our childhood, since the negativity has become locked in our body, we wind up turning these feelings against ourselves. When we are contemptuous or disgusted with ourselves, or hate something about ourselves, this is unformed negativity that we have internalized.

Since we struggle so much with not wanting to see ourselves as having negative feelings, it is often easier to focus on the negativity that is outside of us. We justify or deny our own negativity and then live as victims of all the negativity in the world. We lose any awareness that our disowning these feelings in ourselves adds to the dark and negative energy in the world.

As we become more enlightened and continue the path of accepting our darkness, we can honor our negativity as protector and ally. We can feel how our negativity was a form of safety in relation to the abuse to our needs and dependence, our innocence, our vulnerability and our protest; all of which we had to leave behind as we grew up because these feelings weren't accepted as a necessary and meaningful part of our humanness.

LIFE UNFOLDS

Honoring these protectors of old, we can live into uncried tears, fears, and childhood horrors that we had to harden against. We will also find places of joy and creativity in the darkness that we have had to keep buried. Sensuality that people believed was a sign of our being too alive, also remains buried in the darkness of tight or flaccid bodies. So, too, will there be feelings of power that emerge from our center that we had to hide because it was a threat to our parents. It might have been the power to say "No" or the power to speak our own reality and say our own perception of what was going on in the family. The power that emerges from our center will be different from the feeling of power that has to do with how much we can control ourselves or other people. The first form of power exists without tension and hardness. It is experienced as wholeness and fullness. There is a feeling of aliveness about it. Tension, hardness, darkness, and hostility accompany the controlling form of power.

Our exploration becomes a continuing process of positive experiences followed by the next piece of buried tragedy that has to be dealt with and that, in turn, will lead us to the next place of our aliveness and our spirit. On this path, we will encounter feelings and moods that are part of our defensive structure. For example, when it was necessary to tighten our bodies against an assault like humiliation, the tension itself creates its own uncomfortable feeling.

All of the ways we organize our bodies against the emotional and physical abuse that we received as children make it difficult to accept our deep feelings of joy, sadness, need, anger, orgasm and love. It is equally difficult to give in to the deeper streamings and pulsations in our heart. We have learned to control ourselves to the point of decreasing the intensity of our aliveness or completely negating and/or distorting it.

We learned to tighten our bodies against our feelings, rise above them, or collapse away from them. We had to make our bodies tighter, denser, distorted, fragmented, compressed, depressed, split, or flaccid. We found various ways to organize our bodies away from emotions and experiences that were unsupported and assaulted. We found ways to deal with all the different parts of ourselves that weren't loved and validated. Our life force spontaneously developed these creative ways to help us survive abuse.

That's the good news. The bad news is that to live defensively automatically creates distortions of the emotion that we are now defending against. That is, when we try to get rid of our emotions because we don't have support to allow ourselves to feel them, we distort the simple experience. For example, holding back anger creates spite. Now the anger is no longer so simple and clear. Holding back need can create stoicism on the one hand or create a constant feeling of neediness and loneliness on the other hand.

To live distanced from our inner lives creates less room in our bodies and this then creates more darkness. I mean this literally. A tighter, denser, more collapsed, more fragmented, split, depressed body is energetically darker and has less room than a body where breath and energy flow freely.

The list that follows contains some of the experiences that are the result of our defensive organization. Our defensive stance is like a cage that holds these experiences in our body. They are now distorted and complex forms of simple emotional experiences. The distorted forms that prevent a direct connection to aliveness and

spirit do not feel good. Because of the discomfort and dissatisfaction we try to remain unconscious of them, pushing them further
into the recesses of our defensive structure. As we discussed in the
Chapters on supports, these feelings become our supports and
remain with us until we have a new support that allows us to live
aliveness as it forms in our bodies as emotion.

SOME FEELINGS THAT ARE PERPETUATED BY OF OUR DEFENSIVE ORGANIZATION:

withholding	meaninglessness	spaciness
impotence	depression	craziness
helplessness	confusion	blankness
hopelessness	isolation	guilt
despair	invasion	emptiness
alienation	possession	deprivation
humiliation	desperation	fogginess
compression	devouring	abandonment
embarrassment	formlessness	diffusion
mortification	depersonalization	nonexistence
horror	terror	fragmentation

Here we are! Unable to fully accept and live into all our emotions
of aliveness — joy, orgasm, rage, grief, need, and love — distortions
and combinations of these feelings are created. Distorted feelings
are produced by defending against the assault to life emotions. For
example, anger, need, and sadness being fused in compression
creates a masochistic, complaining whine. Defending against the
underlying anger, need, and sadness with compression perpetuates
a compressed feeling that in and of itself does not feel good and also
further prevents us feeling satisfied, no matter how much we are
given.

We are now stuck in the predicament of wanting to rid ourselves
of these defensive, unpleasant feelings but do not know how to do
this. Often, we are also unclear about where the feelings came from

in the first place. We may feel that they are our flaws, our signs of weakness or of craziness or we may attach some other negative meaning to them. We may become frustrated and disgusted with ourselves for feeling the way that we do. We feel stuck with being unable to change in order to feel more pleasure and satisfaction.

Since we have to live with ourselves and do the best job we know how to, we carry on and survive. We may try to bury these feelings even more deeply, further adding to the vicious cycle of discomfort that we try to rid ourselves of and that even further exacerbates the creation of our personal darkness. We may try to rid ourselves of these feelings by changing our lives, changing spouses or jobs etc., desperately looking for the answer to dissatisfaction. Some turn to substance abuse to try to get away from the pain of living an unful-filled existence.

CASE STUDY

FRANK: THE WAY OUT OF ISOLATION

A summary of a therapy session with Frank illustrates what I am talking about. Frank started one of his sessions by telling me that he felt isolated, and that everything in his life felt as if it had no meaning. I began by providing him with a frame of reference for his isolation and meaninglessness. I told him that isolation was a stuck place where he was suspended between being unable to either separate from people and feel full in himself, or to reach out for contact and feel that he wasn't alone in the world. People get stuck in isolation when the movement between separateness and contact sets off an old assault feeling that has been stored in the body. Consciously or unconsciously, if we believe the assault energies, rather than understanding that they are a part of childhood abuse, they prevent us from moving in either direction. Not until Frank was able to identify these assaultive energies and have the motiva-tion and support to live through them, could his isolation lift. Since he could neither separate in a satisfying way nor take in that he wasn't alone in the world, there was no way for him to feel connected to any sense of aliveness. Without a connection to his life force, it made sense that he would feel meaninglessness.

I asked Frank not to fight the feeling of isolation, but to make room for it. When Frank stopped fighting himself energies were no longer split and he could come more directly into his experience of isolation. Fighting with isolation is like trying to fight your way out of quicksand. It exacerbates the feeling by creating even more tension and disconnection from center. **Moving toward the center of any positive or negative feeling is a movement toward center and aliveness**. That is, to move toward the center of any experience brings us more into connection with our body and with our deeper emotions, more into connection with our life force.

For Frank to focus and bring his awareness to his isolation was to enter a dark, unknown place. This felt like a risk. To take this risk Frank needed to feel that he could support himself in unfamiliar territory. He would need faith that giving up struggling against the isolation could be worth it. He needed some inner feeling of faith that he could survive the experience.

As Frank made room for his experience, I invited him to ask the isolation what it was here for. I further told him not to make up an answer but to make room for the isolation to answer him. The isolation replied that it was protecting him from the fear of abandonment that was the old abuse if he took a step toward being separate, and the fear of being humiliated if he reached out for a connection. I suggested that he honor the isolation for being a safe place against other feelings that had been even more traumatic to experience when he was younger. We began to explore how he had learned to isolate himself rather than feel how he had been emotionally abandoned for his need for separateness, and humiliated for his need for contact. He had been isolated by his parents' response to his need for separateness and his need for love. It felt relatively safer and more comfortable to remain isolated, rather than to feel the old abusive energies. His isolation deserved appreciation for how it had helped him survive a very difficult situation.

In effect, what I suggested to Frank was that he could bring heart and light to his isolation by appreciating it as an old form of protection. The result was that Frank felt kinder and warmer toward himself. The more he could do this, the more his isolation dissolved. What he understood and integrated more clearly was how his isolation had protected him. As he stopped fighting himself, he recognized that he was angry about how he had been treated and sad that his simple need to move between contact and separateness had not been supported. Having supported and entered the darkness created by his isolation, he was beginning to see and feel old emotions of need, anger, and sadness that he had needed to hide.

Although Frank knew that he often felt angry and sad, he was unclear why he felt these emotions. They felt so intense to him that he always considered himself an overly emotional person. He felt disdainful toward himself for being what he considered weak. Because he was still fused with his parents' way of humiliating him when he expressed any emotion, he hadn't been able to accept the buildup of emotion. He had learned to turn against himself in the same way that his parents had turned against him. He didn't have a role model to parent himself differently. He didn't have a way of understanding where his needs and his anger and sadness came from and was therefore unable to have any perspective. Always using his energy to try to rid himself of his needs, the needs grew in intensity. Not appreciating that his anger and sadness made sense, he wound up being isolated from his aliveness and spirit.

Frank wasn't ready to accept his sadness, anger, and need. When I suggested that he make room for these feelings, he changed the subject, instead telling me stories about his childhood. When I pointed this out to him, he started to feel how spiteful he felt. He also felt that to accept his anger was to let his parents "off the hook." He wasn't prepared to do this. He wanted to punish them: he wanted revenge.

As Frank's experiences continue to unfold into consciousness, he was more able to see and experience how each of his emotions were a part of the mosaic of his life, how one feeling related to another. All Frank's experiences became part of the exploration of his "dig." He learned how defending against feeling and not accepting each experience as it unfolded created his isolation and meaninglessness. As he understood the interlinking dynamics for how he was living, he began to feel motivated to accept and take more responsibility for his emotions. He no longer had to live completely in the darkness of revenge and old negative supports. His aliveness now had room to blossom.

BRINGING LIGHT TO THE DARKNESS

To fully accept and appreciate our emotions, including all our feelings of hostility and negativity, brings light to these feelings and therefore, releases them from the darkness. To bring heart to our feelings of cruelty, revenge, spite, disgust, etc., literally transforms these feelings into power. This occurs we no longer have to hide, split off from, diffuse ourselves or act out the way that we feel. We can then simply feel what we feel and share it if we wish to, without attempting to blame or destroy other people or ourselves.

For example, it is common for us as children to say "I hate you" to our parents if we feel that they are treating us unfairly. If our parents accept that this is simply an expression of our upset rather than trying to control us our feelings flow through us making room for other feelings to form. With acceptance for "I hate you," what usually forms is, "I love you."

Keleman states this in a simple and clear manner. "There is no need to bully, aggravate, torment or overpower others when your sense of 'self' is intact."[5] The more we can simply accept all of the negative feelings we have, the more we are adding to an intact sense of "self." So when Frank was able to accept his anger and begin to form his negative feelings of spite, punishment, and revenge, he no longer had to defend himself by remaining isolated from his own and others feelings. The more he accepted himself no matter what he felt, the more power he accumulated and, therefore, the more he experienced a sense of self-possession. Feeling more powerful creates simpler transitions between contact with others and withdrawal into self.

Also, by accepting these feelings, by bringing more light into himself, Frank didn't have to organize his body into a defensive holding pattern. This is true for everyone. As our tense muscles relax, or as we stretch out of collapse, or as a band of tension that causes a split opens, or we form from having been flaccid and unformed, the experiences that are the by-products of our defensive organizations disappear. (See the list: Some Feelings That Are Perpetuated By Our Defensive Organization) We now breathe more deeply and feel the flow of aliveness move through us with each breath. We feel less pressured. Without the chronic tension or flaccidity we also remove the pressure that we have placed on our cardiovascular system and internal organs. Physically we are more in balance. Accepting and containing all feelings helps us remain open to the flow of life. And staying open to our life force, our spirit always moves us in the direction of enlightenment.

Defensive negativity, in Frank's case his spite, originates both as a defense against the abuse with which our hearts have been treated and an internalization of the negativity that was inside of our parents. As children we tried to defend ourselves against the negative, abusive energy. However, because we were fed a constant, chronic diet of abuse the negative energy does get in. If, for example, as children we received contempt and cruelty when we said "No" to our parents, contempt and cruelty become fused with our desire to have and set boundaries. The result is that when we say no to someone, we express our "No" with the energy of contempt and cruelty. In this way we have become like our parents, both in the way that we treat ourselves and the way we show contempt and cruelty toward others. By supporting the truth of how we feel and recognizing that we are reliving the energy of an old assault, we can give up blame. In this way we bring a piece of the darkness into the light and grow beyond our parents.

Giving up blame and being able to take responsibility that it is our own feelings that are being touched, is a critical point in bringing unformed negativity into the light. Blame is simply a form of justification and a way of defending our right to

feel what we actually need no justification to feel in the first place. What we feel is simply what we feel. It is not a sign of good or bad, right or wrong. No defense is necessary. We believe that defensive posturing is necessary when we don't have support for how we feel and expect to be abused in return for our feelings. If, as children, we were abused for feeling angry or negative, we automatically bring the expectation that we will be assaulted for our anger and negative feelings into our adult relationships. We hold onto what we have learned from our formative experiences about how we were treated and project it onto the present and future.

Another example of fusing with negative energy is that as a child, when we were angry, we might have been told that we had nothing to be angry about. By receiving this response, the validity of our anger was denied. We might have wanted to fight for our reality. Yet, if we persisted in expressing our anger, it would only bring angrier reprisals and further denials that we had anything to be angry about. Eventually, we might feel the futility of fighting with a parent who wants to negate what we feel, rather then understand us. The negation and denial of our anger will create confusion and a feeling of craziness since adults are insisting that we have no reason to feel what we do feel. In effect our reality is being tampered with.

The remaining mix of support or abuse from our parents creates the unique way we learn to deal with our anger and our sense of reality. Let's say that on a behavioral level, we join the parent in the denial that there is anything to be angry about. However, on a deeper emotional level, we are still angry. In fact, the underlying anger, like an infection that doesn't heal, can fester and grow. As the inner anger intensifies, it can grow into a feeling of cruelty, of wanting revenge and of the desire to punish. We have now learned how to deal with our anger by not dealing with it. That is, we have created a layer of denial about what we really feel. The denial blocks and numbs us to a piece of our existence (our anger). We have created an internal set in which we move away from center, and therefore, a step away from feeling grounded and in the world. And then in turn, we feel less support for the spontaneous, alive, angry inner child. This underlying, unaccepted anger now becomes a part of the darkness.

If we begin to reverse this process on our "dig" and gain more support and understanding for our angry inner child, we don't have to have our negativity as a defense, as if each situation were life and death. So often this stance of defending our feelings at all cost is what causes the intensification of the feeling in the first place; e.g., simple anger turning into rage or cruelty as we expect not to be understood. If we can reconnect to the truth that our anger and negativity has a context in our childhood experiences and that these feelings are not problems and, therefore, do not need justification, then we can give up blaming other people for how we feel. By accepting our anger, cruelty and rage as our own, we reverse the process of keeping these feelings in darkness where they retain a dark power over us. When we accept our negativity, we bring it into the light. As discussed in the chapter on supports, our anger can become a part of our power to say "no" and a part of our ability to set a simple boundary.

When we blame other people for how we are living and feeling, we have given up responsibility for ourselves. We are living as if our lives are in their hands. Our centers are then outside of ourselves. We are living in reaction to what we expect from someone else, rather than proceeding from our own centers. **A deeper and more abiding truth is that the primary connection to our life is not through other people. Rather, it is in the ability to take responsibility for our own feelings. This occurs as we gain an understanding and a connection with our inner child. The more that we take responsibility for our own feelings and our own aliveness the deeper the connection with other people can be.**

When we are in support of our own life force, we live centered and balanced. When we live from center and balance, we can make room for our vulnerability and innocence. Here, our inner child is welcome, and we can honor that part of who we are. As we direct our attention to feeling and supporting our inner child, we look less to others for approval. The less attention we pay to our inner child when we are adults, the more we unknowingly act like the uncared for child that we once were. If we don't understand that the primary connection to our life is the connection to our inner child, we lose perspective about who is responsible for our life force. Rather than being able to express ourselves clearly, we are more demanding, controlling, bitchy, depressed, hurt, and defeating. In effect, we are acting out our needs through these negative expressions, rather than feeling our needs. Openly or secretively, we live in an energy of entitlement, unable to accept the slightest frustration.

To strengthen the bond to our inner child is an act of self love. It leads us to a direct connection to our heart and to personal power. Being more "in touch" with our heart and power has a direct impact on the feelings that we have been stuffing inside of ourselves. It allows us to express these emotions in a simple and clear way. When we stop blaming other people for how we feel, we find that we can have a more direct and positive connection with others. And this positive cycle continues in that we feel fuller and more alive, so we are often less hostile and negative about things that at one time might have caused us to feel angry. Our feelings of need are easier to live with so they too, do not get stuffed, backed up, and feel overwhelming to us. As we follow this path of opening our hearts to ourselves, we come closer to tasting the nectar and pure bliss of life.

The first of the two aspects of darkness that have been discussed thus far is related to our alienated feelings that are caused by having to stuff our emotions inside of ourselves. A second aspect of the darkness consists of the archetypal experiences that originally had to do with the way early inhabitants of earth experienced the unknown. In this respect, part of our darkness is still related to some primordial place in the human condition where we feel alone, vulnerable, and mortal in relation to the vastness of the universe.

Imagine! There they were, our most ancient ancestors, a small band of people, standing alone in the universe, not comprehending time and space as we have come to understand it from our current knowledge of physics and astronomy. There they were, without any scientific understanding of the flow of life and death. Wild animals and uncontrolled diseases could attack at any time, seemingly coming out of nowhere. These primitive people, living a subsistence existence, where every moment was truly a moment of life and death, were frightened of the vastness of the universe and what they couldn't understand and control. None the less, at some point in their development, they also began to pray to the forces of nature in order to enlist them in their own behalf. Waking up to another dawning, the birth of a child, the experience of a meteor shower, learning about fire, or seeds turning to edible plants, all were experienced as magical. They had not yet learned to defend against their feelings. This allowed for a direct and open connection to the forces of nature, to spirit, to the life force in all living things.

With all our sophistication and knowledge, there is still a primitive and innocent part of us. In many ways the world is still unknown and magical. For example, we can still experience wonder and awe at the birth of a child, or in looking at a star-studded sky, or upon entering a pristine wilderness area. There is still so much magic in being alive, in the unsolved mysteries of biology, cosmology, quantum physics, and consciousness. Even when we are provided with scientific answers, when we are directly touched by disease and death or by trying to comprehend the shift between particles and waves or the ever expanding universe, or with new information about the correlation between emotion and physical pain and illness, we can be awestruck with the magnificence of the interrelatedness and coherence of all of nature. To enter the feeling of the darkness, the mystery, in any of these experiences is to feel a direct and immediate connection to spirit. We can feel the underlying spirit and consciousness in all living things.

Yet, there is a need in many of us to control, regulate and cast out the wilderness, all that is primitive, wild and free, rather than to give into the experience of wonder and awe. We mistake the unknown, the primordial darkness, that which we can't readily see and understand as something to conquer, rather than to simply understand. In this way, we try to conquer the outward wilderness in the same way that we try to conquer our internal wilderness. No matter how much we attempt to rise above nature and control it, natural phenomena are still uncontrollable and unknowable. Weather and natural disasters come in their own time. Likewise, we can't control our process; we can only have some control over how we live our process. In some very basic way we cannot control our own destiny.

Our primitive response to the darkness is quite evident as children. At one time or another, most children are frightened of the darkness. We might have been frightened of getting into bed because we were not sure that we would awaken again. In those early years, we were frightened of disappearing, of becoming nonexistent, of dying.

Nighttime does cast its shadows, its dimmer light from moon and stars. It's certainly a time when criminals can do their work on unsuspecting victims and retire back into the darkness. Besides the obvious danger here, there is still some archetypal fear in us that dates to a time when predators could attack a less protected band of people as they slept. An ancient Celtic prayer I remember hearing as a child expresses this sentiment: "From ghoulies and ghosties and long-legged beasties and things that go bump in the night, God protect us."

As a child I remember many nights lying in bed, frightened of the monsters I saw poised outside my bedroom window. I was sure they were waiting for perfect moment to strike. Each morning when I awoke, I realized that the monsters were the shadows cast by the tree in the backyard. Even though I saw the light of day and the truth about my evening monsters, experience that led to a sense of security in me was long in coming. It took countless mornings to see the same tree in the light of day to reassure me that it didn't turn into the monster as the sun went down and I got into bed.

We have come a long way in understanding our universe and the human condition. We are more intellectually sophisticated than our ancient ancestors. However, our sophistication has moved us away from the simple knowing that there is a spirit in all living things. It has removed us from feeling the magic and mystery of life. It has moved us away from holding in reverence the creativity that is available to us in the unknown. As adults, the darkness can comfort us like being wrapped in a protective cloak. As we enter it, it can become the doorway to expanded consciousness and to our creativity or it can continue to be a place where we feel less protected.

Some continued adult sleep disturbances have their roots in never overcoming our early childhood fears. The way our parents dealt with our concerns upon waking easily could calm or exacerbate and perpetuate these fears. The way that we have learned to deal with our fears of the darkness can determine whether we feel excited of our ongoing exploration or terrified of taking a step into the unknown. One way leads us toward a respectful connection to the consciousness in all living things, the other way leads us to continue trying to control and dominate ourselves and the universe. When we turn against ourselves in any way, we decrease our consciousness and our connection with the unknown.

As we have moved away from feeling a primary dependence on nature, we also find ourselves unable to relate to and align with the consciousness that exists throughout the universe. To be aligned with nature is to acknowledge every part of who we are as natural.

It is interesting that when we organize our life around our intellect, excluding our connection to nature, we often feel awkward, shy, and innocent as we start to feel more of our emotions and live more embodied. We are like the stereotype of "city people," not knowing how to live in relation to the wilderness. Coming upon our emotions, we are like an awkward, new-born colt becoming accustomed to standing on fragile legs.

To support and make room for our awkwardness is to support the emerging inner child that had to rise above his or her emotions and body and depend mainly on intellect to survive. Living primarily from our intellect leaves behind the grounded connection to our life force and removes us from a key element in our ability to feel secure. To live through the awkwardness, shyness and innocence is to return to the feeling of security that comes from the grounded connection to our emotions, body, and spirit, integrated with our intellect. When we bring enough light to our darkness by continuing on our archeological dig, layers of cynicism let go that have prevented us from relishing the magic and mystery of life.

Without cynicism, we can be filled with the experience of wonder and awe. We can touch the magic, fill with wonder and awe and come to know that these qualities are an entry into a deeper spiritually, a deeper scientific exploration, or a combination of both. Either way, the gift of life is beyond an understanding that comes from our usual way of being logical and reasonable.

It is wondrous to see a baby born, to feel people coming together in love and understanding, to view the workings of the human body and the amazing computer that is our brain, to experience other animal species in their never-ending individuality and connectivity, to wonder at the migration of birds and salmon, the fighting for dominance of bull moose, the mating for life of geese, the never ending assortment of colors of animals, fish, and birds, the rush of the wind, the aromas of flowers, how a seed becomes a plant. It is magical to experience the infinity of the cosmos, the feeling of wonder and awe from looking out into space on a star filled night or the infinity that we can experience by exploring the quantum world. And finally, all of these experiences that bring us to mindfulness and oneness with God.

As we explore the darkness, when the circumstances are just right, we can transcend who we are as earth-bound creatures and feel at one with all that we previously considered outside of ourselves. Then we become pure feeling, pure energy, pure consciousness, that merges with all the energy and consciousness in the universe. Then we know all, for we are all. There is no separateness between us and them. We are all a part of universal mind, the universal field of consciousness. All that we need to know is available to us. There is no separateness between internal and external consciousness. We experience that the entire universe is inside our consciousness. Here we have reached enlightenment. We have merged with the darkness, with the unknown. We have moved beyond our archetypal fears and beyond the parts of ourselves that we once believed were intolerable to feel. At this point, we have fully accepted the once alienated parts of ourselves and our ancient fears.

As we pursue our personal archeological dig, living and supporting each experience, we come to a realization that has profound impact upon the way we live and feel. We find that in the darkness is the light. There is no difference. It's all energy. It's all life. One is simply the polarity of the other. Each contains the other, as a complete twenty-four hour cycle contains both the light and dark. One is not better than the other. They are both essential aspects in the flow of the earth around the sun. They are the yin and yang of being alive.

Stanley Keleman[6] presents a brilliant discourse about how we need to allow for the continual transformational process to flow so that there can be a dynamic movement between form, the dissolution of form that leads us into a state of being unformed, then new form being created, that eventually, in turn, dissolves again into formlessness and the cycle continues.

As we continue to bring acceptance to every aspect of our inner life, we continually transform and live based on our own biological self-regulation. We become less bound by out-of-date attitudes and emotions and the physical organizations that we learned as children. We are not bound by needing to defend ourselves against the reality of how we were abused as children. We are able to accept the light of our hearts and our spirit, to accept whatever resides in the darkness.

This transformational process takes place when we allow for the decay and destruction of old, outdated forms that have become a part of both aspects of the darkness that we have learned to hold against. In nature, destruction is a constant, ongoing process that can be seen in the flow of the seasons where the longest, darkest day of the year is also the beginning of the days that contain more light.

At the height of darkness, destruction of the darkness begins to take place. The same holds true as the moment of greatest light brings the beginning of darkness. We also see transformational process in the ecology of a single dying tree or an entire forest that regenerates itself after a fire. The destruction of the single tree or entire forest creates nutrients for the soil that will aid in the preparation of the soil for future development of grasses, plants, and trees. The dying tree also becomes a home for insects and bugs, which in turn provide food for birds and other animals.

The decaying of old forms allows for the continuation of life. In the case of our inner life and consciousness, they allow for our energy to be utilized on behalf of our aliveness and spirit. When we create chronic tension to hold against old internalized assaults, we also hold against the creation of new forms. This is like attempting to control how long each day should be, or tying to control tidal flow, or preventing snakes from shedding their skin, or treating the cater-pillar's metamorphosis to a butterfly as a problem. The essence of all of these transformations is the destruction of one form and the unfolding of another.

We contain elements of both light and dark. Growing ourselves through self-acceptance means balancing the acceptance of our light and dark side, it is understanding that our darkness is not bad. It is knowing that in our darkness is an integral part of who we are, that it is absolutely necessary and essential for our existence and for our connections to ourselves and to all of life.

An example of the importance of the balance between light and dark is observed in the flow of the seasons in temperate climates and the changing season's impact on growth. Spring produces new growth, summer's warmth allows for full bloom, fall's shorter days and colder nights signaling harvest, and winter's darkness calls nature into dormancy that ultimately allows for the regeneration of new growth.

As every part of the year's changing light is necessary and impor-tant, so too, are our various shades of light and darkness. Although we might struggle with our own colder and darker sides, winter reminds us that these qualities are necessary for the growth cycle, and as important as the warmth of summer. We can live winter as the negative time of the year, with its colder days and longer nights, that can cause our bodies to stiffen against the cold and dark. This negative focus and longing for warmth may become our main focus. However, if this is our only focus we ignore winter's message. Winter has its own hard, spare, and crystalline beauty. It is a time of extreme contrast, a time that we need more of our own internal warmth and connectedness to withstand this colder, darker time of year.

Let's enter the experience of winter. Take on its qualities and feel those parts of yourself that are winter like: dark, cold, hard, ungiving, even cruel and vicious at times. The message can be clear. Organismically, we are being directed to move inward and conserve our energies, explore the darker aspects of our being so that we can find our place to rest and replenish. All of nature slows down during the long winter months. When we recognize that we are a part of nature, we can learn that we need not push ourselves out of darkness into a premature blooming.

Our aliveness and warmth will emerge when it is time. Supporting our internal winter spring will come, and we will burst into life. How we deal with this quiescent time of year is what is important. Letting go into a more hibernating state replenishes us. Abel, in A House Made Of Dawn[7] is thinking about the night, "And he did not want to break the stillness of the night, for it was holy and profound, it was rest and restoration."

If we push ourselves to be constantly alive and in bloom, our life becomes like the taste of hothouse tomatoes. These are a flat facsimile of the fresh, vine-ripened varieties that are juicy from being sun-drenched. So, too, forced aliveness may have the form of aliveness, but it does not feel and have the substance of the real thing. And to come full circle, to force our aliveness, is to treat ourselves negatively. To force our aliveness is to split off from our life force and victimize ourselves with the same energies that we internalized as we grew up.

Once again, we return to the question of whether we can let go into ourselves or whether we have to stay away from our centers as a way of avoiding the assaults of our childhood. Can we let go into what at times is the still and quiet darkness, as a bear in hibernation, while at other times is seething like the primordial ooze? Can we continue to nurture ourselves so that we grow and remain vibrant and alive? Only then, can we return to the light, feeling a deep sense of rest and rejuvenation.

We need to be careful to balance our being just the way we are with our exploration on our "dig." Balance comes from exploring ourselves with compassion. It is easy to transfer the way that we usually pressure ourselves to our desire to become more conscious. Our "dig" can be the thing that we now pressure ourselves about. Furthermore, we don't need to pressure ourselves about the way that we pressure ourselves. We only need to stay aware of how we pressure ourselves. Awareness is the key. Once we pressure ourselves to be different, we are assaulting ourselves.

We don't need to be fixed or cured. We need support and nourishment. We need to accept who we are at every moment of our existence, and that includes acceptance of how we pressure ourselves. We need to understand the subtleties of how darkness forms and asserts itself. The energy of abuse can easily shift what it is abusing us about. Our introjected victimizers are always looking for something in us that they can latch onto. They are creative in how they mutate into new ways of abusing us. The bottom line is that however ungiving the words that pressure us to be more alive sound, in reality, they are abusing us for being alive.

At times, the negative energy disguises itself as words that may sound helpful. In this way it is a wolf in sheep's clothing. As we are able to separate the words from the underlying energy, we come to understand the truth of how we were negatively treated and how we still abuse ourselves. As with many archeological digs, we need to be sensitive to clues that break the codes that have been left for us so that we can take the next step in uncovering the treasure of knowledge that awaits.

When enlightened, we possess the pure treasure of knowledge

that comes from experiencing the darkness and fully accepting and becoming one with it. In owning our darkness we transcend our usual way of being.

At first, we experience periods of enlightenment where we live fully in the moment. Stress and pressure melt. We have given up suffering and the voices of the old victimizers. It is worth the trip. Later, more advanced in our "dig," the moments come more often. Pressuring ourselves to reach a transcendent state doesn't work, for it is the antithesis of letting go.

As Buddhism teaches us, we need to find the middle ground, the place of balance. We need to balance living our every day existence while at the same time exploring our darkness and bringing support to each moment. We need to find a practice that deepens our ability to live our life mindfully while clearing out the old victimizing energies. We need to make room in our bodies for our spirituality, rather than using spirituality as a denial of our present personality and life circumstances.

I feel concerned when I see people so totally focused on spirituality and transcendence that it becomes the focus of their lives to the exclusion of living in current reality. Instead of finding a balance between spirituality and our everyday existence, many people live "spaced out" in the name of being spiritual. They have taken on the form of spirituality without any substance. In this way, spirituality becomes a defense against being in the world. It is easy to take on the appropriate words and form of a particular practice to the exclusion of staying real and embodied and accepting our earthly existence. We live in a culture that demands results. To pressure ourselves to be, or act, more enlightened than we really are, is a movement away, not toward enlightenment; it is a movement into perpetuating unconscious darkness, rather than shining light into the darkness.

The pressure to experience a transcendent state can be similar to someone wanting to constantly stay in a drug induced high. Like fusing with the excitement of the drug-induced state, we no longer have as much choice about how to live our lives. This heightened state of being becomes a defense against dealing with the emotions that open when we come down from our high.

For those of us who have not reached a God Realized State, we can open to a transcendent state at times, although, we can't hold the opening. Instead, we spontaneously close against the next piece of assault energy (darkness) that is waiting for us and that we need in order to understand our "dig." Once again, balance is the key. Either using spirituality or remaining stuck and suffering as an addictive defense prevents us from our next step along our path.

It has been my experience that continuing our "dig" is a life-long process. As we gain in the ability to break the codes of our old abusive energies we deepen our ability to shine light onto our darkness and live more consciously. Our heightened consciousness reinforces being able to live mindfully, while our ability for mindful living aids in our ability to bring light to our darkness. When we accept every aspect of our darkness we are more real and down to earth than when we pressure ourselves to be spiritual. The paradox is that not pressuring ourselves to be any particular way is what will enable us to be real and more conscious, more enlightened. We are on a path of embodying our spirituality by accepting and embodying our darkness.

DIALOGUE WITH AN ENLIGHTENED BEING

As we become familiar with deeper places of knowing in ourselves, we can also have a connection with the information and wisdom that is in the universe. We can receive messages from our own deeper place of knowing, from spirit or messages that are stored in the universal energy field, all of which can guide us along our "path." During a deep meditative experience, my wife and business partner, Dr. Naomi Lubin-Alpert, had the following discussion with the spirit of Geronimo, an Apache warrior and chief. The message feels profoundly important in terms of the present discussion about allowing what we usually might consider dark and destructive energies. This discussion brings us a necessary perspective for our "dig" that allows us to balance our light with what we usually consider our darkness.

Two editorial notes about Geronimo's message are important at this point. The first is that, in the following text, *warrior* is defined as someone who lives his or her power fully, not as someone who necessarily has to go to war or who is wantonly destructive. In fact, the violence that is so often a part of declaring and going to war comes from not being able to live through feelings of impotence and helplessness. Violence is a defense against being a true warrior who can have power as he/she backs away from war. Martin Luther King and Gandhi are examples of warriors who neither declared war nor gave into their helplessness. The second note is that his use of the terms *white people* or *white man* fit for Geronimo's culture and the time that he lived. For me, these terms include both men and women and people of all color. Here is what Geronimo said:

"You must be able to *embody* the power of all who are in opposition to you as well as all who are aligned with you, in order to be in full power. You must embody the power of a thief and then contain and not act out that energy, in order to protect yourself from thieves. To have more power than a killer, you need to feel your own killing energy and be able to contain it. By containing the energy of the opposition, rather than acting it out, you will have greater power.

"You must accept the duality of your energy, both light and dark, good and evil. A lesson of ancient cultures is that warriors were loving husbands and fathers, rather than just one or the other. And monks had to learn martial arts in order to balance their masculine and feminine energies. In newer cultures this lesson has been lost. People (and their energies) have been divided into categories. People have lost the teachings of how to pull all their power together.

"Because white people did not own their full power they had to own what they believed was 'good' and disown and act out what they believed was 'bad.' It is the white man's problem to disown the warrior inside. This is basically a Western phenomenon. White men throughout history have wanted to dominate while denying they wanted to dominate. They rationalized that they were acting in the name of 'good.'

"White men are not warriors and have no respect for warriors.

Warriors are no longer honored opponents; there is just destruction. Not accepting that good and evil exists in all people causes the split which produces non-warriors. Rather then respecting all things, they have divided all things into good and evil.

"Christ was trying to balance the cruelty and greed in the world with compassion. He was a prophet with so much light that he was killed by the opposition in the name of goodness and righteousness. Gandhi was a warrior, not a prophet. He knew exactly how to steal the power of the opposition.

"The gift that you have been given by your parents is that they have opened the way to your being a murderer, a thief, and a rapist. They have provided the doorway to being a warrior. Warriors have these energies. They don't act them out. Your parents acted them out on the innocent. They didn't save the murderer's energy for the murderer, the thief's energy for the thief, or the rapist's energy for the rapist." (Geronimo is talking about Naomi and her parents, although his words apply to many of us and clearly elucidates much of what I have been saying about the Body-Centered Gestalt Therapy process). He continues: "In Western societies there is no model for the energies you need to be able to contain or how to contain these energies to be a warrior.

"The land is raped in the name of good and progress. This happens because man disowns his evil side. He sees others as bad and evil, rather then feeling that aspect of himself that is the rapist (or evildoer) and he does not contain these feelings in himself. To contain these feelings is to be a warrior. Not to contain them is to act out the evil.

"This is both a time of energetic murder, as well as actual physical murders in the world.

"White men, again, all people who have grown up in western society, are dangerous in that they don't see the evil of what they do. They do it in the name of good."

TRANSFORMATION

Geronimo's message is telling us that it is essential to transform how we think about what we now believe to be bad or evil parts of ourselves. We need to acknowledge and flexibly contain, that is, breathe into, the negative energies that we usually keep hidden from others or buried in our own unconscious. We need to accept these energies as a part of our humanness so that they may become a part of our power. Remember that acceptance leads to integration, alignment and, therefore, more personal power. Conversely, rejection of any part of our self leads to splitting of and disintegration and, therefore, less personal power. To accomplish this, the destruction of the old forms we learned as a way of dealing with these negative energies is necessary. For example, we have to destroy old forms of rigidity, frozenness, collapse, withholding, being above our centers. We need to find new ways of understanding and appreciating how our negativity was created by our aliveness being assaulted, and then assaulted again when we protested the abuse.

Our new understanding based on Geronimo's message will help us come to the center of what we usually label as negative and unacceptable. In the past we have often tried to destroy, rather than accept our negative energies. This never works. Trying to destroy a part of ourselves is like a double negative. We feel negative about our negativity and therefore bring negativity to our negativity. Like this sentence, we go around and around, remaining stuck in the negativity. By finding support and acceptance for our negativity we allow for the transformational process to occur. We proceed on our "dig" by meeting our dark places with compassion in order to build a strong and flexible enough container so that these energies transform into power and aliveness.

Earlier, I mentioned that Martin Luther King Jr and Gandhi are examples of warriors who did not act out their aggressiveness by going to war. Neither did they become overwhelmed by helplessness, becoming passive and collapsed. In order to develop the passive resistance they practiced, they needed to contain their feelings of impotence and helplessness and become energetically and emotionally larger than these feelings. They needed the perspective that it was useless and destructive to meet bigotry, repression and violence with greater violence. They didn't need to rise above feelings of powerlessness and strike out at their enemies as a defense against their helplessness. This enabled them to live the power of their hearts and their spirits and not have to act out destruction. They contained whatever negative and angry feelings they had and transformed these feelings into passionate action. The enormity of their hearts, spirits, and power came from that containment. Like Martin Luther King and Gandhi, when we do not act out our darkness, the energy that comes from our hearts and our spirits has the power to change the course of history.

We all become more powerful if we are able to contain our feelings of impotence and helplessness and not rush to avoid and deny these feelings by rising up into violence. We have been trained to feel and believe that to feel helpless and impotent is a sign of weakness. There are many real situations that produce an appropriate response of impotence and helplessness. To be able to understand that and not have to avoid these feelings allows us more time to deepen our ability to live mindfully so that we can discover the creative, nonviolent option. Flexible containment of our emotions is the key. Containment then leads to balance and the ability to live without being bound by stereotypes. This is freedom. Peace begins inside of us in the acceptance of our darkness. In accepting our shadow side, we transform the threat of war into peace, both on a personal and global level.

THE IMPORTANCE OF THERAPISTS LIVING THEIR "DIG"

As psychotherapists, we are not immune to needing to understand our own darkness, to deal with our own "unfinished business." It essential for us as therapists to be able to live with and through all the various forms of our own negativity: our cruelty, in all its guises, violence, humiliating, shaming, our impotence, helplessness, powerlessness, not knowing, and confusion. Without this ability, we will act out and become controlling, negative, overprotective, easily frustrated, or live as if we really are impotent and unable to help our clients continue their "dig." We will be corralled by what is unfinished in us without a way of living these experiences that help us return to center and ground.

The fullness of life is about living the entire range of our feelings. As therapists, we need to be able to acknowledge and accept all of our feelings in order to allow us and our clients to come to a deeper level of consciousness. We need to be actively living into our own personal "dig" in order to help our clients proceed with theirs. Being a therapist is not just a matter of knowing the right words and techniques. Like the hot house tomatoes, there is a difference between providing our clients with an energetic invitation to go deeper into themselves and offering a facsimile of it.

There is a profound difference for our clients as we live more embodied and more conscious. It is the same as when we were children growing up and our parents were living "as if" they were alive. We then bond with the "as- ifness" of our parents. "As if" is so very different from "real," open-hearted, direct, authentic, and immediate.

As therapists, when we intimately understand how we have organized ourselves into rigid, dense, collapsed, or flaccid structures in order to avoid how impotent, sad, angry, in need, frightened etc., we felt when abuse came at us as children, we are able to meet our clients with true understanding. We all defended ourselves, therapist and client alike, in the best way that we could. Knowing this about ourselves also leads us to feel more understanding and respectful of our client's defenses and what they needed to do in order to survive. In this way, as therapists, we are always exploring ourselves as we help our clients with their own exploration. We are always involved in our own "personal dig" as we are helping our clients explore theirs.

RETURNING TO OUR DIG

One of the pieces of attitudinal equipment that is necessary for a successful "dig" is to be in a process of suspending judgment and control. When we give up control and judgment, we release old structures that were our allies in our life long battle against our childhood abuse. When we begin to explore how we judge ourself and keep control, we are immediately in our "dig."

As we enter the darkness and explore our personal archeology, letting go of some of our control and judgment about what we imagine may happen can lead us into feeling that there is nothing to hold onto. We might feel that we have lost sight of why we thought this was a good idea in the first place. We don't see and can't know how it will all turn out for us. Old structures may not fit as well any more as we let go of pieces of old chronic tension and the old attitudes that were set in the tension. We need to make room for the experience of strangeness that newness brings. This is the way it is with any exploration into the unknown. Developing our ability to open our breathing and to strengthen our ability to live mindfully is very important at this point. We are building personal power and our new power will increase our ability to stay centered. It will enable us to fit the pieces of emotional artifact and pottery together. This, in turn, will enable us to see how one hidden chamber opens to the next, allowing the mosaics of our history to unfold and to form.

Containing the truth of who we are brings more understanding, meaning, and light to our existence. We are developing an inner compass and gyroscope, finding direction and balance as we develop more personal power. We, in turn, increase our ability to be intimate in our relationships, and can hold our societal and environmental concerns with caring and passion. As we breathe and become accustomed to this process, a feeling of having more room in our bodies develops. In short, we feel fuller and freer.

I want to re-emphasize something here. As we continue our "dig," we are confronted with the orderly and efficient unfolding of body memories that carry us through a cycle of

victim and victimizer, impasse and aliveness. What we begin to see and understand is that there is an organismic reason for every experience that we feel. What we are experiencing is never a sign that we are bad or wrong, inept, worthless or stupid.

Our traumatic, depressing, devastating, debilitating feelings are always some event in our current reality touching past body memories in the unfolding process. The significance of this is that each feeling is worthy of appreciation and understanding, no matter how difficult or unpleasant it is. Our feelings are never a sign that something is wrong with us; they are a sign that something wrong was done to us as children and that we are now reliving that experience. In fact, that we are reliving the experience is a sign that we "work right," that our bodies are attending to a sore spot that needs attention in order to heal so that we can achieve a state of inner peace. When we stop bemoaning our fate and bring support to any feeling, we become larger than it and transformation takes place.

In bringing this chapter on darkness to its conclusion, my thoughts return to the environmental darkness that we have created on our planet. External darkness is woven together with the darkness that exists in each of us. Each of us has had a part of creating darkness on our planet by the pollutants that are the by-products of our consumption. Our consumption adds to the smog that darkens the sun, decreases the ozone layer, and dirties our rivers. We are part of producing the endless non-biodegradable garbage that darkens the land. We treat our planet in a self-destructive manner and, thereby, pollute the earth and air beyond any point that is healthy for all the species that inhabit it. We have learned to treat ourselves and our planet in the same self-destructive manner.

What I have experienced with myself, my friends, my colleagues, and people I have treated in therapy, is that reaching a fuller, more centered and peaceful place within ourselves through the acceptance of our darkness, reduces how we abuse ourselves and our planet. Personally and planetarily, we become less self- destructive. The more we honor our own internal process, and make room for organismic self-regulation, the more aware we become of how we and others are negatively treating our planet.

I don't believe that by supporting and appreciating ourselves, we become more self-absorbed. It is in the failure to nourish ourselves that we become narcissistic and self-centered. Caring about ourselves in the way that I have presented leads us away from egotism. To give up polluting our internal experiences is an important step in accepting that each individual is related, interconnected, to family, community, plants, animals, Earth, and the universe. On the path toward enlightenment, the experience grows within us that there is a planetary, animal, plant, and personal kinship with all that exists in the universe. To treat ourselves with heartfelt caring is to see and treat the world with an open heart. A statement in a book by Susan Weed is a fitting end to this chapter. "The thread of love and acceptance can lead us out of the bonding with self hatred, planetary destruction, and war."[8]

CHAPTER NINE

Faith

ALL OF NATURE IS CONSTANTLY TRANSFORMING. LIFE IS not static and set. The forming, unforming and reforming of the universe is a fact. From the moment of conception, our growth and change are automatic, like the rest of nature. In whatever way our life force actually regulates our growing, we don't have to tell it how to do its job.

I have faith that the energy, the life force of the universe, is perfect. There are no mistakes. We are being called to this perfection. Spirit, universal consciousness, is constantly calling us to awaken. It is beckoning us to clear ourselves of the abusive energies of our childhood and whatever ego identifications prevent us from reaching enlightenment. The more awareness we have of the perfection of nature and the universe, the more we move toward a conscious and intentional merging with this perfection.

Look at a butterfly or a flower. Look deeply! Bring as much of your consciousness as possible to becoming involved with the butterfly or flower. Feel its perfection! Let go and see if you experience an inner tug to stay with the butterfly or flower. Be aware of whether you can allow for the feeling of magic to open inside of you, the magic of life. This magic is beyond our linear and intellectual way of trying to understand the world. Also, be aware that you may feel uncomfortable as you observe the perfection of life. You may want to quickly move away from the experience. Perhaps it touches a feeling of contempt or of wasting your time and energy. Or perhaps it opens a feeling of sadness, or of wonder and awe.

The more we clear out the old assaultive energies from inside of ourselves the more we can join the magic. We can allow our energy and spirit to join the perfect energy and spirit of the universe. Universal consciousness is waiting for us. So, too, is the experience of the interrelatedness of all animate and inanimate beings. Thich Nhat Hahn, a Vietnamese Buddhist Monk, calls this interbeing.

Imagine what it would be like to live our lives surrounded by the energy of these beliefs, to be surrounded by the energy of faith. Imagine absorbing the positive, loving energy of the universe and then releasing all negative and toxic energy inside of us. In this chapter I want to discuss the effects that having or not having faith has on the way that we live.

Ask yourself the following questions. Were you raised with faith that growth and transformation are a natural part of life? Do you have faith in your ability to be guided by your own deep inner wisdom? Do you feel faith that the universe, without interference, is as it should be? Do you feel faith in how you are a part of the perfection of the universe? Do you have faith that each experience you encounter is here to help you in your transformation?

If we are not overly abused as children, we flow continuously through stages of being formed, unformed, and reformed. We are supported and remain alive in our transformations. The process of forming, unforming, and reforming is one that we see in nature all the time. A frozen river melts under the spring sun, it doesn't remain frozen forever. Its banks shift through the years.

When I spent time on Nantucket Island some years ago, I would marvel at how the island was continually changing. Sand dunes grew, diminished, and shifted. One side of the island was growing while the other was being eroded by the sea. The records of the island showed that the reverse growth and erosion pattern had occurred in the previous ten to twenty years. The same is true of mountains that are constantly growing, shifting, and changing. Nothing in nature remains exactly the same.

All animals that live in the wild, live an instinctual life where their energy, movements, and behavior are derived from a continuous inner flow. Whatever structures they do create enhance and protect their species. They do not create rigid structures that stop energy flow as a way of accommodating their parents or their society. I have a sense that the more animals are tamed and domesticated, the more chance they have of taking on the fears and rigid structures of humankind.

The same is true for us humans where the domestication of our true nature can be an excuse for abuse. The assaults to our life force interfere with our faith that we are a part of the natural order of the universe and its transformational process. It is only the human species that, after its formative years, sets itself into a structure that limits and is destructive to growth. As you have read many times by now, fixed, stereotypic structures occur as a result of protecting ourselves against the assaultive energies of our childhood. And the harsher the assaults were that limited emotional, energetic, and bodily movement, the more we live with a sense of not trusting and not having faith in our own organismic process. The abuse we received as children interferes with our faith that our life force will lead us to the lessons that we need to learn in our lives. We lack the faith that living a conscious process will lead us to greater aliveness, directness, and clarity.

Our life force has a natural intelligence when it comes to growing us and moving us in the direction we need to go. We don't have to teach our life force how to work. We don't have to use our will and conscious minds to tell cells how to divide or decide which ones should be striated muscle tissue for the long muscles of our body, and which ones should form into smooth muscle tissue for our heart. Our life force not only grows us physically but also leads us in the direction of greatest satisfaction with the least amount of pain. I remember, years ago, reading a research study that demonstrated how children who were left at a buffet table over a period of time would automatically choose the right foods for their health and nutrition. When we are not abused for our choices, we naturally choose the appropriate items for our continued and healthy growth.

Our life force does not only grow us physically. We also feel the perfect and necessary emotions that are expressions of our life force. These emotions are either expressions of how we are already in balance or expressions of an imbalance. An infant cooing from contentment or crying because something is wrong is the earliest example of this. There is wisdom in the flesh, and in the embodiment of our spirit, in the way that our life force directs us and is expressed through us.

Since our life force knows how to grow us, it is assaultive for our natural processes to be interrupted. We need support to remain connected to the intelligence in the universe that allows for the transformational processes that occur in the universe to flow through us. We need validation to feel how we are a part of the universe and that we are connected to all natural phenomena, to the flow of life and death, and to the experience that there is a planetary, animal, plant, and personal kinship with all that exists in the universe.

When our connection to these natural biological rhythms is interrupted, we create rigid or collapsed structures that reinforce degrees of hopelessness, despair, alienation, and depression. The assaults teach us to be angry and they disconnect us from a sense of community and earth. We therefore become separated from our own process of self-regulation and the transformational process that is an intrinsic part of nature. **All traumas distance us from the feeling of faith that allows us to trust our self regulatory process. We are distanced from feeling some basic, nonverbal, primal connection that everything in ourselves and in the universe is as it should be.**

Stories of the way people connect to the earth to reinforce their experience of faith are a part of many non-technological cultures. We need stories like this that are handed down from generation to generation. We need to build ways of feeling the earth beneath us into our culture so we treasure it as we would want to be treasured. When these ways of living become more a part of our daily existence, our reverence for ourselves as a part of the earth will be built into the fabric of our lives. We will create our own stories of connection based on ritual and ceremony that can be passed on, generation to generation.

Native Americans' traditions of living as stewards and guardians of the land rather than as possessors of it, offer guidance as we relearn reverence for the natural world. These traditions, expressed in stories, teach us another way of living.

In the book *The Man Who Killed the Deer*, by Frank Waters,[1] a father sends his twelve-year-old son into a kiva, a ceremonial room that is going to be used to help the boy in his transition to manhood. The father explains to his son the meaning of some of the experiences the boy will have:

"Hence you will be taught, as those Old First Ones were taught, that the pine tree, the corn plant, have a life as we, but that they may be used and that they accede to their sacrifice for the maintenance of all life. You will be taught that the eagle, the trout, the deer, each has a life as we, but that they may be used and that they accede to their sacrifice for the need of progression of all life.

"But through all these truths will run the one great truth: the arising of all individual lives into one great life, and the necessary continuance of this one great life by the continual progression of the individual lives which form it.

"You will learn that this continuous progression seems to extend infinitely into time. But you will learn likewise that time also is an infinity.

"And that is life. Life must be lived, not learned from. And that is why in full consciousness only there is freedom. And that is why you learn awareness; to live life, in full consciousness, in freedom."

And earlier, the father said, "Listen, son. In your mother's womb you were conceived. From an individual human womb you were born to an individual human life. It was necessary, it was good. But individual human life is not sufficient to itself. It depends upon and is part of all life. So now another umbilical cord must be broken-that which binds you to your mother's affections, that which binds you to the individual human life she gave you. For twelve years you have belonged to your lesser mother. Now you belong to your greater mother. And you return to her womb to emerge once again, as a man with no mother's hold on him, as a man who knows himself not as an individual but as a unit of his tribe and a part of all life which ever surrounds him."

And as the father says his final good-bye: "Now I, the father, say good-bye to his child.

We will meet again, but as brothers, as men together, as equal parts of one great life, no longer separated, but in that consciousness of our oneness which gives us our only freedom."

Stories like this one validate our connection to the universe, to the flow of life in and around us. When we know of the truth of our connection to all living things, and live within that experience, we automatically want to make room for all that exists in the universe. We therefore make room for other people's existence, as well as that of other species and our planet.

To have trust and faith in our life force, our organismic process allows us to fully live each experience as it unfolds. To regain our faith is to open ourselves again to the belief that everything is as it should be. To have faith also allows us to feel that everything and everyone we encounter is an experience for us to live in terms of where and how we need to grow.

In saying that "everything is as it should be" I do not mean to imply that the world is all light and beauty or that there is no evil and cruelty in it. I am referring to the natural laws of the universe, not to the way that humankind distorts itself and the universe for its own ends. Neither do I ignore the existence of disease, problems of the homeless, drugs, crime, war, environmental pollution, close-minded politicians, or corporate greed. And I certainly don't believe that we should meet the world with passivity and acquiescence.

There are polarities of light and dark, cruelty and open-heartedness that we all need to come to grips within ourselves. Each of us needs to decide whether to live a life based on ethical and caring behavior or acting out in a destructive and egocentric manner. Not only do we need to decide how to balance these issues within ourselves, but also we need to consider what part we want to play in dealing with these issues in our society. The consequence of the statement "everything in the universe is it should be" is that we are always presented with the difficult and sometimes painful challenges that we need to grapple with in order to allow for growth and transformation that will lead us to a more enlightened state of being. The beauty and elegance of the universe are there for us to bond with and to feel a sense of oneness with it.

The choice of which way we will move and grow is constantly being presented to us. Each moment of our existence can be an experience that we live mindfully and, therefore, we are moved closer to our center and to the center of caring for ourselves and the earth. Or we can hold onto outdated beliefs that are based on childhood teachings that interfere with our life force and our connection to all that is alive. If we hold on to outdated beliefs we resist any new mind-body reorganizations. Then our current experiences reinforce old beliefs that the world is still only the assaultive place that it has always been.

Building our internal support enhances our connection to faith and the direction we move in our lives. Our spirit is fighting for us to survive and wants to show us the way.

Two poems I wrote some years ago address these issues.

To Carlos Castenada

I've known the world to be cruel and unyielding.
So it is when I indulge
my loneliness and fear.
When all that stands before me is
self pity
and my refusal to let go.
I grasp the unyielding ground,
feeling a shallow safety
in its familiarity,
then I hold on even more tightly,
fearing the unknown.

I've known the world to be warm and beautiful,
to embrace me in its graceful yielding.
So it is when I let go of my
Self-importance,
and accept what is.

An Old Ending...A New Beginning

There's a world out there
that doesn't care
what I do
where I am
or how I feel.

The clouds and sky don't care...
they don't mourn
my closings or
shine for my openings
and deeper breaths.

The trees and flowers...
all living rooted things don't care
whether I watch them
through their openings and closings
with an open hearted oneness
of life processes
or flat on my back in despair.

The squirrels, rabbits or fawns don't care
if I watch them play
and feel their movements inside of me
so that their play is mine
and mine is theirs
or that I walk through the woods
ruminating my lack of spirit.

The mountains, streams or oceans don't care
whether I flow with the rains moving toward the seas
or build barriers against the world
not to see
not to feel-
they don't care.

The quiet winds, squalls, hurricanes
sun, moon or stars...or the center of the cyclone don't care
about my moodiness and intensity or
peacefulness and calm.
Their movements or stillness don't depend on me.

And in all of nature's disregard for me
lies her grace and beauty.
She doesn't care,
she doesn't project,
she doesn't reject,
she lives.
And when I experience her living
and not caring
I experience her eternal waiting and patience for me
To return to my sense of oneness...

Our spirit fights for our survival and always shows us the way to enlightenment. I am constantly asking myself and my clients what the message is in whatever event is happening in my or their life. I am asking the same question in relation to what I am or they are feeling. (Although I continue in these paragraphs talking about my clients, I just as easily can continue referring to my own experience).

I may also have my clients ask whether the message is from their spirit or whether it is a message from a victimizer. The voices that we hear inside us at times can be the old assault energy. The more we tune into the deeper places in ourselves, the more sensitive we become in differentiating which energies and messages come from assault and which ones come from our spirit. I ask my clients these questions when the event that has occurred is entirely an internal emotional or physical experience or even when there is a serious disease process that they are faced with or an important traumatic event has happened to them. I ask them to contact the event (internal or external) and then to ask the questions: "What are you here for?" "Do you have a message for me?" "Is there something that I need to see or learn?" "What do you need from me?" It doesn't matter what the person or event is. There is always a message from our spirit if we are open to hearing it. Our spirit is ready to help us receive the lesson that we need to integrate from each of our experiences. It is worthy of repetition to say that **each and every experience that we have presents itself to aid us in our transformation and our continued movement toward enlightenment.**

We manifest and co-create our lives from the totality of the energies that are in us. Each experience in our lives is an expression of our own energies. We can enjoy the positive, joyful parts of our lives and learn from the difficult, traumatic, and painful experiences that unfold as a way of allowing the flow of life to continue. When we have faith to live in this way, we are than constantly meeting life with power, rather than as a victim.

The desire to become ever more conscious comes from the power of our spirit moving us toward the quiet center of our being where we can connect to universal consciousness. In our quiet center we are in perfect balance, not overly controlled or overly passive as a way of avoiding what we feel. The message from our spirit is always about acceptance and compassion for all of our experiences. Acceptance and compassion are the essence of our spirit. Acceptance does not mean that we should always passively accept whatever comes our way and just learn to breathe into powerlessness. Acceptance of powerlessness can mean feeling our anger and our pain and not acting out. As was expressed earlier, living into our powerlessness means that we can either be more assertive and stay in the arena or we can give up and separate from an impossible situation.

We need faith to feel grateful for what we have and not have to suffer and feel tortured for what we don't have. We need faith to understand that no abuse of power will ever lead to wisdom. In fact, balance and harmony are the foundations of wisdom. We need faith that bringing light to the darkness, rather than struggling against it, allows for balance and harmony. We need faith to know that we are moving toward the ultimate experience of having the entire universe inside of our consciousness. We need faith that, without an open and loving heart, we can never taste the nectar and pure bliss of life.[2]

We also need faith for those times when we struggle with our faith. In the following personal, unpublished essay, Dina Fisher, once a teacher and school administrator and now a psychotherapist, writes about how she lost her faith as a child and then regained it (and how she keeps losing and rediscovering it) through her own "personal archaeological dig." She also writes about the difference this made in her life.

"When I was at a church in Chimayo last summer, a place of spiritual power near Santa Fe, I received a message that said I needed to learn what faith is, and then teach others. I was deep in cynicism at the time, and the message seemed ironic and inappropriate. It is curious that I want to write about faith, since mine seems so low so often. Nevertheless, I feel compelled to respond to the message, because it is just possible that I have something to share. Some force wiser than I am says that I should.

"I have spent my life helping others. I'm the administrator of a school for autistic children. I have gained a great deal from that, but I also left a lot of dreams behind. One of them was about becoming a writer. Just writing this brings many feelings up for me because I never had enough faith in myself to pursue my creative side. I followed what I thought was my path to survival by working in schools.

"Teaching was something I fell into. I always expected that I would be a teacher, since my best friends through childhood and adolescence were my teachers. They liked me. I was good and quiet and smart. School was an escape for me, and I found once I'd left it, academics seemed boring to teach.

"Organizing the administration of a new school that I helped start was easier. I had an endless capacity for responsibility and very hard and mostly mindless work. I also did care about special children. What I didn't know then was that for someone without boundaries, the needs of the children and their families would be limitless. I had the energy to continue for nearly 14 years. I see now how the work drains me and gives me very little support for anything but more effort.

"Six years in therapy, and training to become a therapist, has changed my life. For the first time, I am beginning to consider my own needs, to dream new dreams and recapture old ones. After ten years of caring for severely handicapped children, I have given up being a foster parent. After the grief came an incredible sense of freedom. It was a big step for me. But I am still very frightened to change most of my day-to-day existence. I endure! In other words, I don't seem to have a lot of faith, faith that there is something better to do with my life.

"So how can I tell you anything about faith? What I know is that faith is about trusting yourself - your intuition, your emotions, your path. Faith is knowing that whatever you've done in your life is what you needed to do, and that taking another step for yourself, despite terror, grief, spite, or regret, or whatever else you have to feel, is what you needed to do. That step may seem small – like telling someone "no" for the first time, and enduring the assaults that make you feel as if you'll go crazy. Or it may seem very, very big - like leaving an abusive relationship, or giving up an addiction or quitting a miserable job, and feeling as if you won't survive."

"I can't tell you what form that faith will take for you. Maybe it will take the form that knowing that, no matter what, there is someone in the world who loves you, and will support you in your growth. It could be a religious or spiritual belief that tells you that you have a right to exist and to find your own path. Maybe it's knowing that we all die, and that there is a purpose, our own purpose, to find and live before our lives are over. There are signs to follow, and helpful friends and guides, both real and spiritual that will help you along when we are open to them."

"Our lives touch others, and move them along their paths just as they move us on ours. So there really are *no mistakes* we make along the way, no wasted moments. We find when we look back that our darkest hours contributed fully to the brightest. We can't really have one without the other. It is impossible to be real and not feel pain, and only the most dedicated defeater of life never feels pleasure. It has been the most profound relief to me to begin to understand that each feeling has its polarity. As deeply as I feel hurt, I feel joy to the same degree, and the distance between these seemingly opposite feelings are sometimes only a breath apart. My bitter cynicism protects my tenderest compassion; I am only tough because I am also gentle and vulnerable. I can be blank and boring, or fascinating and poetic. Every rich feeling is available to me, and none are good or bad, all are simply human."

"I hope that something in my words will resonate in your spirit, meet your experience or offer you insight and hope. I suppose that's a statement of faith that words, perhaps even my words, can heal and inspire. Certainly my therapists and guides have moved, inspired and helped me heal. But when I'm deep in the assaults that insist I have nothing to say and nothing to offer, I feel no such faith."

"Even when I'm in the middle of this issue and deep in withholding, I can recognize that as a child what I would have said, had I not been viciously silenced, would undoubtedly have had value. What is more delightful to the open-hearted parent than the free and simple expression of a child? Sadly, my parents' expressions were too destroyed and blocked to allow them to hear mine, and I have been and still am remarkably silent in my life. Until my therapy, I had almost given up believing I could ever be heard and understood. That faith has been restored. I am very grateful for that, and very angry that this piece of faith that everyone needs to have, was almost completely destroyed in my childhood."

"It is easy for me to slip into feeling that I know nothing, have said nothing. But I also have some faith, so I know that what I've written, which may be a little piece of nothing, is really a little piece of everything. I hope that you can find the faith that permits your expression and growth."

In Dina's story we see how she, like most of us, was raised in the tradition of believing that we could only exist in "role layer," rather than having faith that our life force could lead us. **Even though we have grown up trusting form more than substance, we can begin to reconnect to faith in our life force by appreciating and embracing this very moment, this very breath**. The following experiment is an example of what I am referring to.

Focus on whatever you are experiencing. Don't attempt to change it. Simply allow it to exist. Be aware of your breathing. Allow for the possibility that there is a good reason for whatever you are feeling. Again, simply be aware of how you are breathing. See if you can allow room in your body for the statement that "there is a good reason for whatever I am feeling." As much as you can, and without pressuring yourself, feel that statement and be aware of your breathing. Even if you wind up saying, "I feel terrible, or this is ridiculous," allow for the possibility that there is a deeper reason for even these feelings. Breathe! For a moment, don't go to your thoughts to give yourself reasons for why you feel the way that you do. Stay *in the experience* that there is a reason for your feelings. Breathe!

As you do this experiment, that is, as you suspend judgment for a moment and have the experience in your body that what you are feeling has meaning, then for this moment you are living with an experience of faith. Can you appreciate that doing this same experiment with each successive moment, with each successive breath, would lead to living more embodied and more within the experience of faith? The more faith that we develop for our process, the more we feel our connection to all living things and to the earth. Our faith then can spread outside of us to encompass the universe.

The more we can live in this way, the more we can live life as a ceremony, honoring each moment as it unfolds. We can honor and appreciate all of who we are. We can honor our defenses as allies, as being with us because they helped us survive the assaults of our childhood. We can begin to appreciate our lack of or loss of faith and our cynicism as a part of our process. We can know that all of our experiences are expressions of our life force and have meaning.

Faith not only allows us to honor ourselves, it also allows us to honor all people, all living things on earth, the earth itself, and all the experiences that we have in our life. During the summer of 1988, and for the following ten years on and off, I spent some time with Berniece Falling Leaves, a spiritualist and Native American Hocule, (a term for a medicine woman) at her home in Arizona. Berniece was remarkable in the way that she honored everything that existed in the universe. When a bird flew by she would raise her hand and say, "Welcome, thank you for coming." She would honor all animals in the same way. There was even a reverence in the way that to she related to clouds, trees, plants, and rocks. Each of these parts of the universe had equal billing for her, for she could feel the spirit in each one. She was also fully aware of the movement of the rising and setting sun and the flow of the seasons. She had simple ceremonies to honor these daily and yearly transformations. In this way Berniece lived each day as a continual process of connection to an ever-changing universe. Her life was and still is a ceremony.

The more we honor and celebrate life, the more we bring a balance and harmony to ourselves and those around us. We are building our personal power to enable us to move in the direction of enlightenment where there is no difference between inside and outside.

All of life is energy. Different forms of life are only the various manifestations of this energy. We are all a part of this universal energy. We are all one with the universe. The question we have to answer is whether we are going to recognize

this truth. Eventually, living within the experience of how we are energetically one with the universe leads us to living life as an ongoing meditation.

This doesn't mean the same as being removed from life, spaced out, in some meditative cloud. Nor does it mean that we become so introspective that people and relationships are unimportant. The entire emphasis of this book has been on allowing for deeper and more satisfying relationships and on embodying experience. Therefore, within this context, meditation is meant as the focus toward possessing each moment in our body, not removing ourselves from the experience. Living every day with this kind of awareness, we live life as a blessing. A life continually blessed becomes a beautiful circle that is never ending. A one-word Native American prayer, "HOH," was shared with me by Berniece Falling Leaves. The prayer honors the tradition of faith in the circle of life that connects everything in the universe.

HOH honors the...

...Sun
...Sun Behind the Sun
...Creator
...The Power of Creation
...Greatest Light in the Sky
...Oldest and Wisest Energy form in our System...The Universe
...Power of the Seasons
...Sacred Ceremonies
...Power of Growth and Transformation

HOH is a...

...Sacred Circle
...Sacred Circle of Life
...Birth...Power...Wisdom...Death
...Circle of Healing
...Symbol of Dependability

...Symbol of Guidance
...Sacred Path
It is the spiritual counterpart of earth
It is where some of our relatives came from
HOH
Oh Great Spirit, ever present
Great Spirit of all knowledge
Great Spirit of all understanding
Great Spirit of all wisdom
Great Spirit of all right action
Guide my footsteps as I walk the path of heart
Teach me to walk softly
Help me to harm no one and no thing
Let me be part of the sunset, the rainbow and the starry sky
HOH

FAITH IMPACTS THE WORLD WE LIVE IN

We are perfect in the way that our life force, has formed us in order to survive! Life is a continuous circle where everything is interrelated! If more of us lived our lives from a perspective of caring and support, in which each moment had the potential of being a ceremony, it would seem that deep consideration for our planet and for our humanness would go into each decision. Decisions would be less likely based on how to manipulate life, to use the resources of our planet until they are depleted, and to avoid litigation by finding loop holes in environmental laws. It would be interesting to speculate what kinds of governmental and corporate decisions would be made, in relation to environmental, health, and other human issues, if faith in life could be brought to each decision.

Although much of our society claims to be caring, law abiding, and ethical, there seems to be much hypocrisy in these claims. A great deal of lip service is paid to faith in our society. Attending church, or espousing the name of God or goodness in our actions, is often only form without substance. Words of faith become something to hide behind as we are intolerant of other's beliefs and justify our own actions and beliefs. Where is our heart if we are not allowing ourselves to acknowledge our own darkness and accepting people of all faiths and beliefs? There is a difference between faith that dictates a rigid form and one that is open to the process of our own and other's humanity.

The more rigid individual, governmental or societal forms are the more violence is the outcome. Rigidity is a form of violence. This is true of the terrorists in the world as well as our own government. I don't accept the use of violence and terrorism as a means to whatever end is being espoused. However, I still want to understand the factors that would lead people to have beliefs that violence is the only way to express themselves. I want to look beneath the surface of their acts and see if I can put myself in "their shoes." I still hold onto my faith that even though I feel that their acts are inhuman, I know there is also violence in me, even if I live it differently. I wonder how I would respond if I grew up in their world. I want to own my darkness and not use what is going on in the world to deny my violence and instead see only the darkness as "out there." I feel the same way about the use of violence by our government.

What we don't accept and can't embody, we project onto others. We then live in the unreal world of our own making believing that we are good and other people are bad. When we love a life where we have faith in emotional/biological process, we feel how we are similar to others rather then holding ourselves separate from them and feeling that we are superior. Embracing all of who we are leads us to faith, not away from it.

The more we alienate ourselves from these feelings in ourselves and only see others violence, the stronger, not the weaker, they become. We fuel their acting out with ours, rather than containing these feelings in ourselves so that we can spread personal responsibility and peace. Murderers and terrorists, for example, split off from their anger and negativity. They are unable to contain anger in their bodies. The emotional and energetic charge becomes too much to embody. Besides needing to deal with these issues of acting out of violence in its extreme forms of terrorism and murder and our violent response to it, the same issues hold true in our daily acts of uncaring that have an underlying energy of violence in them.

Faith in process and in our humanity leads us to taking responsibility for ourselves and our actions. Once we start living in this way, there is a force that propels us to continue this path. It is a force that knows that it is leading us toward a fuller, more satisfying way of being. The path toward enlightenment is a path all can walk. It is not only for the rare few who have time to spend hours each day meditating in silence. It is a path of respect and kindness that all people can choose to take. It is a path that does not naively or judgmentally wipe out others, or ask us to stuff any experiences or any emotions. It includes all of life. We can even move toward enlightenment while supporting our anger or our cynicism. If we fully accept these feelings and live into the center of them, we move to what is in the center of any feeling: pure energy.

The path toward enlightenment is also a path to be walked that doesn't measure how far we have come or how far we have to go. It is equally concerned with our everyday existence, as it is with our spirituality. The following quote speaks to this last point. "The magician does not worry about attaining enlightenment. He/she is more concerned with getting the laundry done. The sacred mandalas of Tibet have no more capacity to raise consciousness than the shirts and underwear falling past the window of the dryer, nor is their capacity to quicken spiritual development any less."[3]

Living with support for each moment, and exploring our own personal archeology, is necessary in order to move us along the path toward enlightenment. To live in this we need support for our individuality. However, currently, we are living in a world where individuality is often suppressed so that we lose the instinctual base that binds us to the earth and to spirit that is the basis for this kind of support.

Instead, we live in a culture where our thoughts and allegiances are sought after. Image makers attempt to seduce us to think or buy what they are selling. The attempted manipulation of our thoughts

only serves someone else's power or profit. We are numbers in many
computers, on credit lists, on companies' market analysis. In war, we
might be considered part of the permissible number of casualties. We
are losing personal freedom to our government's way of fighting
terrorism and to the religious fundamentalists' way of believing that
their view of faith is the correct and only one that leads to the good
and pious life. The forces for and against conservation and sustainability are at odds.

Yet, paradoxically, we are also living in a world where there is
possibly more respect for individuality then ever before in history.
Our right to live our own lifestyle is protected by law even if there
is an erosion of that law recently taking place. Also what we think,
write, or speak is both protected and at risk now. Still, the sanctity
of a human life is considered precious by many people.

There is an increasing body of writings about life and spirit.
Unified theories that move to bring cosmology, quantum physics,
biology, environmental sustainability, consciousness, and culture
together are being developed. People are exploring the boundaries
of life and life after death. We are living an exciting and threatening
time in our history.

Statements made by Chief Seattle in 1844 and 1855 are still relevant in their expression of concern about the need and importance
of an attitude of stewardship toward the land. He speaks of honoring,
respect and freedom. "How can you buy and sell the sky, the warmth
of the land? We do not own the freshness of the air or the sparkle of
the water. Every pine needle shining in the sun, every sandy beach,
the mist hanging in the woods, every clearing, each humming insect,
and every part of the earth is holy in the memory and experience of
my people. We are part of the earth and the earth is part of us.

"The white man is a stranger who comes in the night and takes
from the land whatever he wants. The earth is not his friend but
his enemy, and when he has conquered it, he moves on. He treats
his mother, the earth, and his brother, the sky, as things to be bought,
plundered, and sold like sheep or bright beads. His appetite will
devour the earth and leave behind only a desert.

"You must treat the animals of this land as your brothers. What are human beings, without animals? If all the animals should cease to exist, humans would die of a great loneliness of the spirit. Whatever happens to the animals will soon happen also to the human beings.

"Teach your children what we have taught our children. The earth does not belong to us; we belong to the earth. All things are connected, like the blood which unites one family. Mankind did not weave the web of life. We are but one strand within it. Whatever we do to the web, we do to ourselves. All things are bound together."[4]

Each time I read Chief Seattle's words, I am deeply moved. His statements strike "home," they reach to the heart of the matter. His words resonate to a frequency that says "yes" to life.

In some ways, we are being torn apart by opposing forces that surround us. In other ways, there is a necessary battle taking place that may move us in the direction where we can integrate the best of all worlds. We have to be more diligent and determined to live ourselves with authenticity.

And now, I would like to dream with you. I would like to dream of a world of faith, where people can exist in their common humanity and in their individuality. It is a world where having a heart for ourselves and for others is not seen as weakness and our power is not used to control. It is a world that recognizes anger and negativity as the raw material of our power and not as emotions that should be hidden and treated like lepers of old. It is a world that recognizes that all of who we are is worthy of caring and support. It recognizes there is nothing about ourselves that we have to get rid of. All of who we are can be transformed through our acceptance. It is a world that honors the perfection of the universe and that honors the call of our spirit moving toward that perfection. And therefore, let's continue our dream of a world that honors the earth we live on and the universe that we are a part of, that honors that the earth needs as much of our acceptance as we need for ourselves. That is the dream that I would like to have with you. Come dream with me.

Epilogue

(This Epilogue is from the original edition of this book).
Harmony and Struggle are a Breath Away

I RECENTLY LED A WEEKEND TRAINING AND PSYCHOTHERAPY workshop for psychotherapists. As I began the workshop, something was missing in me. I quickly realized that I didn't feel any fear or insecurity. I hadn't even felt stage fright prior to the workshop. Instead, I experienced an inner calm. Nevertheless, twice during the two-day workshop I felt myself losing my centered, flowing, easy place. Something that occurred in the group had touched an old feeling that I was going to be annihilated and for having so much aliveness and an ability to follow my own path. My back began to tighten, and I could experience myself begin to feel one-dimensionally. Both felt like defenses against an old assault. I knew that I could continue leading the workshop from being tight-backed and one-dimensional. However, it would then feel like a burden, rather than an exciting event that I was participating in.

Very soon after I felt these things, I shared with the group what was going on in me. I told the group that I believed that I must be projecting that they were going to be contemptuous and angry with me for being so alive. Sharing helped me be clear and experience that the basis for my feelings was my childhood reality projected onto the group. It helped me separate my childhood reality from the current reality of the workshop. Actually, the group was quite friendly and supportive of my experience.

Prior to my sharing myself with the group, I felt an injunction in me against doing this, that I shouldn't have lost my centered, easy feeling in the first place, and if I had, I shouldn't share it with the group. There was a belief that with all the personal therapy that I have had that I should be beyond such a loss of center. I could feel how these messages were actually part of the killing energy I was trying to get away from by tightening. If I followed the messages as if they were true it would only cause me to withdraw even further, the result being an even tighter back where I would become more disconnected and more one dimensional. I needed to be aware of the negative energy of the message, rather than just the message itself. The very act of sharing was a way of breaking the fusion with the negative energy and my sharing allowed me to become more three dimensional.

The theme of the workshop was The Good, The Bad and the Ugly. It was a way of saying to people what I have been writing about throughout this book; let's see how everything about us is worthy of support, has been an ally for us, and can be transformed into more aliveness.

The events that I am describing here happened very quickly. The way I dealt with them also brought me quickly back into balance. I have been working with my self-acceptance for a long time. I couldn't always share myself and return to a balanced state as quickly as I did in this workshop.

There are still other issues in my life where I don't fully accept what I am feeling. Although, intellectually, I know that these are the places where I don't want to fully take responsibility for my own life even though I need to, I still struggle. These are the places in me that I would like to blame others for what I'm feeling. Wisdom for me, like for so many others, is achieved step by step. Intellectual knowledge, easily acquired, takes time and effort to be transformed into emotional, embodied knowledge. I'm working to uncover the remaining sources of my discontent. I can feel my faith that my "dig" is about to bring the next shard of emotional pottery out of the darkness. I can feel how I am struggling to open another chamber of my psyche and body that has been long closed. An old familiar feeling happens in me when I feel myself getting close—that something that has been off-balance is about to right itself.

What I am also aware of is that the more that I deal with how my "old reality" intrudes on my present life, the less I analyze myself. I am here to live my life, not to think about it as a way of avoiding my life. A poem I wrote many years ago expresses this sentiment.

> Months of coping with loneliness, sadness, and tightness
> have paid dividends.
> "Stay with the feeling,"
> "Keep your breathing open,"
> I would often hear myself say.
> Scrupulously,
> I experienced my suffering,
> my despair.
> Faith was then all I had,
> that staying with myself would work.
> Now,
> the warm burning embers of tobacco
> in a corn cob pipe
> glow quietly,
> peacefully-
> so, too, my heart.

I'm curious about where my life force is going to lead me now that I am finished with this book. Actually, there's a warm feeling of excitement and satisfaction that I have just finished a difficult job. I feel at one with the world, and my life is now more inside of me. I recognize that fullness comes from an embodied connection to my history, feeling myself in the reality of my present life, and the recognition that there is a future. For the moment, I feel myself in harmony.

Postscript

NOW THAT I'VE FINISHED WITH THE REVISIONS, I FEEL
satisfied and excited. It was worth the effort I put into it. Some victimizing energies appeared, but nowhere as intense or as often as they
were when I first wrote the book many years ago. In fact, these
victimizing energies were more like a flash thundershower that was
over very quickly, rather than the old hurricanes that would last for
days at a time. As I finish this last paragraph, I feel excited to
continue on the journey of returning to the book that Naomi and I
have already begun. I can move onto the new theories we are developing about physical pain and illness and how to work with these
issues.

> In Beauty may we walk.
> All day long may we walk.
> Through the returning seasons may we walk.
> Beautifully will we possess again.
> Beautifully birds...
> Beautifully joyful birds...
> On the trail marked with pollen may we walk.
> With grasshoppers about our feet may we walk.
> With dew around our feet may we walk.
> With beauty may we walk.
> With beauty before us may we walk.
> With beauty behind us may we walk.
> With beauty above us may we walk.

With beauty around us may we walk.

In old age, wandering on a trail of beauty, lively may we walk.

In old age, wandering on a trail of beauty, living again, may we walk.

It is finished in beauty.

It is finished in beauty.

Navajo Night Way Prayer
Stuart Alpert, April, 1992
September, 2005

Notes

Preface

1) List: *What To Do Until Enlightenment*. This statement that is paraphrased from a brochure by Hedy Schleifer announcing a workshop: *"Laughing Your Way to a Loving Relationship"* presented at a conference in Saratoga Springs: "The Positive Power of Humor and Creativity."

Chapter One

1) King, Serge, *Kahuna Healing*, The Theosophical Publishing House, Wheaton, Illinois, 1983

Chapter Two

1) I want to give credit for the ideas, and some of the wording in the last two sentences, to a brochure advertising David Grove Seminars.

Chapter Three

1) Nabokov, Peter (Editor, *Native American Testimony*, New York, Harper & Row, 1979 Note: Today this is relevant to all people, including women, not just the white man.
2) Hesse, Herman, *Siddartha*, New York, Bantam Books, 1971
3) Bly, Robert, *Iron John*, Reading, Mass., Addison-Wesley, 1990
4) Weed, Susan, *Wise Women Herbal Healing*, Woodstock, New York, Ash Tree Publishing, 1989
5) Rifkin, Jeremy, *Time Wars; A new Dimension Shaping Our Future*, Utne Reader, Sept./Oct. 1987

Chapter Four

1) Satir, Virginia, *Peoplemaking*, Palo Alto, CA, Science and Behavior Inc., 1972
2) *Keleman, Stanley, Emotional Anatomy*, Berkeley, CA, Center Press, 1985

3) Vonnegut, Kurt, *Slapstick*, New York, A Delta Book, 1976
4) Verny, Thomas, *The Secret Life Of The Unborn Child*, New York, Delta Books, 1981
5) This paragraph was written by Sherry Osadchey. She originally wrote it into her personal journal.

Chapter Five

1) Williamson, Marianne from *A Return To Love: Reflections on the Principles of A Course in Miracles*, Harper Collins, 1992. From Chapter 7, Section 3

Chapter Six

1) Satir, Virginia, op. cit.

Chapter Eight

1) For more discussion of these views read Keleman, op. cit. and
2) Lowen, Alexander, *Bioenergetics*, New York, Coward, McCann and Geoghegan, 1975
3) Santayana, George, *From Life Of Reason*, Vol.1, Reason In Common Sense, 1905-1906, New York, Scribner, 1981
4) Sams, Jamie and Carson, David, *Medicine Cards*, Santa Fe, Bear & Co., 1988
5) Keleman, Stanley, *Your Body Speaks Its Mind*, Berkeley, CA, Center Press, 1981
6) Keleman, ibid.
7) Momaday, N. Scott, *House Made Of Dawn*, New York, Harper Row, 1968
8) Weed, Susan, op. cit.

Chapter Nine

1) Frank Waters, *The Man Who Killed The Dear*, New York, WashingtonSquare Press, 1942
2) Sams and Carson, op. cit. The thoughts and much of the wording in this paragraph were taken from this book. I did not use quotes as a convenience, where some of the wording and sentences are my own.
3) Sandbach, John, *Astrology, Alchemy And The Tarot*, Birmingham, Michigan, Seek-It Publications, 1982
4) Nabokov, op. cit., and written material from Native American Rights Fund, Boulder, Colorado

INFORMATION ABOUT
HARTFORD FAMILY INSTITUTE

Recognizing and respecting the power of the human spirit and body to heal itself emotionally and physically, Stuart Alpert and Naomi Lubin-Alpert, two of the co-founders, created HFI in 1969. Naomi and Stuart developed Body-Centered Gestalt Therapy. They continue to refine, practice, and teach the therapy.

HFI is a private psychotherapy practice and training institute where individuals (both adults and children), couples and families are seen for therapy and come to train in Body-Centered Gestalt Psychotherapy. We have grown to where we are now nine partners, two associates, and more than 20 Independent Practitioners. Besides psychotherapy, HFI also provides massage, movement therapy, yoga, Reiki, Qi Qong healing, Alexander Technique, and Cranial-Sacral work. We welcome other psychotherapy and energy healers to lead workshops.

TRAININGS AT HARTFORD FAMILY INSTITUTE
From A Taste To A Total Immersion

Professional Training Program in Body-Centered Gestalt Therapy (A program for psychotherapists and healers that is a total immersion)

Weekend Training Program for those people who want to study with us and who live out of town. This program is similar in content to the Professional Training Program, although less intense. (Students in the Both Programs can receive coursework credit for either a Doctor of Psychology or a Doctor of Ministry at the Graduate Theological Foundation)

Four Hour Monthly Seminars (A program for psychotherapists and healers that provides a taste of Body-Centered Gestalt Psychotherapy

Human Relations Training Program (A program for the general public who want to learn about being more human)

To learn more about these programs or more about Hartford Family Institute, visit our web site at www.hartfordfamilyinstitute.com

There is also a training program/therapy group in Kansas City led by Stuart and Naomi and a New York City supervision/therapy group led by Stuart.

For information about these training programs, call or write:

Hartford Family Institute

17 South Highland Street

West Hartford, CT 06119

Tel. (860) 236-6009

Training programs in Kansas City and Germany led by graduates of the HFI training program.
In Kansas City:
Gestalt Psychotherapy Offices Contact:
Pennie Cohn: (816) 531-4490

Soulworks Contact: Sam and Garth Matthes:
Tel. (816) 753-2396

Between 1977-1998 Stuart and Naomi led training/therapy groups in Germany. The students in these groups formed their own institutes and have developed clinical practices and training programs.

Analytisches Gestalt Institut Bonn Contact: Dr. Wolfgang Heinz 0228/210166

ISPG (Coburg) Contact: Dr. Prof. Helmut Pauls

Daumling Institut (Siegburg/Bonn) Contact: Norbert Sattler Tel. 022441/53102

A NEW BOOK IN THE WORKS

Naomi, my wife, business partner, and co-founder of HFI and co-developer of Body-Centered Gestalt Therapy, and I are in the process of co-authoring *The Soul of Psychotherapy: A Psychotherapeutic-Spiritual Approach To Wholeness*. In this new book, we share where we have come to in our understanding of human growth and behavior and how we understand and work with the emotional and energetic roots of physical pain and illness. We also present our understanding and work with depression, addictions, an energetic perspective of clinical issues such as suicide, anorexia, and bulimia, as well as writing about various other clinical issues. We share more about faith and the meaning of having a connection to spirit in regard to our emotional and physical health. All of these issues will be part of understanding the evolution and the development of Body-Centered Gestalt Therapy.

We continue exploring how openness breeds openness and repression breeds repression. We understand that we see the world through patterns of energy that surround us as children. The molecules, atoms, subatomic particles that give energy its unseen form swirl around us. As the finest of mists, the energy enters any crack or crevice in our body. It even enters through the pores of our skin. As a magical sandstorm, this energy affects perception and senses, creating beliefs, influencing the way we come to know ourselves, deeply affecting our connection to spirit, deeply affecting our emotions, psyche, body, and mind as it teaches us how life should be lived.

INTRODUCTION TO

The Soul of Psychotherapy

The earth does not belong to man, man belongs to the Earth. All things are connected like the blood that unites us all. Man did not weave the way of life, he is but a strand in it. Whatever he does to the web he does to himself. —
Chief Seattle

Introduction to The Soul of Psychotherapy

The soul is the spark of divine consciousness that lives in each of us. It is the essence of each being that continues beyond all lifetimes. The soul of psychotherapy is the energy in each therapy session that is beyond words, beyond personality, beyond techniques. It is the force in every psychotherapy session that transcends the personality of both the client and the therapist. The soul energy in each session allows a meeting beyond knowing, where spirit brings messages of what is necessary for both client and therapist to move toward wholeness, toward enlightenment.

The spiritual imperative within each therapy session is the place in psychotherapy where the client and therapist are given the opportunity to understand that each movement toward wholeness, toward homeostasis, is a movement toward spirit. The practice of psychotherapy can be more than working on personality, physical pain and illness, and relationship issues. It can be a shamanic experience where "breaks" from spirit for both client and therapist can be

227

healed if the therapist recognizes that a connection with spirit is possible.

The spiritual component of this therapy was integrated with Gestalt and Bioenergetics after we were apprenticed with Native American Healers, other Medicine People, and Masters of Eastern traditions for more than fifteen years. As it exists at this time, the spirituality of Body-Centered Gestalt Therapy is a nondenominational connection between each individual's spiritual experiences integrated with a grounded experience of body and emotion.

As was discussed in "Enlightenment" we see how all the cells in our body contain the memories of the childhood support and abuse that we received from our parents. They also contain the energetic memories of the experiences of our grandparents, our great-grandparents, and our ancestors, as well as the caring and abuse that we received in this life from teachers, colleagues, and friends. These cellular memories can be brought to consciousness through the work of Body-Centered Gestalt Therapy to help each client let go of the past and to live mindfully and, therefore, to live what is real in the present.

It is essential to understand that Body-Centered Gestalt Therapy is so much more than technique. It is a therapy of realness and relationship. It is a therapy where the therapist is providing the client with an energetic invitation to explore how he has learned to organize his body, emotions, energy, and spirit to survive the abuses of childhood. This "combing out" of old realities from personality releases energy into the body that had been used to store and hide trauma away from consciousness. With the release of energy from tension, relaxation occurs and aliveness flows through the body, bringing a feeling of well-being and internal harmony. It also moves us closer to spirit and gives us a connection to the energy of soul.

Clinically, we hold the understanding that the creation of emotional distress and suffering is based on childhood trauma. Deepening this understanding we can observe how abuse structured in our body becomes an important component in the creation of physical pain, illness and disease. All of these issues are held in the belief that the energy of soul is at work in each session.

Body-Centered Gestalt Therapy incorporates a view of pain, illness and disease that is based on our experiences with clients and our view of process. This belief system is based on Einstein's theory that $E = mc^2$. In other words, energy and matter are convertible; that is, energy can be converted to matter and matter can be converted back to energy. With this understanding, tumors, breast masses, and other illnesses and diseases are results of energy that has been blocked and stagnated. With the introduction of healing light into the area of blocked matter, Body-Centered Gestalt therapists have had significant success in converting matter back to energy, resulting in masses disappearing before scheduled surgery and the remission and/or cure of many illnesses and diseases. This in no way means that we feel that every condition can be cured. Rather, it is an example of our belief that every illness and disease is a message from spirit about either the physical, emotional and/or spiritual healing that needs to take place. The illness and disease are also messages of where energy is blocked in the body and a way that our spirit is bringing our attention to the block. As spirit seeks to heighten our awareness of where we are blocked, we have the opportunity to heal a spiritual/emotional wound that can allow the blocked energy (matter) to be converted back to flowing, healthy energy.

Index